Off the Grid

Steven W. Smidesang

PAGE PUBLISHING, INC.
New York, NY

First originally published by Page Publishing, Inc. 2019

ISBN 978-1-64544-854-9 (Paperback)
ISBN 978-1-64544-853-2 (Digital)

Printed in the United States of America

Thanks to Mom for the constant encouragement and
thanks to Lord Jesus for the generous wisdom.

Chapter 1

Brady Witek was not smiling as his attorney, Sydney Brandenburg, guided him into a small glass room with his hand on the small of his back. Sydney pulled out a chair for Brady. "I don't like the look on your face."

Brady waited for Sydney to close the door before responding. "Their offer has the student loan in it again, and I won't pay for it. I'm drawing the line."

Sydney smoothed his hand over his bald head. "I agree. You guys borrowed the money for the benefit of the marriage, and then your wife ended the marriage. The benefit is over for you."

"Are you sure they can't hear us in here?" Brady gazed around the ceiling.

"Stay with me, Brady. You need to be strong in there. You're a small fish, but they plan to filet you, and remember, the judge wants a settlement."

Brady crossed his arms. "I won't pay for the student loan."

"The appellate court said a new spouse's income can be considered for support. I intend to argue the arrangement Jolene has with this new guy… What's his name?"

"Aaron."

"Aaron provides for your wife and kids, while at the same time, you send them forty percent of your take-home pay. If it goes to court, I have something to argue, but for now, we need to negotiate. Now, shake it off and let's get in there."

They made their way to the conference room where Jolene, Brady's wife, and her attorney sat at a glass table. No one stood when they entered.

Sydney nodded at the attorney sitting to the left of Jolene. "Franklin."

Franklin nodded. "Sydney."

"We have a new offer," Jolene said. "You can throw out the one from last night."

A clerk passed a paper to everyone in the room. Sydney nodded at Brady. Brady set his paper aside and placed his leather bag on the table to pull out a file. "Let's approach this a different way this time. Take a look at all my accounts, and Jolene gets half. We can end this, and then Jolene can go back to committing adultery."

Franklin raised his hand. "There's no need for that type of talk, Mr. Witek. We'll look at your accounts."

"You got it, Frankie boy." Brady arranged his documents on the table. "This row here represents my current accounts—credit card balances, checking, investment funds, et cetera." He waved at the other row. "Here are my pay stubs for six months and my last two tax returns." He made a sarcastic bow. "As you can see, I am not in the same tax bracket as Bill Gates and won't be passing Warren Buffet on the rich-guy list."

Franklin collected the documents, perused, and passed them to the clerk who wrote down totals and took notes. Jolene joined the process checking out each paper. Ten minutes went by.

Franklin looked at the clerk. "James, can you give us the numbers?"

James tore the page off his pad and handed it to Franklin. Franklin's expression flattened after he read and slid the paper in front of Jolene. Jolene's eyes widened. "Bullshit, he has more than this."

Franklin pulled the paper back in front of him. "Yes, your estimation of your husband's finances was higher than this amount."

Jolene pointed at Brady. "I want ninety thousand dollars."

"Mr. Witek, you must reveal all your accounts, or you will be found in contempt of court," Franklin said.

Sydney took over. "A couple of things… First, we just gave you the list of all of Mr. Witek's accounts, so you can knock off the threats. Second, there's a reason for the smaller figure on James's paper, and the responsibility falls on your client."

Jolene said, "That was five years ago."

Sydney continued. "Mr. Witek was denied a new credit card five years ago. When he checked his credit, he found six new cards were taken out in his name by Mrs. Witek, and that was after she'd acquired balances totaling over forty-eight thousand dollars. Subsequently, my client was required to take out a home equity loan to pay off the balance."

Franklin rubbed his face.

Sydney turned to Brady. "Go ahead."

"You'll get half of the money on James's paper, but I'm not going to pay your student loan, and I won't sign the divorce papers otherwise."

Jolene crossed her arms. "You're going to give me ninety thousand dollars and pay for the loan, all fifty thousand dollars of it. And the court will give me a divorce even if you won't agree, so save your empty threats."

Sydney and Brady exhaled at the same time.

Sydney said, "Franklin, get us a court date."

They stood up to leave.

"Yes, indeed." Franklin let James clear the papers.

In the hallway, Brady strode away ahead of Sydney, who sped up and grabbed his arm. "Hold on now." Sydney led him down a side corridor and sat down with him on a bench by the wall.

"I know I need to calm down."

"Yes, and remember what former alcoholics like to say-accept the things you cannot change."

"I never wanted my family broken up. I won't sign the divorce papers."

"And like I've said over and over, the court will still grant the divorce. Jolene used mental abuse as grounds, so she doesn't have to stay separated from you for two years."

"So another guy gets my wife and kids, and I have to pay for it? I'm not feeling the justice here."

"Do you want to counter file? We can still do it."

Brady got up and paced in front of Sydney a few times. "It would be pointless, and I'm almost out of cash. I'm living like I did in college. No, let's end this thing, but get rid of the tuition. I won't pay for it."

"So I gather. I'll do my best, but you're not going to win very often in Illinois. This is a bad state for a father to get divorced in."

Brady held out his hand and pulled Sydney up from the bench. They walked side by side out of the building.

◊　◊　◊

Thursday Evening
Roger's Park
Chicago, Illinois

Brady circled the block in his Chevy Trailblazer, finally squeezing into a spot two blocks from his building. He carried his leather bag full of work stuff through the courtyard where buds filled the trees in the early spring. He let himself in to his World War II–era apartment on the third floor of a building in the Rodger's Park neighborhood of Chicago near Devon Avenue.

He had one decoration, a large painting of gray shapes dominating a small orange square. Occasionally, he would stand and contemplate the meaning of the picture.

He took his bag into the smaller bedroom—his room—tossing his wallet, keys, and loose change on the dresser before changing into shorts and a T-shirt, and then he finally quit stalling and turned on his phone.

As expected, Spencer Moss had sent six e-mails and two text messages demanding to know what was taking him so long to respond. Brady read the oldest e-mail and worked his way up. Spencer couldn't figure out why a user sent e-mails to several people, and they always returned. He replied to use semicolons to separate the names instead of commas. What a numb nuts.

The girls would stay with Brady tomorrow. He walked into the master bedroom to inspect the bunkbeds on each side of the room. Reading lamps were clipped to the bed frames. Four old dressers sat side by side at the end of the room. He'd installed a full-length mirror nearby.

In the kitchen, he took a beer from the fridge and took it to the living room to watch TV.

He only had the girls every other weekend, and lately, behavior problems were developing. He never wanted to lose his family in the first place.

The Bulls played on TV. The apartment buzzer sounded, so Brady got up, pushed the button, and cracked the door, sitting down to wait for his friend Paul to come up the stairs.

Paul entered, off after working all day as an associate pastor at the Methodist Church. "What's the score?"

"They're down by ten, third quarter."

Paul took a diet soda from the fridge and flopped next to Brady on the couch. He drank and belched. "I really want one of those beers."

"Have a tough day?"

"Mrs. O'Neil passed away. It wasn't a surprise, but she was such an awesome lady. Won't be the same without her."

"She was an awesome lady."

"She stopped talking two days ago, and then this afternoon, her hands turned blue. Doc said time was up. The blue went up her arms to her neck, and then the machine whistled—she was gone."

"We were in her rec room when you finally got me to accept Christ."

"Yup. So what happened in your hearing?"

Brady took a long drink of beer. "Jolene decided the moon is not enough. She wants the stars too."

"Listen, Brady, I'm not here as your pastor, but I have to say something."

"Go ahead, man."

"The deal where you cashed out your stocks and converted the money into certified checks, I'm not on board with it."

"They requested information on my accounts, and the checks are not in any account. I have them in a safe-deposit box."

Paul punched Brady's arm. "You know Jesus is a great crapola detector."

"If I give Jolene that money, I'll be broke in no time."

"If she did that to you, would you buy it?"

Brady shrugged. "They asked for a list of accounts."

Paul took a long drink of soda and let a long whisper of gas escape through is lips. "As your friend, I need to say more."

Brady turned down the volume. "Let me have it."

"Your talk about leaving town and getting a new identity, you can't do it. Forget about what you see in the movies. God never asks people to do bad things."

"I understand." Brady rubbed his forehead. "But it's complicated."

Paul stared at Brady for a moment. "If you leave, I won't have a regular-guy friend anymore. Sometimes I need to shoot the shit."

"Let's see what the judge says. Maybe things will work out."

◊　◊　◊

Friday Morning

Brady left for work, walking up to his Trailblazer. Winter salt had rusted the fenders like cancer, not a good look with white paint. The Trailblazer had needed trading in before his family fell apart, but now he was stuck with it. Lately, when he hit the gas, blue smoke came from the exhaust. The door creaked as he got in. The engine coughed to life, and Brady joined the traffic heading to his office in Harwood Heights. Most commuters headed east toward down-town in the morning, but he drove west toward the suburbs. The sun glared behind him both ways on the twenty-minute drive.

In the Polyglomerate Container parking lot, one spot remained. A yellow Corvette flashed in front of him, causing him to screech his tires and mumble a few choice words before reversing to park in the street. Spencer jumped out of the Corvette with a sarcastic salute.

Brady gave him the finger, and Spencer grabbed his crotch. Brady let the jerk get inside the building before he went in.

The building had none of Chicago's architectural charm, institutional in design with plain cement walls and square windows. Going in the front door, Brady nodded at Lexi, the receptionist, and took the stairway to his third-floor office, already hot inside.

With computer servers located in his office, he could never cool down. Fans blew hot air into the hallway, but the thermostat was installed right outside, so the hot air kept the heater from turning on. Cold employees, usually women, constantly sneaked over to turn up the thermostat.

Today, he had a plan. He hung up his coat and loosened his tie, knowing Spencer would come in at any time. Footsteps came down the hallway, and Spencer barged in. "You need to take care of my e-mails as soon as I send them, Witek."

"I was in court yesterday, and you know it. Next time you pull in front of me in the parking lot, I'm going to forget where my brake pedal is."

"If I want lip from you, I'll unzip my pants."

Brady waved him off. It wasn't worth it. The aging hipster would force him into a screaming match, and Brady couldn't stand it when his face got red and he barred his brilliant white capped teeth. He hadn't bothered to tie his hair in a ponytail yet—it flowed down his back, blond with gray streaks. His Tommy Bahama shirt had the top two buttons undone, and the gold chains and big-faced watch were too much. At least the asshole looked like an asshole. People weren't too surprised when he came on strong.

Spencer turned to leave, but Brady couldn't help himself. "Can't figure out where to put a semicolon, give me a break."

Spencer paused for a few seconds and then slipped out.

Brady wiped his forehead and began to work on the heat problem. With the open ceiling, the walls did not go all the way up. He took an extension cord and tied one end around a stapler to toss it over a metal beam. He clanked the first try.

Someone in an office nearby said, "What the hell was that?"

He tossed again, the stapler dropped over the bar, and he wiggled the cord to lower it. He untied the stapler, tied the cord around the handle of a box fan, and hoisted it up to the top of the wall. He tied the other end of the cord around a table leg. When he plugged in the power cord to the fan, it blew hot air from the top of his office toward Spencer's office.

When he turned around, Mark Seivers, the president of the company, stood watching with a smirk on his face, shaking his head.

He handed papers to Brady. "Here are some configuration changes for the reports. I need these by noon. Spencer said you could do them."

Brady looked them over. "Boss, I have no time for this. Have Spencer do them."

"Why don't you sit down, Mr. Witek?" Mark motioned, and Brady sat. "I know Spencer can be unpleasant, but you have to work with him."

Spencer was protected, dressing like a gigolo and cursing in front of women, nothing ever happened to him. It was pointless to complain.

"All right, but my other projects will be late."

"Just get it done." Mark left.

After fixing the configurations, Spencer strode into his room ten minutes later. "You really fucked up the reports, hotshot. Now you get to fix them again. Here are the errors in red."

Brady noticed sweat on Spenser's brow. The red markings meant he would need to undo many of the changes he'd just done. Spencer didn't understand the database structure.

"You don't know what you're doing. Why are you my supervisor again?"

The red in Spencer's face grew dark, looking like he was about to let loose, but instead, he turned to leave, bumping into the HR director in the hallway turning up the thermostat. "Get out of my way, Sherry. Fucking cow."

◇ ◇ ◇

Friday Afternoon

Brady drove to pick up his girls in Crystal Lake, about an hour's drive from Chicago near Rockford. Both he and the girls were getting used to weekend custody, and while the younger two daughters, Crissy and Laurie, seemed to enjoy themselves, the older two, Ashley and Britney, were giving him attitude and would rather have fun with their new friends in Crystal Lake.

Sixteen-year-old Britney, his adopted daughter from Jolene's first marriage, had been a lot of trouble. Brady made the effort to treat her as his own daughter, and until recently, things were fine. Ashley, age twelve, worshipped her older sister. Six-year-old Crissy and eight-year-old Laurie were still his buddies and thought the bunk beds were great.

This weekend should go better. The church had fun things planned for the weekend, including a sleepover on Saturday night.

His phone rang. He put in his Bluetooth. "Brady."

"I'm switching weekends," Jolene said. "They're not coming tonight."

"What? You can't do that."

"We're going out with Aaron to a nice restaurant, and we have reservations. The girls will come next weekend."

"Jolene, I'm almost there. They're coming with me."

"Lower your voice, or I'll get a restraining order."

Brady's tires hit the rumble strip on the side of the road. He jerked the car back to the center of the lane. "Hold on a minute."

"Hurry up."

Brady pulled to the shoulder. "Speaking of court orders, I'm supposed to get the girls at six thirty tonight."

"Not going to happen." Jolene hung up.

Brady took deep breaths as the car rocked when a big truck went by. The weekend was ruined. He called Sydney.

"Hi there, Brady. Happy Friday."

"Same to you, but I have a problem. Jolene won't give me the girls for the weekend. They're going out to eat instead."

"Sorry this is happening, buddy. I want you to go back to Roger's Park and file a complaint at the police station."

"Can't you do something?"

"No, the police won't get involved."

"I guess not."

A truck hauling a crane blasted by Brady's car.

"Are you okay? What was that noise?"

"I'm on the shoulder of the expressway. I better get going."

"Please do. Go to the police station and file the complaint. We'll talk on Monday."

Brady ended the call and accelerated into traffic, driving ten miles to find an exit to turn around.

Brady entered the police station an hour later and got the attention of the desk sergeant. "I need to fill out a complaint. My wife didn't bring my children for visitation."

The sergeant grabbed a form. "Just fill it out and give it back to me when you're done."

"Will you do anything about it?"

"No, but your lawyer probably wants it on record. See those guys back at the table?" He pointed to the back.

Brady turned. Five men filled out forms.

"Those guys are filling out the same form as you. Nothing will happen to their ex-wives either."

Brady took the form.

Chapter 2

Later Friday Night

Because it was still early, Brady parked and walked two blocks to the courtyard of another apartment building. He pushed a button at the entrance.

A voice came from the speaker. "Who is it?"

"It's me, Brady."

There was a pause. "Are your girls with you?"

"No. Jolene screwed me over. Can I come up?"

Nothing happened for thirty seconds. Brady wondered what the problem was, and then finally, the door made a buzzing sound. He went up the stairs to the second floor and into the hallway, passing by a young guy. Cindy, Brady's sister-in-law, opened her door for him wearing a robe and looking like she was settling in for the night. Brady gave her a kiss on the cheek and gave her three-year-old son, Lane, a high five.

Cindy said, "Sit down and tell me what happened."

Brady sat on the couch. The cushion was warm like someone had been sitting there. "I was halfway to Crystal Lake when she called. They're going out to eat instead."

"I thought you had a custody agreement."

"We do, but she knows she can get away with breaking it."

Cindy sat close to Brady, took his hand, and put her head on his shoulder. "Lane and I will keep you company."

Brady leaned his head against hers, feeling weird snuggling with his brother's wife before the divorce was finalized. After Tom disappeared, the judge had to allow fair time for a response before proceeding.

Brady reached into his jacket and pulled out an envelope. "I was going to give you this tomorrow."

Cindy took the envelope with five hundred dollars inside. "Thanks so much, Brady. I know things are tight for you."

"It's okay. Things will get better someday…" Cindy was young and nice looking. Someone had to raise his brother's son. "I haven't eaten yet. Why don't I get take out from Repita Pita?"

"Great."

◊ ◊ ◊

Sunday Evening
Crystal Lake, Illinois

Jolene Witek sat in Aaron Gilbert's lap on the back porch in Crystal Lake. He let her hold a glass of scotch for him to sip. Jolene enjoyed her sexy new boyfriend, no more button-down Brady.

Aaron spat the straw away from his mouth. "That's enough. I have to go in early tomorrow."

Jolene set the drink down and went to another deck chair. "I want to talk about the new house."

"The new house? Just a second." Aaron drank the rest of the scotch. "Go ahead."

Jolene smacked his arm. "Funny guy. Don't you think the house on Aspen Street is great?"

"You don't have to sell me. The pool is awesome. The girls get their own rooms. We can park four cars in the garage. One thing sold me right away, can you guess?"

"The exercise room on the back of the garage?"

Aaron touched his nose with his finger. "On the nose." He put his hands behind his head and flexed his biceps. "Got to keep the dogs runnin'."

Jolene felt his bicep. "We need to make an offer tomorrow."

Aaron turned. "Babe, you haven't gotten your divorce done yet. My house hasn't sold, and I'm borrowed up to my eyeballs at the gym."

"Don't worry so much. I'm getting fifteen hundred a month from Brady, and I'll be teaching soon. And remember, I'll make sure Brady chokes up another ninety grand."

He bent forward for a kiss. "And I get a hot new lady with four pretty girls. Life is good."

"That's what I want to hear."

◊　◊　◊

Monday Morning
Seward, Kentucky

The rock wall rose thirty feet high in front of Kacey Farrell's car. The Winslow-Carnac Corporation had cut a hill in half in Seward, Kentucky, to build their headquarters, leaving a new feature in the landscape. Kacey allowed his eyes to trace the patterns in the rock before going into his office. Natural layers lay horizontal, but the machines left vertical grooves, perfect for his eyes to wander as he separated from himself to think.

Today was no different from others in relation to the wall. He spent time in the same parking spot every morning, but last Friday, he'd missed work because of marital problems, spending part of the day in a jail cell. Mrs. Lambert would feel the need to stick her nose in, calling him into her office this morning, and he must decide ahead of time whether or not to blast off her nose with the 9 mm pistol in his glove compartment.

He popped open the glove box and dropped the pistol into his briefcase, paused, and then loaded in two spare clips of ammunition, planning to see how things went first but prepared to go all the way.

As he walked past the foolish modern sculptures in front of the building, coworkers converged on another sidewalk heading for the entryway. They chatted away, seeming not to notice Kacey, but then slowed down to avoid him. He walked faster and entered the building ahead of them, speeding through the foyer, past Freddy the guard to the stairs. As he entered his office, his foot slipped on a piece of paper, causing him to dance foolishly. He regained his composure and checked the hall. No one had seen him. He picked up the paper, a note from Mrs. Lambert. "Please come to my office first thing."

Normally, his belly would tighten and his face would become warm, but instead, he remained calm because of his preparation at the wall, a technique he'd developed while touring in Iraq. Now during civilian life, he continued to find the technique useful, maybe more so because of the complexity of human relationships.

Kacey spun the note into the trash can and took his briefcase up another flight of stairs to the management reception area where Jill sat at the desk. "I must meet with Mrs. Lambert."

Jill picked up her phone. "Kacey Farrell is here… Okay." She put down the phone. "Please wait for a moment."

Kacey took a chair. Footsteps came down the hallway, and one of the young male accountants, a large muscular fellow, walked in the direction of Lambert's office. The phone on Jill's desk beeped. "You can go in now."

Kacey stood in front of the chair. It seemed Mrs. Lambert needed a large young man in her office when she spoke to him.

Jill's eyes peered over the counter. "Are you okay, Mr. Farrell? You can go in."

Kacey nodded and passed through the reception area to the hallway. Four doors down, he entered Mrs. Lambert's sitting area and knocked on her office door. A voice told him to enter, and as he walked through the door, the young accountant spoke. "Yes, Mrs. Lambert, we have the account set up for you." *Lousy acting.*

Mrs. Lambert stood and shot out her hand. "Kacey Farrell, how are you this morning? Thanks for coming in."

Kacey shook her hand and said nothing.

"Please sit." Lambert turned to the accountant. "Jason, I must speak with Mr. Farrell for a few minutes. Will you please wait in my sitting room?"

"Certainly, Mrs. Lambert. I'll be right outside the door."

Jason nodded at Kacey and left the room.

How was Lambert in charge of so many people without a spine?

Lambert opened a desk drawer, took out a file, and removed a printout, handing it to Kacey. "This article is about you, Mr. Farrell, and how you assaulted your wife last week."

Kacey glanced at the copy of the newspaper article, decided to not respond, and handed back the printout.

"Do you wish to make a comment?"

"This is a family matter. Why do I need to comment?"

"When you were hired, you signed a morality agreement. Spousal abuse is listed as behavior that cannot be tolerated by Winslow-Carnac."

"So I *must* comment, if I read you correctly."

Lambert nodded.

Kacey felt his temper rise, but he thought he should be able to speak. He crossed his legs and folded his hands on his knee to appear thoughtful. "Last Thursday evening, my wife, Billie, and I engaged in a physical altercation, as you have already learned. My wife suffered minor bruising."

Lambert looked away for a few seconds. The paper in her hand shook. "What was the cause for this altercation?"

"Billie had been drinking and became physical with me. I subdued her. A neighbor alerted the police, and I was taken into custody."

"Have you been charged with assault?"

"Yes, but I retained a lawyer and will contest the charge."

"Very well, thank you for being candid." Lambert took another paper out of the folder and handed it to Kacey. "You've been a reliable employee for six years, Mr. Farrell, and we want to be fair with you. You will take one week off with pay while this matter is investigated, and then you'll be told your fate."

"You don't need to send me home. I have deadlines to meet."

"I must follow procedures. Thank you for your willingness to cooperate. I will see to it your deadlines are moved back a week."

Kacey uncrossed his legs and placed his hands on the arms of the chair.

Lambert read his body language and stood up. She offered her hand for a shake. "Hopefully, we will settle this matter soon."

Kacey stayed seated, looking down at his briefcase on the floor. "Hopefully, you will."

He picked up the briefcase and ignored her hand. *She damn well better settle this soon.* He did not suffer fools.

Jason sprang to his feet in the sitting area as Kacey passed through. "Continue setting up the account, Jason. You're a credit to the company."

◇　◇　◇

Later in the morning, Lambert arranged her sitting room around a coffee service cart, straightening books on the shelf and wiping dust with her hand. She took a seat and breathed, attempting to appear at ease. Frank Whiteside, the company president, strode in, nodded at Lambert, and fixed himself a coffee. "You met with Kacey Farrell?"

"Yes, sir. The meeting went well."

"What did you do to him?"

"I gave him a week off with pay and told him we would look into the matter."

Whiteside sipped and set down his cup. "Don't get defensive, Geraldine, but are you afraid of Mr. Farrell?"

"The man is not normal, and the US military agrees."

"What does the military have to do with this?"

"Complaints were made by employees a few months ago. I pulled his résumé and made some calls. A staff member at his last posting spoke off the record. Farrell may have a mental disorder."

"Why didn't we know about this when he was hired?"

"I was not employed here at the time."

Whiteside picked his cup back up and took a long drink. "We distribute engine parts, Geraldine. Should be a stress-free environment."

"The domestic assault is cause enough to get rid of him."

"What were the complaints from staff?"

"People who cross him suffer, like their computer system crashes or their electricity at home is cut off. One person had pornography magazines delivered here at corporate after arguing with Kacey about where he hangs his coat. But there is nothing concrete I could pin on him."

Whiteside paused for a moment. "Farrell keeps the accounting systems running. The board thinks highly of him. Let him come back to work in a week, and manage him. Am I clear?"

Lambert nodded.

Whiteside went to the door. "Thanks for the coffee."

When Whiteside was gone, Lambert smacked her fist into the palm of her hand.

◊   ◊   ◊

Monday Morning
Harwood Heights, Illinois

Brady rumbled his Trailblazer into the company lot, keeping an eye out for a yellow car, believing a wrinkled fender would give his Trailblazer more character, but Spencer was nowhere to be seen. Mark Seivers grabbed Brady's arm in the hallway as he made his way to his office. "We'll meet at eleven in the conference room. There's something big to talk about."

"Can you give me a hint?"

"We acquired Jenkin's Container. You'll be a busy man soon."

"Wow. Don't worry, boss, we'll get the job done."

Mark let go of Brady's arm. "I know you will."

Brady entered his office and plugged in the fan on top of the wall, blowing hot air toward Spencer's office. Spencer barged in as Brady was booting up his computer. "Did you hear the news? We're taking over Jenkin's Container in Terre Haute."

Brady motioned at his guest chair. "What accounting software do they use?"

Spencer skootched his chair closer to Brady, hitting him with his Aqua Velva aftershave. "They sent a package to look at in the meeting. Remember how Mark was so stressed out a few weeks ago?"

Brady nodded.

"Well, the merger should get us out of trouble. Our management structure will stay in place, and we'll take all their clients and manufacturing." Spencer looked over at the door and then back at Brady. "Keep this quiet. We're the big winners here. Jenkins management will get the axe."

Brady was glad he didn't know the company was in trouble—he had enough to worry about.

Spencer waved his hand in front of Brady's eyes. "You in there, fool? We just got a reprieve. The governor called. We get to live. Got it?"

"I had no idea we were on the brink."

"We don't tell guys like you. You'd jump ship like a rat."

"So how should I get ready for the meeting?"

"You'll be window dressing. I'll do all the talking."

Spencer got up to leave, tucked in his floral-print shirt, dropped his gold chains in the front, and buttoned up. He tucked his pony tail into the back of his shirt. "Got to look like a businessman."

Brady chuckled.

◇　◇　◇

Later, Brady checked his e-mail, finding a message from Spencer with the subject "Get your ass to the C-room."

He checked his watch, grabbed a legal pad, and went down to the conference room. He didn't recognize two men and a woman, likely Jenkin's people, and they didn't appear to know their days were numbered. Spencer and Mark talked at the front of the room with their backs turned, so Brady went over and shook hands with the new people. The Jenkin's IT guy was named Bigham—he didn't give his first name. Brady took him aside to talk shop, and Spencer barged in between them. "Brady, you've met Bigham. Now go sit at the end of the table. We're about to start."

Brady noticed the startled look in Bigham's eyes. *Enjoy getting to know Spencer.*

Mark noticed Brady sit down. "Let's get started. Get coffee first if you like."

A dozen people sat down around the conference table. Bigham tried to sit with Brady, but Spencer steered him to a spot next to him. Accountants, controllers, and supervisors waited for Mark to start. When he looked up from his papers, the room got quiet.

"First, we want to welcome our friends from Jenkin's Container: Stacy Goodman, Jack Westburn, and Bigham…just Bigham." Chuckles went around the table. "An eleventh-hour deal was struck between Polyglomerate Container and Jenkin's Container, much to the relief of everyone involved. Mr. Westburn can attest to our long, sometimes-heated discussions."

Westburn nodded. "But we're all still friends."

Everyone chuckled. Mark saluted. "The attorneys closed the deal early this morning."

Everyone clapped around the table.

Brady got into the excitement. *Maybe things would get better.*

Mark slid a folder down the table to Brady. "Take a quick glance at the top page, and give us your reaction."

Brady opened the folder to a list of bullet points. Jenkin's infrastructure was summarized—e-mail system, payroll software, sales database, web interface, inventory system, etc. Below was a list of hardware, presumably hosted at Jenkin's headquarters in Terre Haute.

A hand gripped Brady's shoulder. Spencer reached down and snatched the folder off the table and took it back to his seat. He patted Bigham on the shoulder. "Let's take a look at this. Mark, take better aim next time, the big boys are over here."

Mark's lips tightened. "My smart guys will all have a chance to review systems."

Brady said, "Their accounting software uses the same version database as ours, so we can link much of the data over the internet, but the other databases will be a problem, we'll have to convert column by column."

Spencer smacked the table with his hand. "I need to check out everything first. And you can't connect accounting software like ours over the internet."

"Your payroll does. It's linked between the plant and the corporate office."

"It is not. Shut your mouth, Witek, or you'll need to leave."

Mark stood up. "Enough!" He rubbed his forehead. "Why don't you guys go into the lunchroom, have some doughnuts, and talk about what the rest of us can't understand."

Nervous laughter came from around the table.

Brady headed to the lunchroom. Spencer grabbed the folder and scurried ahead of him. Bigham paused for a minute and followed. Spencer banged the door on the wall as he left. By the time Brady and Bigham got there, Spencer continued through and left the room.

"Let's you and I have a meeting," Bigham said. "I have another copy of the summary. This Spencer guy is wound up a bit too tight."

"That must be how they say 'asshole' in Terre Haute."

◊　◊　◊

Later that afternoon, a knock came from Brady's door, and Sherry entered. "What are your plans after work?"

Brady leaned back. "What do you have in mind?"

"I want to talk about the merger. How about five at Ernie's?"

"I'll be there."

Sherry left. She'd been director of HR for decades, and now in her late sixties, employees were like family. She wanted to stay in her job for as long as possible.

At a quarter till five, Brady took the stairs down to the reception area.

Lexi hung up her phone. "Where are you going?"

Brady stopped. "Going to have a drink with Sherry. Good night." He headed for the door.

"Don't you want to invite me?"

Brady stopped again. "Maybe Sherry and I have something going on."

"Okay, I believe you."

Brady turned but waited this time.

"So I can't go?"

He strolled over to her desk. "You've already turned me down twice. I have to consider my dignity."

"Well, if it's important to you, then I understand."

Brady put his hands on the counter. "Do you want to join us for a drink?"

Lexi looked up. "No, thank you, I have plans."

Brady shook his head and headed out the door.

◊　◊　◊

Sherry had a booth in the back of Ernie's, crunching from a bowl of chips. Brady sat down across from her, ordered a beer, and grabbed a chip from the bowl. "You guys did a good job keeping this merger a secret."

"You were one of the reasons we didn't talk about it."

"I can keep a secret."

Sherry crunched a chip. "We didn't want you, the engineers, or the developers to know the company was in trouble and find new jobs."

Brady's beer arrived. "How bad was it?"

Sherry sighed. "After acquiring Jenkin's Container, we should stay afloat, which is why I wanted to talk to you."

Brady held in a burp with his fist, nodding for her to continue.

"You spent a couple of hours with the Bigham guy. How does the merger look from your point of view?"

"It's doable, but we'll be much bigger afterward, so we'll need to keep some of Jenkins's people."

Sherry sat for a moment. Finally, she shook her head.

"If you make cuts, then get rid of the people that deserve it."

"Spencer is staying." She crunched. "I'm ready to retire if things go wrong."

Brady reached across the table and squeezed her wrist. "No, you can't leave."

She gave him a weak smile.

"Sherry, I have to ask—"

"You want to know why Spencer is bulletproof?"

"He doesn't know what he's doing, his behavior is unprofessional, and he gets paid way too much money."

Sherry leaned in. "That's been a mystery for years, but I know one thing."

Brady leaned in. "Let's hear it."

"Spencer lived in Mark Seiver's guesthouse for a few years. The rest is up to your imagination."

◊　◊　◊

Later in the evening, Brady met Cindy and Lane at Burger King for dinner. Cindy looked nice. After he dropped them off, he parked in the middle of a blue cloud of smoke by his building. When he switched off his motor, his cell rang. "Yeah."

Jolene said, "You'll get the girls this weekend."

Brady didn't feel like arguing. "Fine, I'll be there."

Jolene hung up. He popped open the car door and his phone rang again. "Yeah."

"This is Sydney Brandenburg's office. Is this Mr. Brady Witek?"

"It is."

"You have a court hearing at 8:00 a.m. on the Tuesday of next week."

"Got it."

Chapter 3

Thursday Afternoon
Lewisburg, Kentucky

Kacey Farrell needed a new place to stay.

Earlier in the week, his wife met him at a coffee shop accompanied by a social worker. It went well, but Billie wanted him out of the house, so getting the week off had worked out in his favor.

Kacey continued to search on Thursday, parking at the supermarket facing a cinder block wall. He allowed the pattern to take hold of his mind, and once the annoying emotions disconnected, he considered how he was he having trouble finding a place to live. He'd met with unsophisticated landlords, worn-down interiors, and roaches, but his hotel had the same things. He should have settled on the least offensive unit by now.

The answer wouldn't come, so he stepped from his Sonata and headed into the supermarket. Inside the automatic doors was a rack of free fliers. He took one and stood by the front window for light, turning to a section advertising apartments for rent. One caught his eye, located on Ridge Road in Seward, close to the office. The advertisement seemed to glow brighter than the others. He took the flyer back to his car, called the number, and Beatrice Herman answered. He set up an appointment and got directions.

Driving over, the right turn for Ridge Road was familiar—he drove by it every day going to work. It cut through the forest like a tunnel, giving Kacey the thrill of claustrophobia. After a mile, the road curved to the left, and then after two miles, the road ended at an orange plastic mailbox marking a gravel driveway. The box had the correct number on it. The drive was another tunnel of trees. The dense growth thinned out to an open area with large tree trunks and a three-story white house surrounded by old barns and sheds. A cement stairway led to the front door.

He stopped the car to admire, already knowing he wanted to live here, when an old lady wearing sunglasses opened the front door and came down the cement stairs tapping a white cane with a red tip. Kacey's instincts lit up.

He pulled the car close to the steps and parked. The lady waited patiently for him, not looking at Kacey's vehicle, suggesting she must be completely blind, not merely impaired.

Kacey got out. "Hello, might you be Beatrice Herman?"

She raised her hand. "Yes, I might. Please call me Bea. Would you be the gentleman calling about the apartment for rent?"

"Yes, I'm John Wilson. Nice to meet you."

Bea held her hand straight out. Kacey reached around and shook it. Bea nodded. "Good handshake, firm and dry. Come inside so we can talk."

"Certainly."

Bea climbed the stairs with no trouble, likely having lived here many years. She took notice of handshakes. She would notice things others didn't, so he would need to be careful. She led them to an open kitchen area with plain wooden floors and no decorations. The walls were white, and so were the trim and doors. The appliances were fairly new. No lights were on, but the windows let in enough light for him to see.

"Turn on whatever lights you need, dear. As you can see, I don't need them myself." She sat at the kitchen table. "Let's get to know each other."

Kacey pulled out a chair, careful to keep it from screeching on the floor. He sat down and folded his hands on the table. How did he smell today? "I'm a grocery store manager in Lewisburg. Fifty-seven years old. My wife passed away a few years ago, and now I wish to live in a quiet setting, free of the city bustle."

"Your voice sounds young for a fifty-seven-year-old."

Kacey knew he was risking it, but he needed to establish a different persona right away. He was really thirty-four. "Thank you. A person's voice is something you would notice, I suppose."

"Yes. I lost my vision years ago. It can be a burden at times, but I've adjusted. Just as you had to adjust to the loss of your wife."

"Indeed."

"Do you have children, Mr. Wilson?"

"None. My wife wasn't able."

"A shame. You sound like a steady fellow, but I can detect a bit of loneliness. Would you like to see the apartment?"

Kacey caught himself nodding and said, "Yes, I would."

Bea found her cane and got up. "Follow me."

She went to the base of a stairway in the middle of the house, started to climb, and then stopped to flip on a light switch. She took hold of the railing and headed up. On the second floor, she turned and followed a railing, which led over to the next flight.

Kacey inspected rooms on the way. The house was sparsely furnished. Wide-open spaces dominated the house. Bea must relish the freedom of movement.

They headed up the next flight to a hallway that crossed the house from side to side with windows at each end. Bea opened a door on the right, and Kacey followed. The apartment looked like the rest of the house—wood floors with white paint all around. The kitchen furnishings were simple and sturdy. Two doors on the left side were for a bathroom and bedroom.

Kacey took his time, despite already making the decision, strolling the wood floors as Bea followed with her ears. He tapped on surfaces, turned on faucets, and opened cabinets. The windows opened without sticking, and the closets had plenty of room.

"There's more storage for you in the back area on the other side of the hallway, and you'll have a separate entrance from the backstairs. What is your opinion, Mr. Wilson?"

"Could I park my car in one of the buildings?"

"Oh, yes. The buildings are no longer used. You can keep your car out of the weather. Also, the last tenant had cable TV and internet installed."

Kacey found a wall in the living room with cracks, chipped paint, and nail holes. "This is just the place I was looking for. I want to become your tenant, if you'll have me."

"Yes, Mr. Wilson. Welcome home. Let's go back downstairs and work things out. It will be good to have a man in the house again."

◊　◊　◊

Friday Evening
Crystal Lake, Illinois

Brady waited at the designated meeting place: the shopping center parking lot on Route 14 in Crystal Lake. He arrived at 6:00 p.m., and when Jolene showed up with the girls at 6:20 p.m., Brady helped transfer weekend bags to the back of the Trailblazer while Jolene stayed in her car to avoid contact. The air was cool in early spring, and Brady noticed the girls weren't wearing coats. He went over to Jolene's window. She rolled it down. "What is it?"

"I need the girls' coats."

"I guess they didn't remember to wear coats. Too late now." She rolled her window up and drove away.

Brady stood in the lot. *Why did this have to be so hard?* He wasn't the one ending the marriage. He could be a horse's ass, but he never wanted to break up the family. For the hundredth time, he searched himself for what he'd done wrong. After the answer didn't come, he got in, started the engine, and cranked up the heat. "Does anyone have jackets in their bags?" He turned the rearview mirror from face-to-face, watching three of his daughters shake their heads. He looked down at Crissy in the front seat next to him.

"No, Poppa. Momma said not to bring them."

"Shut up, Crissy," Britney said. "Remember what else Mom said?"

"She said to not talk about it. Oh…"

"Brilliant. I'm glad I'm not your blood relative."

"Please, no more of that." Brady put the car in gear. "We'll have to stop at the secondhand store and get some coats."

"What is a blood relative?" Crissy asked. "Is that like a vampire?"

The girls in the back seat giggled.

"Yes, but you're too little," Brady said. "We would still be thirsty after drinking your blood."

Crissy giggled.

Brady drove out of the parking lot to head back to the city. The girls talked in the back seat while Brady caught up with Crissy's adventures in first grade. Traffic was still heavy inbound, so Brady exited for the Goodwill in Niles.

"You were serious about buying used coats?" Ashley asked. "I'm not going to wear a scumbag's old jacket."

"I'll wait in the car," Britney said. "I'm not cold."

Laurie asked, "Do they have arts and crafts in there?"

"Everyone comes in," Brady said. "Let's go."

Britney said, "I just said I'm not going in, are you deaf or just stupid?"

The car got quiet. Brady turned the rearview mirror to look at Britney. "That was harsh."

"I'm sorry. Let's go look at the latest in homeless fashion."

"That's better." He put on a goofy look. "What! Homeless fashion? Ah, man."

The girls laughed. Britney smiled. Brady got out and rounded up everyone in a group before they headed into the store.

◊   ◊   ◊

Later that evening, Brady and the girls left the Indian Palace on Devon Avenue. Brady enjoyed the moment as each girl wore a jacket from Goodwill, modeling in the restaurant window. Jolene's attempt to screw with him had turned into a fun time.

On Devon Avenue, people from all over the world shopped in ethnic stores. They went into an Indian grocery to look at tea sets, inspect strange looking vegetables, and try crispy snacks with a spicy zing. Afterward, they piled into the Trailblazer and drove to his apartment. Inside, they trooped into the bedroom to set up for the weekend, hanging up their new coats, filling dresser drawers with clothing, setting purses, brushes, and makeup bottles in the top drawer. Brady enjoyed the operation standing in the doorway. After only a few weekends, the girls had settled into routines.

"Who thinks they can beat me in Golf?"

"It's already ten o'clock," Britney said. "I have to get these two in bed." She nodded at Crissy and Laurie.

"It's Friday night. If they start to go to sleep, we'll poke them with a fork."

Crissy and Laurie said, "Nooo…"

"No? Okay, but a steak knife could be dangerous."

"No, Dad," Crissy said. "You won't do that."

"Mom said to be strict, or you'll try to spoil us." Britney put her hands on her hips.

Brady rubbed his chin. "So what's wrong with that?"

"Right," Laurie said. "What's wrong with that?"

Britney sighed.

Brady led them to the kitchen table and brought over decks of cards from a kitchen drawer, along with a pad of paper and pencil. "Whoever wins gets out of garbage duty for the weekend."

Ashley said, "Now you're talking."

Brady kept them up until midnight, playing cards with chips and sodas. Britney loosened up but wouldn't talk about herself like the other girls. Later, Brady had no trouble getting everyone to bed. For the first time, Laurie demanded a night light in the room, so Brady brought the one in from the kitchen. He kissed them all, even Britney. The bunkbeds made the room like an army barracks. He listened at the door for a minute outside as the girls talked quietly on the other side, and then he headed to bed wondering about tomorrow and what more fun things he could come up with for the rest of the weekend.

◇　◇　◇

In the morning, Brady stayed in bed until 8:00 a.m., knowing the girls would sleep in. He headed to the bathroom before the line formed, washed up, and got dressed before waking the rest up. When he tried the door knob, it was locked. He jiggled and frowned and then tapped on the door with his knuckle. Rustling noises came from the other side, and maybe a low voice.

"Unlock the door, please." He tapped again.

The other side of the door got quiet. They weren't supposed to lock the door—he needed access to the little ones. He scratched his head and went to the kitchen. After getting along so well last night, he didn't want to start with trouble first thing in the morning, so he took out eggs and bacon to start breakfast, making coffee for himself. He set the table, filled up bowels and platters with food, and poured the juice.

Still no girls, but they had to come out eventually, even with their young bladders. He stood in the hallway with his hands on his hips, deciding whether or not to bang loudly and holler like a fool or stick a screwdriver in the lock. Instead, he found his phone and called Paul. Luckily, Paul had just driven away from his house and could detour toward the apartment. Brady kept his ear on the bedroom door while he waited. Crissy spoke out loud once and got shushed.

The intercom buzzed. Brady pushed the button to let Paul in and went back to the door to listen. Pairs of feet hit the floor with some whispering noises.

Paul came in from the hallway. "They still won't come out?"

Brady shook his head.

Paul made heavy footsteps, walking through the kitchen and raising his voice. "Well, you're right, Brady, the girls left all this food for me to eat. Since they need to sleep all day, I'll be glad to eat everything."

Crissy and Laurie giggled on the other side of the door and then stopped as if hands went over their mouths.

Brady raised his voice. "Oh no, you won't, Paul. You may be the girls' favorite, but I will eat half of their food, and then you can leave without visiting anyone but me."

The door handle wriggled once. A whispering argument could be heard, and then Crissy said, "They're going to eat my breakfast, and I want to see Uncle Paul."

Britney said, "Fine then, go."

The door opened, and three girls charged out to surround Paul. He laughed and patted their backs. Britney stayed in the bedroom.

"Girls, you can mug Paul after breakfast," Brady said. "Let's eat before the food gets cold."

Everyone went around the table to take a seat. Brady took Ashley's arm. "Fix a plate for Britney, and take it to her, okay?"

Ashley nodded. "Okay, Daddy."

◊　◊　◊

Sunday Evening
Seward, Kentucky

The old wooden dresser smelled like cedar, and it was clean, so Kacey filled the top drawer with his socks. The second drawer was for undershirts and shorts. Pants and shirts went down lower. The old furniture suited his tastes—plain, sturdy, and didn't belong to him. Nothing was picked out, cared for, or familiar.

On some level, he knew he should feel regret for his failed marriage, but he didn't, just like how Billie nagged him all the time about his emotional distance; she'd been right all along. The twinge of guilt sent him into the living room and in front of the wall, where a settling foundation had cracked the plaster, requiring patch jobs. Nail holes spotted the area, peeling paint revealed previous coats, and ripples of wallpaper glue were painted over. The convenience of having a wall like this right in the apartment would make life easier. He arranged the living room furniture with a chair in a proper viewing spot, sitting down to try it out, letting his gaze wonder.

Tomorrow, he would either return to work, or if Lambert terminated his employment, he would respond in his own special way, and she would pay a serious price. A shame, after he found such a great place to live.

Kacey sat for an hour at the wall and then went to bed, separated from his emotions.

◊　◊　◊

Monday Morning
Seward, Kentucky

Lambert walked into the reception area and up to Jill's desk. "Please arrange for Kacey Farrell to meet with me again."

Jill looked up with wide eyes. "Mr. Farrell is in your sitting room."

Lambert paused, looking down the hallway. "Is Jason here? Never mind… I'll see Mr. Farrell right away. For your information, we will retain Mr. Farrell's employment and only issue him a warning for his conduct."

Jill sighed. "Good."

Lambert marched toward her office, tired of spooky Kacey Farrell. During the drive in this morning, she decided to stop the intimidation. If she was stuck with him, then he would need to fall in line. In the sitting room, Kacey stood in front of her office door, staring with his hands folded behind his back. She stopped dead in her tracks with a grunt.

She recovered. "Mr. Farrell, how good to see you this morning. Allow me to unlock my office so we can discuss your future."

Kacey nodded, picked up his briefcase and stepped to the side. He followed her in and stood by a chair in front of her desk. She motioned for him to sit. "Straight off, I want to ease your mind by saying you will remain employed at Winslow-Carnac, despite violating your moral agreement. Mr. Whiteside suggested that a warning is enough."

Kacey took the briefcase off his knees and sat it on the floor beside the chair. "Thank you, Mrs. Lambert. I would like to return to work and catch up."

Lambert tilted her brow at Kacey. "Certainly… I don't want to pry into your affairs, Mr. Farrell, but we would be happy to find you some counseling. You're not a worker drone to us. We care about our people."

"Thank you, and I will let you know if I need help, but getting back to work would benefit me the most."

"Indeed. Please do so, and my door is always open for you."

"I'll keep that in mind." Kacey got up and walked out.

◊   ◊   ◊

Tuesday Morning
Chicago, Illinois

Judge Jurgons, in her late fifties with close-cut gray hair, turned to Jolene Witek on the witness stand. "Please continue."

Jolene testified to rumors of Brady having an affair, and Sydney shouted out an objection for hearsay. The judge upheld the objection. Next, Jolene's attorney, Franklin, asked about mental cruelty.

"Many times, Brady would raise his voice when he didn't get his way. He wanted dinner prepared a certain way, or the bathrooms cleaned a certain way. No bicycles should block the garage. When things went wrong, he would verbally abuse me and the children."

Franklin asked, "Were you ever afraid for your safety or the safety of the children?"

Brady sat forward, and Sydney put his hand on his arm.

"More and more... I worried that his temper would lead to something worse. Yes, I became concerned for our safety."

"Can you describe an incident where Mr. Witek lost his temper?"

"Last year, we decided to have a private Thanksgiving with just our family. We roasted a twelve-pound turkey and set a nice table. When it came time to serve, our youngest daughter got underfoot, causing our oldest daughter, Britney, to drop a bowlful of mashed potatoes. It went down Brady's pant leg, and he screamed at the girls to the point where dinner was ruined. I had to get between him and the girls for protection, and then he then yelled at me for raising an irresponsible child."

"Will you please explain the reason he said this?"

"Britney is not Brady's biological daughter."

Sydney stood up. "Objection, Your Honor, this is speculation."

"Your objection is noted," Jurgons said. "This isn't a criminal trial. I can sort things out."

Franklin said, "That's all I have, Your Honor."

Sydney walked in front of the witness stand. "Did you prepare the mashed potatoes, Mrs. Witek?"

Jolene looked at Franklin and then at Sydney. "Yes, I boiled the potatoes and mashed them up. Britney scooped them into a bowl and carried them to the table."

"Would you say the potatoes were hot from the stove?"

"Of course, they were."

"So when my client began to scream, did he immediately impugn the responsibility of his adopted daughter?"

Jolene frowned. "Well, no. He screamed in pain first."

"Did he ever say, in direct terms, that the incident was caused by your lack of parenting skills, or that he held resentment for his daughter Britney because she was not his biological daughter? And remember, you are under oath."

Jolene glanced at Franklin. "No, but I could sense it in his tone. He stormed out of the room and came back when we were already eating."

"Did his leg require treatment?"

"I put aloe on his leg."

"But then he returned to dinner, even with a burn on his leg?"

"Yes."

Sydney turned to the judge. "Nothing further, Your Honor."

"Would your client like to testify?"

"No, Your Honor."

Jurgons wriggled her fingers at the two tables. "Please approach. Come on up."

The two lawyers guided their clients so they were standing well away from each other.

Jurgons said, "Now that we've finished debating the great mashed potato accident, I'm ready to rule on the divorce decree." She turned to Brady. "Mr. Witek, you've not signed the papers. Has your counsel explained this will not stop the divorce from becoming final?"

"Yes, Your Honor. Can I ask a question?"

"Go ahead."

"Mrs. Witek stood before the Lord and swore to stay married to me till death do us part, and now you're going to end the marriage because of a bowl of mashed potatoes?"

The judge glared. "Starting up trouble with me will do you no good, Mr. Witek. Your marriage is about to end for many reasons, all of which you intimately understand."

"I object to that. I don't understand why I'm losing my family, and I sure as hell don't know why I'm the bad guy, but since you call the shots, then so be it. For the record, I don't agree to any of this."

The judge continued to glare at Brady and then at Sydney before she scanned the room and looked at the clock. "Okay… It's in the record. Now that you got to run your mouth, let's finish."

Sydney breathed.

The judge signed the paperwork. "The clerk will have the rest of the paperwork for the distribution of assets. Child support and custody will continue as currently set." She banged the gavel and pulled over paperwork for the next case.

The attorneys thanked the judge and led the clients away to different exits.

Brady said, "Let's get the paperwork. I need to find out how bad it's going to be."

◊ ◊ ◊

Tuesday Evening
Chicago, Illinois

Paul found Brady in the sandwich shop they frequented. It didn't seem to have a name, just a sign advertising Vienna Beef. Brady sat with a partially eaten combo of Italian beef and sausage, struggling to open his mouth wide enough for the next bite.

"That looks good. Let me get one, and I'll join you."

Brady grunted and nodded.

After a few minutes, Paul sat down with his own giant sandwich. "Don't forget you have plans on Friday night with Serena Haynesworth."

Brady grunted and nodded again.

"Good, get back in the saddle. Should I call you 'Brady the divorcee' now?"

Brady made a big swallow and washed it down with beer. "That you can. Never thought I'd be one of those guys."

Paul picked up his sandwich, considered it for a moment, opened his mouth like a crocodile, and bit off a huge bite. People at other tables paused to watch. He covered his mouth with a napkin while he got the bite under control.

"That's the spirit."

Paul bobbed his head and saluted around the restaurant.

Brady took a bite using his system of alternating angles. With his mouth full, Brady pointed at a green pepper on Paul's shirt and grunted. Kids laughed.

Paul grunted and flicked the pepper off his shirt. It landed on Brady's arm. Brady made a wild face and picked it off with a napkin. Kids laughed again.

"So, Paul"—Brady pounded his chest to swallow—"you should notice how I'm not drowning my sorrows in booze. Instead, I'm burying my sorrows in sandwich."

Paul stretched his neck and swallowed. "They hit you hard, eh?"

"Sydney warned me about getting divorced with four girls."

"Maybe Sydney is a lousy lawyer."

"No, he's good, or at least expensive, but I already knew how things were in Illinois."

"What about the student loan?"

Brady rubbed his forehead. "I can't believe I have to pay, Paul. Sydney tried to argue that the loan was taken out to benefit the marriage, and now that means nothing to me."

"But the judge ruled against you?"

"She said because Jolene got her master's degree two years ago, I did benefit. The fact that she still doesn't have a job doesn't matter. With four daughters, she can't handle the payments."

"You're going to have to suck it up." Paul watched Brady.

Brady sighed and shook his head. "We live in a new age, my friend. Everything is politics. It stopped being about right and wrong a long time ago. Jolene and I should be raising those girls together, but Illinois offered her an easy way out, and somehow, I've gotten what I deserve."

Paul contemplated his sandwich. "There are two sides to every story. I spoke with Jolene a number of times."

"Keep going. I want to hear this."

Paul looked up from the sandwich. "You have a temper, and you have a problem with authority figures."

"Fair enough, and I offered to go to counseling, but when she hooked up with the pretty boy, that was it."

"So why didn't you sign the divorce papers?"

"Breaking up the family was wrong, and I wasn't going to put my signature on it."

Paul glanced at Brady's sandwich. "Will that be enough to ease your pain?"

Brady lifted the sandwich. "No, this is way too much." He opened wide and took a huge bite, unable to close his mouth all the way.

Paul lifted his sandwich. "I'm here for you, pal." He growled and took a huge bite.

Everyone in the restaurant laughed.

Chapter 4

Wednesday Afternoon
Harwood Heights, Illinois

Spencer banged the door open to Brady's office and plopped down in the chair by his desk. "You need to quit screwing around and get your ass to work. This merger is a load of work, and I can't do everything myself."

Brady kept typing on his keyboard. "But I enjoy going to court so the judge can flush my life down the drain."

"Hah. Why did you get married in the first place? All you did was give the custody of your nut sack to some broad."

"What do you want?"

"I need a status on the merger. Bigham won't return my calls."

Brady cracked his knuckles and leaned back. "I'm starting with their payroll system. Bigham is doing the inventory. What are you doing?"

"I'm in charge, remember? I'm going to set up VPN tunnels to remote in to the Jenkin's systems."

"That should take like five minutes. I need help with the accounting servers."

Spencer stood up. "You do payroll, taxes, purchasing, sales, and I'll keep track of the progress."

"You can't dump all that on me."

Spencer left, banging the door closed. Brady went back to writing scripts. The merger was a new thing, not an everyday responsibility, but if he missed a deadline, employees wouldn't get paid. The pressure was on.

His intercom buzzed.

Lexi said, "Hey, Brady. Heard your divorce is final. Does this mean you'll sexually harass the secretaries even more?"

Brady's mouth dropped open. "Are you recording this?"

"No." She giggled. "Maybe I should."

"Then let's get a drink at Ernie's after work."

"Sorry, I'm busy." Lexi hung up.

Brady chuckled.

Sherry tapped on the door and came in. "May I?"

Brady waved at the chair.

"I had to decide which half of the Jenkins people to let go."

"That sucks." Brady turned in his chair. "But you have to keep Bigham. Tell me he gets to stay."

Sherry made a weak smile and shook her head.

Brady slapped the arm of his chair. "Ouch! Does he know yet?"

Sherry shook her head again. "And you don't know either. We'll tell him after the merger is done."

Brady slumped in his chair. "If there's anything you can do to keep the guy on, please do. Otherwise, my workload will double, and I haven't gotten a raise in years."

"I know you haven't. We may hire an entry level guy to work at the Jenkin's warehouse in Terre Haute."

Brady noticed Spenser in the doorway from the corner of his eye. "Why don't we keep Bigham and get rid of Spencer?"

Spencer flipped him off.

Sherry watched him leave and clapped in delight.

◊ ◊ ◊

Friday Evening
Roger's Park Neighborhood
Chicago, Illinois

Brady pulled hamburger wrappers and empty soda cans out from under the seats in the Trailblazer to prep for his blind date. He drove toward Lake Michigan on Lawrence and found a parking place near Starbucks. Inside, he searched for a woman he'd never seen before, wondering how this would work, gave up, and ordered black coffee. When he sat down, he paid attention to a table with a woman sitting alone, but she wouldn't make eye contact.

A deacon at the church had asked if Paul could find a date for his daughter. Paul was uncomfortable with the request, but the deacon, Winston Haynesworth, donated large sums of money to the church, so Paul asked Brady to help him out. Brady should have asked Paul to e-mail him a picture of Serena Haynesworth.

When he went to google her on his phone, he felt eyes on him. The woman sitting alone was checking him out. He looked over and smiled. She wiggled her fingers at him for a green light. Brady picked up his coffee and went over.

The woman said, "Sit down. It's Friday night. People need to socialize."

"I agree." She looked great—maybe Paul did him a favor. "I haven't been out for a while. The judge just cut me loose this week." He realized he still had his wedding ring on, gave the lady a guilty smile, and pulled it off. "Forgot to take this thing off."

She laughed and clapped her hands. "You know what, I really believe you. No one can fake an expression like that."

"Thanks, you're a good sport."

"Keep that move for the future. You look cute when you're embarrassed."

"Good advice… You're not what I expected."

"How is that?"

"I thought I was doing someone a favor, being here tonight, but you're awesome. I'm Brady." He held out his hand.

The lady frowned and shook his hand. "Right, I'm Allison."

The bell over the door rang, and a middle-aged woman walked in, dressed in a loose black outfit, with voluminous frizzy hair. Her tanned face had lines, making her handsome. She recognized Brady and walked up to the table. "Hello, Brady, I'm Serena." She shook his hand. "Who's your friend?"

Allison got off the stool with her drink. "Please take the table. I'm…late for an engagement." She smiled at Brady and left the coffee shop.

Serena took the stool. "Nervous girl… Do you know her?"

"Well, I didn't know what you looked like, and she checked me out, so I assumed she was you."

"Oh… Funny. She was very attractive. Interesting…"

"It was a simple mistake, and now the correct attractive girl has arrived."

Serena gazed at him for a moment. "Aren't you going to buy me coffee?"

Brady jumped off the stool. "Oh, sure. What can I get you?" He felt stupid for sounding like a waiter.

"Get me a soy caramel latte extra foam and a dash of cinnamon. Put a couple of ice chips in first."

Brady paused. "Caramel foam latte with extra cinnamon."

Serena sighed. "No. Now listen this time." She repeated.

Brady went to the front counter, muttering to himself. The barista took his order. He thought he got it right; otherwise, he planned to tell her to just drink the damn thing. He brought the drink back to the table.

She took a sip. "Are you sure this is soy?"

Brady shrugged.

"They can't seem to do anything right in here." She took the drink back to the front counter.

Brady checked his watch, drank down the rest of his coffee, and took the cup to the garbage. Serena sat on her stool sipping her drink when he returned. She got foam on her upper lip, maybe on purpose, but he didn't comment.

"Tell me about yourself," Brady said.

"You first."

"Okay, I work in the IT Department for Polyglomerate Container. I have four girls, ages six to sixteen, and my divorce was just finalized. I stay in Rodger's Park."

"Four girls, eh? That's a lot of estrogen to deal with. Do they live with the mother?"

"Yes."

"So about me…I live in the guesthouse of my father's home. He's forgetful and needs me around to keep track of him. We love to attend the Chicago Symphony—we have season passes. My favorite car is Bentley, but I'm driving an Alpha Romeo. The company is making a comeback in the states. I'm a huge fan of Hillary Clinton, but don't worry, I won't go on and on about her record. She has time for a comeback. Nothing bores me more than these young millennials and their 'Oh, woe is me' attitude. Now that I'm in my forties, I can appreciate an adult point of view. Why is everyone bothered by Obamacare? They should get a cheaper smartphone and pay the premiums. Maybe they don't need the latest Xbox—maybe they need to get a checkup first. Sure, my father pays for our health care, but it doesn't cost that much. This outfit is from Kohl's by the way. I've been slumming for a while after my last court experience. Don't get me started about that. Everyone is so into suing people for the dumbest reasons. A guy thinks I'm pestering him, so I need to call my attorney? Maybe there are no real men left on the planet. Are you a real man, Brady?"

"Huh? I'm not sure. What was the question again?"

"Never mind. You're polite, and that's a good start. And you have your shirt tucked in. That sends a message these days. Talk about the fall of society. No one even wears a tie to funerals anymore. My friends say I make the effort to look good. I mean, we try to look good for each other, and when someone dresses like a slouch, it's like they're telling the rest of us that they just don't give a damn. And don't get me started about punctuation. Texting led to the end of being able to read what the hell people are trying to tell you. Messages are one big glob of words. We could read what they're saying in half the time if they remembered what a period or a comma is. And no one capitalizes anymore, not even their own name. Do you capitalize your name, Brady?"

"Yes. I agree—"

"And where did holding a door open for someone go. I'm not saying women should be treated like the weaker sex, but having the door whack you in the nose is ridiculous. People are making a statement by letting the door slam. They can't figure out there're other people around them. Just the other day, I flagged a taxi, and a guy tried to jump into the car ahead of me. What are we supposed to do now, rent the bikes for an hour in the pouring rain? Driving is no good when you have to pay six dollars an hour to park."

Brady looked at his watch.

"What, am I boring you?"

Brady looked up. "No, you just reminded me of parking. How about we continue our conversation at the burger joint down the street?"

"Do they serve tofu burgers? I can't stand the thought of eating flesh. Flesh! But fish is okay. Maybe they serve a salmon burger. Fish just don't have the personality of a cow. Chickens should be left alone, and pigs are cute, but they let off too much methane. All fish do is swim around and eat each other. We can ask the manager if—"

"We should be able to find something for you." Brady got off his stool and stood sideways, suggesting she walk out of the coffee shop with him.

Serena looked down at her drink. "I just have a few more sips, and then we can skedaddle." She put the straw in her mouth.

Brady sat back down.

"Now, let me tell you about my Hillary Clinton memorabilia collection."

◇   ◇   ◇

After dinner, Brady made sure to open the door for Serena when they left Joe's Burger Joint. "Are you sure you don't want an ice cream cone or something? I'm sorry they didn't have fish."

They went down the sidewalk back toward the Starbucks.

"I had plenty to eat, what with the salad and the fruit bowl, but I better take a Gas-Ex pill later, if you know what I mean," Serena said.

"Where are you parked? I'll walk you over."

"Is the date over? I thought we were just getting started."

"I'm not a kid anymore." Brady faked a yawn. "Let's call it a night."

"Oh, well, I'll try to get a cab. I didn't drive tonight."

Brady took a few more steps before responding. "Let me drive you. I'm parked up ahead in the street."

Serena elbowed him in the ribs. "Okay, sly one."

Brady frowned and opened the passenger door to his Trailblazer. Serena paused to pick at the rust around the fender and then grabbed the handle above the door to swing herself in. Brady watched cabs go by, but it was too late now. He went around and got in. "Tell me where we're going." He pulled into traffic.

"Oh, I'm sure you know where you're going." She winked.

"Ah, Serena… We attend the same church. A pastor arranged this date."

Serena crossed her arms. "Seriously? You're a prude? It's a wonder you have so many kids."

A bus stop was up ahead, but he couldn't just drop her off. He drove over the river and turned north on McCormick.

Serena said, "Hey, we could walk on the walking path. Turn here into the park."

Brady drove past the entrance to the park.

"So I guess the night is over. Sorry to disappoint you."

The silence in the car became uncomfortable. "Please don't feel that way. I'm going through a merger at work, my divorce just became final, and my daughters are giving me a hard time. I'm out of energy tonight, but I appreciate your company."

Serena stayed quiet.

"I need to know where to drop you off."

Serena gave him her address but didn't offer any directions, so he pulled over and put the address in his phone. The female voice on the phone told him where to turn and filled in for the lack of conversation in the car. When they pulled up in front of the mansion, he got out to open the door for Serena, but she jumped out and met him in front of the Trailblazer's headlights, putting her arms over his shoulders. She pulled his head forward and planted her lips on his mouth, inserting her tongue.

Brady pulled away. "That was a surprise. Good night."

Serena grabbed his arm when he tried to go back to the driver's door. "I'm sure you want to have a drink with me inside. You can get a tour of this big mansion." She caressed his arm. "You can see what my bedroom looks like."

Brady tried to respond when a miracle took place—his phone rang. "Just a sec." He answered, and Spencer was on the line. Brady said, "Hello, dear."

"Hi, sweetheart. You need to work tomorrow, and I don't care if it's Saturday. If we don't stay caught up on the merger, you'll be working every weekend."

"Did you tell Mom? She can put a cloth on it to stop the bleeding."

"Are you talking to me?"

"When will she get back from the store?"

"Who's at the store?"

"You have to be brave, honey. I'll be there soon. Stop crying."

"Brady, are you fucking with me again? You're coming to work tomorrow."

"Have your sister put a wet towel on it, and I'll be right there. Bye-bye."

"Brady, you stupid ass—"

Brady hung up and turned to Serena. "I have a problem with one of the girls. I need to go."

Serena held out her hand. "Can I see your phone, please?"

Brady sidestepped over to the car door and yanked it open. "My daughter needs me. Thanks for the nice time, Serena." He jumped in the car and put it in gear.

Serena came up to the window and yelled. "It was a magical night, Brady. I'll always remember!"

Brady sped away, leaving Serena in the middle of the street. In a few blocks, he pulled over to call Spencer back.

Spencer answered. "What's wrong with you, nutjob? Did you lose it?"

"Are you working tomorrow?"

"No. You need to catch up, not me."

"You're the head of the department. If you're not going to be there, I sure as hell won't be."

Spencer hesitated. "We know the judge won't reduce your child support payments if you quit. You have to legitimately get fired. So knock off the bullshit."

"You better hope the quality of my work doesn't decline."

"I can move you to the office by the toilets. Hell, there are a number of things I can do."

"I'll be in the office tomorrow, but if you're not there, I'm informing Mark, and then I'm going home." Brady hung up. Now he really did need to get home early. He dialed Paul's number.

Paul answered. "Yo, Brady. How did the date go?"

"You owe me, big-time."

"Ouch."

◇　◇　◇

Saturday Morning
Harwood Heights, Illinois

No yellow Corvettes were parked in the lot when Brady arrived at work on Saturday morning, so he considered just going home, but Mark's Lincoln Navigator was there, so he went in and headed straight to Mark's office. Mark looked up. "Witek, glad you came in."

"Spencer is head of IT, why isn't he here?"

Mark set down his pen. "He said he would be in soon. Just focus on the merger. You have plenty of work to do."

Brady's face grew hot. He took a couple of deep breaths and turned to walk out.

"Hold on, Witek. You look ready to blow a fuse. Just focus on your own work. I'm in charge of Spencer."

"Why don't you let me say a few things?"

Mark leaned back in his chair and put his hands behind his head. "Speak, but don't cross any lines."

Brady sat in front of his desk. "Spencer said you guys know I can't quit because of my child support. He threatened to make my life miserable."

Mark leaned forward. "That fucker." He shook his head. "Spencer doesn't speak for me."

"Then fire him. He's useless anyway."

"There, that's the problem. You don't respect authority."

"Respect needs to be earned."

"Of course, it does. Do you respect me?"

Brady paused.

"Your hesitation is answer enough." He picked up his pen and slid around some documents. "We need to focus on the merger right now. It's vitally important."

Brady frowned, took more deep breaths, but couldn't cool off. "So you and Spencer really need to keep the bucks rolling in. Good for you."

Mark's eyes went wide.

Brady continued. "For me, the merger is just a lot of extra work. Seems like my pay won't be affected."

Mark flipped his pen on the floor and glared at Brady. Brady glared back, focused with anger. After a long stretch, Mark's face softened, and his breathing slowed down. "You don't hold back, do you Witek? But then again, if I had to give forty percent of my pay to the broad who walked out on me, I would try to get fired too. I'm right, aren't I?"

"No, you're not. Not only did I show up to work on Saturday, but I actually do the job right."

"I'm not going to give you more money—no one gets a raise right now. And if you could find a better job, you would have."

Brady laughed. "I guess you're right, big guy. And if the money is so tight, then make some cuts. Spencer makes twice what Bigham does and accomplishes half as much."

Mark chuckled and rubbed his eyes. "Shit, get out of here, Witek." He got up to find his pen. "Go catch up on your work, and I'll have lunch brought in. Go."

"Don't order lunch if Spencer doesn't show up, because I plan to leave." Brady went to his office and plugged in the fan on top of the wall to make sure Spencer's office was toasty when he came in.

As he sat down to work, he considered how everyone gave him shit lately, yet he still had to live paycheck to paycheck. That was before making payments on the student loan. Something had to give. He'd promised himself he would never pay for it, but now what? Guys went off the grid in movies and had a lot of fun, but he'd probably end up sleeping outside and eating garbage. Then again, the checks in the safety deposit box could go a long way if he lived the simple life. Maybe he really could leave all this crap behind.

But then there was his new faith in God. Leaving his responsibilities was probably a sin, but then on the other hand, doing all the work so other people could benefit didn't sound right either. His family now lived with a rich guy, his bosses made a bundle, the rent on his apartment was sky high, and he helped support his brother's wife and kid.

And now the student loan…

Spencer's office door slammed.

Brady checked his watch; the guy just made it.

◊　◊　◊

Monday Lunchtime
Seward, Kentucky

Down in the basement of the office building, Kacey Farrell carried his lunch in a brown paper bag down a hallway, around the boiler room, and into a large room used for document storage. He'd arranged some of the shelves to keep one wall open, one with plenty of cracks, water stains, and ripples from concrete forms. He sat in a metal chair twenty-feet from the wall, took a sandwich from the bag, and let his eyes wander as he ate.

His job at Winslow-Carnac would end soon. It was inevitable. Lambert was afraid of him, and no one wanted to live in fear. He was still here only because he kept the systems running, same as in the military. When he turned bad guys into dead guys better than anyone else, the officers left him alone.

His eyes followed a seam in the wall and diverted to a crack with a trickle of water. Finding a new job would be difficult. He had trouble appearing normal in interviews. Fitting in with new coworkers drained him. He needed a plan.

Voices echoed down the hallway, probably maintenance staff. Kacey finished the last bites of his sandwich and went back up to his office.

◊　◊　◊

Monday Afternoon
Harwood Heights, Illinois

Brady used remote access to observe Bigham's computer in Terre Haute as they spoke on the phone and collaborated on the screen. He heard a beep in his earpiece—another call coming in. He ignored it to concentrate on the project.

Bigham stopped scripting. "So how long do you think I have?"

"How long for what?"

"Don't play stupid."

"I don't know your status, man."

"I'll try to stay to the end to partake of the unemployment insurance."

"Understood, but if they didn't tell me about the merger." That was all he would say—he didn't want to lie.

"All right, we've done enough for today. Why don't we hook up again tomorrow?"

"Sounds good. Later." They hung up.

Brady went to the phone log and dialed the missed call.

Serena Haynesworth answered. "Hi there, sexy, do you miss me? I guess I didn't rank high enough for you to answer the first time."

"How did you get this number?"

"Ancient Chinese secret." She laughed too hard.

"Sorry, Serena, but I'm really busy today. I need to go."

"Don't brush me off, Brady. You can't just throw me away. I deserve a little respect."

Brady pulled his Bluetooth out of his ear as her voice got loud, sticking it back in when he heard his name over and over. "The boss is calling. Goodbye." He hung up.

His phone rang—Serena's number. He disconnected, blocked her number, and headed to the hallway. Insulting Spencer would calm him down.

◇　◇　◇

Monday Evening
Roger's Park Neighborhood
Chicago, Illinois

Brady arrived at Cindy's building at 6:30 p.m., and she buzzed him up. Inside, a teenage babysitter held Lane's hand. She would take care of Lane while Brady took Cindy out for dinner. Brady took Cindy's hand while they walked; she let him, and it felt nice. They walked down to the restaurant called Repita Pita. Cindy liked the saffron rice, and Brady liked to make a pita sandwich. Cindy sat next to Brady on the same side of the table where they shared an order of stuffed grape leaves. The red sauce made Brady's head sweat. They didn't speak during the meal, comfortable in the silence. Brady bought an order of baklava for Cindy.

She didn't seem to put on weight, even with all the carbs. Brady noticed her hair was different, shaved on one side—it made her look younger. When Cindy finished dessert, she took Brady's arm in her hands and leaned against him. "Thanks for getting me out of the apartment. Dinner was good."

Brady held off a burp with his fist. "You can't beat a pita. And then you repeat a pita."

"We can repeat a pita anytime you want." Cindy sat up straight. "I need to tell you something. Are you ready?"

Brady turned.

"The divorce is set to go through."

"How can you afford a lawyer?"

"I'm not using one. The judge had me take an ad out in the paper. Tom never came forward, so the divorce will happen."

Brady shook his head. "He used to be a good person."

Cindy looked at him for a moment. "It doesn't matter he's your brother. You've been great."

Brady took her hand in both of his. "How weird would it be for you to have a relationship with your ex-husband's brother?"

"Weird, but let's keep hanging out and see where it goes. Maybe I won't have to change my last name on my driver's license."

"There you go, always looking on the bright side."

She looked down at his hands. "Lane will warm up to you eventually. He's scared he'll never see his dad again with you around."

"I understand. We'll spend more time together."

Cindy sipped some water.

Brady asked, "Want to walk on Devon?"

"Let's go."

◊　◊　◊

Thursday Afternoon
Seward, Kentucky

Kacey spent half his workday in the server room located on the second floor of the Winslow-Carnac building, down and around the hallway from his office. A hard drive had died in a server this morning, and the team worked on a hot swap.

His supervisor, Vijay, and coworkers Jen and Rich stood back as the server rebuilt information before running full speed. Kacey fixed his eyes on the blinking orange light. The human beings in the room had simply removed the new drive from the plastic container and inserted it in the slot. The server did the complicated restoration on its own. Most companies no longer had server rooms after moving their systems to the cloud. Server farms handled the hardware, safe from fires, weather, and intruders.

Human beings still had jobs coding and configuring, but artificial intelligence programs were on the way to take over even those duties. Human beings—with their bad attitudes, health care costs, retirement costs, and most importantly, their tendency to make mistakes—will be out.

Winslow-Carnac had decided to move systems to the cloud, and he was assigned tasks to make it happen, but he didn't plan to just sit idly by, knowing the big picture.

The flashing orange light turned green, interrupting Kacey's thoughts. Vijay said, "Good to go. Jen, will you please order another drive?"

"Will do, boss."

Vijay turned to Kacey. "I read your memo about the database conversion. I agree we need to update to the latest version of MySQL, but won't that cause downtime? It could take more than a day."

"Yes, with our server. When we go to the cloud, we can pay for more bandwidth and complete the conversion in as little as three hours."

"Good idea." Vijay went to leave and turned back. "Hey, Kacey, are you feeling okay? Lambert didn't tell us why you missed a week."

"I had a family issue."

"Got it. Let me know if you need anything." Vijay headed to his office. The others split up for their desks.

Kacey headed back to his office in the front of the building, thinking it ironic for Vijay to offer him good tidings. With the plan he had in mind, Vijay would not be as gracious in the future.

◇   ◇   ◇

Friday Evening
McHenry County, Illinois

Brady drove north on Route 31 to Crystal Lake, driving north from the Jane Adams Expressway through a sparsely populated area near the Fox River. Boats and RVs were for sale in several lots along the way. Traffic backed up as people headed to their weekend playgrounds, causing Brady to come to a stop next to a gravel lot with RVs for sale. As he gazed down the line of vehicles, one caught his attention—an RV with a front end like a van, a Type C if he remembered correctly. It was plain but sturdy looking with flat white paint and one gray fender. He wondered what it looked like inside, and then shook his head. He couldn't just drive away and leave the girls, despite all the trouble lately, and then there were Cindy and Lane.

The car behind him honked when traffic started moving. Brady accelerated, anxious to pick up the girls for the weekend.

◊   ◊   ◊

Friday night
Seward, Kentucky

Kacey didn't want Bea to notice how much time he spent in the storage room at the back of the house, so he spread out a Persian rug he found in the stored items to deaden the sound of his footsteps.

At seventy-six years old, Bea was consolidating her belongings, clearing out most of the clutter. Many of the closets in the house were empty, as well as most of the bedrooms, but Bea could be found sweeping the floors anyway. Kacey put himself in Bea's perspective, considering how open spaces in a big house would create a little world to move around in.

When he first entered the storage room upstairs, junk was still stored in there. Bea asked him to describe what he found and place old pieces of furniture, clothing, and assorted items out for the Disabled Veteran's charity. He kept a dresser, a desk and chair, picture frames, and the rug. The walls were exposed wooden studs, which were acceptable, but not suitable for his meditations.

Tonight, he walked softly across the hall to the workroom and lifted the back window for a nice breeze. A doorway led outside to a narrow landing leading to the external stairway on the back of the house. He stepped out for a brief look around the grounds. All was quiet, except for the crickets in the wooded area.

He went back in to the desk and booted his computer, now connected to the internet. Find another job and start over? Negative. He'd had enough of regular civilian life. The time had arrived for a big change, and that required money. Fortunately for him, Winslow-Carnac had plenty of money, and they'd put him in charge of it.

Using remote access, he logged into the company server and began coding. His goal was to transfer funds from Winslow-Carnac, after which, he would make the money and himself disappear.

Chapter 5

Saturday Morning
Roger's Park Neighborhood
Chicago, Illinois

Time ran out for Brady while Ashley and Britney occupied the bathroom. He danced into the kitchen, badly needing to pee, and glanced at the kitchen sink. He couldn't do that, and he could get arrested for peeing in the alley, so he dug down in the garbage and found an empty coffee can, took it into his bedroom, and set the can in his desk chair to fill, sighing with relief. When he finished, he leaned in for a shake and then hid the can under the desk. Back in the kitchen, he washed his hands and sat down with Crissy and Laurie at the table.

Laurie asked, "What did you do with the coffee can, Daddy?"

"I put some pencils in it."

Crissy and Laurie colored with crayons. Brady read the sports page from the *Tribune*. He planned to take the girls secondhand shopping, giving each girl ten dollars to spend. After twenty minutes went by, he put down the paper. "Crissy, what's taking them so long?"

"It could be fingernails. It could be hair. It could be makeup."

"Britney has something happen to her once a month, just like Mommy does," Laurie said. "I'm not sure what it is, but it will happen to me someday."

Brady picked up the paper. "Got it."

Ten more minutes went by, and Brady went to the bathroom door and tapped. "Come on, guys. We're going shopping."

Britney yelled through the door, "Go away!"

"Are you okay in there? Ashley, is she okay?"

Ashley yelled, "Leave us alone!"

"I can unlock this door." No sounds, only silence.

He went to the kitchen drawer and brought back a screwdriver. "Ready or not." He went to stick the screwdriver in the lock, but a click came from the handle, and the door burst open, smacking him in the face. He staggered back into the kitchen.

Ashley followed. "We didn't mean to hurt you, Daddy. Are you okay?"

"I think so. Can you get me a Band-Aid?" Blood dripped from a cut to his eyebrow.

Ashley went to get the first-aid kit. Brady put a napkin on his forehead and went to look for Britney in the bedroom, but the door was locked. He used the screwdriver to open. Britney stood by her dresser wearing panties only. She covered her breasts. "Get out!"

Brady turned and shut the door. Blood ran down his cheek as he returned to the kitchen.

"Sit down, Poppa," Ashley said. "Let me fix your eye."

He obeyed and let her work. She applied ointment to the cut.

Crissy asked, "What's wrong with Britney, Poppa?"

"I don't know. I just don't know."

◊　◊　◊

Sunday Morning
Chicago, Illinois

Brady had gotten things under control yesterday morning and salvaged the day by shopping. The girls demanded to eat at a restaurant with a salad bar so they wouldn't get fat. After shopping in four different secondhand stores in the afternoon, they went home for pizza and a movie, where they forgot about getting fat, enjoying the pizza. Today they attended church—Sunday school, morning service, and then youth groups. Paul worked with the young people.

Brady still had issues to deal with. Britney had mostly stopped talking to him—no mystery as for why, and Serena could be at church today, so he intended to lie low.

Paul spotted him in the hallway. "Yo! Brady."

Brady stopped and bumped his fist.

"Are the girls with you this weekend? What's with the eye?"

"They're all in Sunday school." He touched the Band-Aid. "I literally ran into a door. But right now, I'm going across the street for coffee."

"No Sunday school for you, eh?"

"No. Have you seen you-know-who around?"

"Serena? Yes. Go get that coffee. She's looking for you."

"Oh boy. See you later."

Paul sped off to teach his class, and Brady went to hide from Serena in the restaurant.

In the morning service, the minister gave an interesting message about how God punished your sin by causing you to run back to Him for help. Before he came to know the Lord, he thought Christians were prudes and just wanted to keep everyone else from having fun. Now, as he built a relationship with his Savior, he had a new outlook on life, a more positive point of view. Christ was God of the planet, and a guy like himself could get to know Him, incredible.

At the end of the service, Brady led the girls through the line to shake the minister's hand before they made their way to the dining hall for coffee. Crissy needed supervision at the cookie tray. Britney joined a group of teenagers clustered by the stage. Ashley spotted a group her age. Crissy and Laurie always stayed with him. Brady found a table shared with another family with young kids.

As he visited with the girls, hands clamped down on his shoulders, causing him to drop his coffee cup. Coffee ran across the table and dribbled down on Laurie's dress. She gasped and fell backward. The father of the other family twisted around to catch her before she hit the floor. When he sat her back up, she had a big brown stain on her light-blue dress. Brady bent over the table and pulled the fabric away from her skin. "Did it burn you?"

"I'm okay, Daddy, but I need to change clothes."

"We'll go in a minute." Brady turned around, thinking Paul stood behind him, but found Serena instead.

"Hey there, butterfingers. Remember me?"

Brady leaned back. "You just made me spill hot coffee on my daughter."

"Oh, is this your daughter? She's so cute." Serena headed around the end of the table.

Brady caught the eyes of the other father across the table. The father climbed out of the bench and blocked Serena from coming up behind Laurie. "Ma'am, we need to clean her up a bit. Give us a moment."

Serena turned to Crissy. "This must be your youngest, Brady. She's adorable."

"Please don't—"

Serena picked up Crissy under her arms, causing Crissy's plate of cookies to fall on the floor. Crissy began to cry. Serena set her feet down on the bench and strode out of the dining hall. Brady reached over and held Crissy to calm her down. After a few minutes, he took her back to the cookie tray for a rebuild. When he got her back situated at the table, he offered his hand to the other father. "I'm Brady, thanks for the assistance."

The father shook his hand. "I'm Bob, happy to be there for you."

◊　◊　◊

Sunday Afternoon
Crystal Lake, Illinois

On Friday, the seller accepted the bid, and the closing was set for next week. Aaron drove Jolene down Aspen street to savor their new house as Jolene bubbled with excitement. She squeezed his bicep. "We got a great new house. Aren't you happy?"

"The house is great. The bidding war was not so great."

She popped the door handle. "Let's walk around the yard. Come on."

The spring grass was professionally maintained to golf course quality. They admired the stone walls of the house. The pool glimmered bright blue in the sun. They sat together on a bench built into the deck around a fire pit.

Aaron turned to Jolene. "The bank called me on Friday. The loan will go through, but I'll have to drain all my accounts for the down payment."

Jolene shook her head. "Is that what you're worrying about? Relax, we've got this. I start work next week. Support payments are coming in. We're going to be fine."

"I now have two mortgages. The Tan Tax is killing me at the gym. We may have to dump the tanning beds."

"I understand, baby, but you're an important person in this town, and you got that way by taking risks."

"What about you and me? We just bought a house together, and we aren't married."

Jolene paused. "I'm not pressuring you into anything."

"Yeah, you been great. After what happened with my last wife, I just don't want to get married again."

"I know, baby, my marriage fell apart too. We're two broken people, lucky to find each other in this cruel world. Now, you, me, and the girls are going to start over, and we're going to enjoy the good life together."

Aaron wobbled his head and grinned, despite himself.

Jolene pinched his chin. "Now that's what I wanted to see."

◊　◊　◊

Sunday Evening
Seward, Kentucky

Once he stole the money, the name Kacey Farrell would go on the most-wanted list, meaning he would need a new identity, so Kacey logged into the Dark Web, considering how his intuition had paid off. Because he hadn't used his real name, he could remain John Wilson and continue to live right here in Bea's house after the crime. Bea would tell the police a fifty-seven-year-old John Wilson lived upstairs. She couldn't describe him, and if he were not around when they searched, they would likely believe Bea's account and move on. He would leave pictures of an older guy in the apartment to seal the deal.

Bea had trusted him too much. Besides a rental agreement, she required no other paperwork—no references, no identification. He'd simply signed the agreement, gave her a deposit of five hundred dollars cash, and she never thought twice. But now he needed John Wilson documentation if the police checked further. Twenty years ago, a new identity was easy: you only had to assume the life of a dead person by tracking down social security numbers, billing information, and applying for a new driver's license.

Currently, three quarters of the states had joined the Electronic Death Registration System, but New York had not yet joined, and finding a dead John Wilson of the correct race and age should still be possible.

The Dark Web used Tor browser to defeat tracking measures. Kacey took the extra step of connecting through a proxy server in Russia. The connection was slow, but it would be impossible to trace back to Bea's house. He opened the IceRocket search engine to search for Doxing sites. Getyourman.onion looked okay.

The Get-Your-Man site had no graphics, only a white screen with a black box and instructions on how to make a request for their service. Kacey typed information into the black box and uploaded a picture, listing a new Gmail address for reply. When he submitted, the information disappeared from the box, and a message in red letters said, "Thank you for the request. You will receive communication within five days."

He closed Tor and cut the proxy connection, needing to work more on the theft. The plan was coming together: hidden scripts in the accounting server would alter payment transfers, redirecting money to his bank account while correctly logging the transfer to a vendor. As with most embezzlement schemes, he was a trusted insider. But the amount he would steal was large and would be noticed quickly, requiring a diversion for escape.

◊   ◊   ◊

Sunday Evening
Roger's Park neighborhood
Chicago, Illinois

The girls were back in Crystal Lake, and Brady's thoughts drifted to the road while he sat at his desk at home. If he left town, the name Brady Witek could easily be tracked, and Illinois put guys in jail after missing several child support payments, but if pretty boy Aaron got to have his family, then he could pay their bills.

Research showed Wisconsin had not joined the Electronic Death Registration System, so he researched how to use the Dark Web to acquire a new identity. Being in the IT field, he knew about security, and if he purchased a used computer on eBay and connected to a public Wi-Fi, authorities would not be able to track his activities.

As he logged into eBay to shop, he still didn't really believe he would go through with it, but then he couldn't stop working on it either. Dreams of the open road kept popping into his head while he found and purchased a used laptop before going to bed.

In the morning, a swishing sound came from the other side of the door while Brady got ready for work. He pulled the door open. His landlord gasped and put her hand on her chest in the hallway.

"Good morning, Mrs. Fitzgibbons, can I help you?"

She pointed at a plastic bag hanging on the doorknob. "Your new contract is ready. Just sign it and put it in the slot."

Brady unhooked the plastic bag and took out the contract. The monthly payment was increased by three hundred dollars. "You've got to be kidding. I can't afford this."

Mrs. Fitzgibbons put her hands on her hips. "You can thank the mayor, sugar. Property taxes went up again."

"Please give me a break. I pay child support for four girls."

"This is a business, not a charity. Sign the contract and put it in the slot."

Brady tossed the contract on the kitchen counter. "Hold on, can you keep the current contract going for a little while?"

"Sure, there's a clause where you can add a three-month extension, but the rent will still go up, and there will be a thousand-dollar fee."

"That's highway robbery."

"You signed the contract, honey. Maybe you should read before you sign this time."

Brady sighed. "Good day, Mrs. Fitzgibbons."

"Sign it and put it in the slot." She walked down the hall.

Brady rubbed his eyes. He had ten days before he had to sign for another year, and the extra three hundred per month would hurt badly. He'd need to disconnect the cable. No more air conditioning at night. When it got cold, he'd have to wear long johns. No more eating out.

The checks in the safety deposit box were his last hope, but if he lived off the money, hope would run out. The math didn't lie. More money would go out than came in, and then what?

His current salary was actually pretty decent before it was split up and handed out, but now he'd have to find a better paying job. Or as a last resort, he might have to flip burgers at night.

He leaned on the counter with his head down. Everyone took from him, but he no longer had enough to give. And according to his watch, he would be late for work.

He left the apartment at a fast pace.

◊　◊　◊

Monday Morning
Harwood Heights, Illinois

Spencer followed Brady to his office, berating him for being late. Brady tried to shut the door on him, but he pushed his way in.

"You need to step it up, shithead. Mark doesn't like how the merger is going, and we're running out of money."

Brady set down his briefcase. "So try doing some work for a change."

"I came in on Saturday."

"And did what? Catch up on your pornography?"

Spencer shook his head. "You won't get to talk like that forever."

Mark walked up to the doorway.

"Then fire me." Brady poked him with a finger. "I've been insubordinate."

Mark cleared his throat. "Spencer, go to your office. Witek, get back to work."

Spencer left. Brady spoke up. "Just a minute, boss."

Mark turned back.

"I can't keep up with my bills any longer, and I haven't gotten a cost of living increase in four years."

Mark sighed. "Like I told you before, no one gets a raise, but after we merge and get rolling again, we'll see what happens."

"Put something in writing. Otherwise, I'm not feeling well. I better take a sick day."

"Go home. You'll get paid again when you come back to work."

"Fine. Instead of working, I may use my time looking for another job, even a sucky one."

"Do you remember signing a paper when you started working here? A noncompete?"

"I signed it, but I believed I wouldn't get the job if I didn't sign."

"Understood. I hope you still have money for that lawyer of yours, because I'll give you a fight."

Brady glared at him and then sat down at his desk, resisting the urge to put his fist through the monitor.

"And for the time being, you now work every Saturday. Get used to it."

"I have custody every other weekend."

"Then your girls can do their homework in the lunchroom." Mark left the doorway, turning up the thermostat before heading to his office.

◇   ◇   ◇

Monday Afternoon
Seward, Kentucky

Kacey's office phone rang. "Yes."

"Mr. Farrell, this is Roger Cantwell, your wife's attorney. How are you today?"

"What do you want?"

"Your wife is filing for divorce. She would like you to remove your personal items from the house."

Kacey heard the squeak of a shoe outside his open office door.

"She can have what I left behind, and she can have the house and the car and the savings. Let's end this quickly."

"Billie will be pleased."

"Aren't you supposed to hand me a subpoena?"

"We're all adults here, Mr. Farrell. You don't plan to hide anything, do you?"

"No, but I'm not making a trip to your office to sign anything. Send someone to my office." Kacey hung up the phone and skipped around the front of his desk and out into the hallway. Vijay stood near the wall. "Hear anything interesting, Vijay?"

Vijay stammered. "I… It's… I came by to give you some configurations. You were on the phone. I wanted to—"

"Listen in on my phone call?" Kacey took a step toward Vijay.

Vijay stepped back. "Calm down, Kacey." He handed him a paper. "You'll need this to start testing cloud connections."

Kacey stepped toward him again, taking deep breaths.

Vijay walked backward, stumbled, and fell to the floor. Kacey continued toward him. Vijay climbed to his feet and jogged away in the other direction.

Kacey stopped, turned to the wall, and allowed his gaze to wander for a minute on the painted cinder blocks. His breathing slowed. He went back to his desk.

He was glad to get Billie out of his life. She needed to be free of him. He looked over the configuration sheet and brought up the router interface.

◇　◇　◇

Monday Evening
Crystal Lake, Illinois

Aaron sat staring at a spreadsheet in the gym's office. The number at the bottom of the last column was too small. Tanning wasn't generating enough revenue, even with state-of-the-art equipment.

The Tanator Turbo tanning bed analyzed the client's skin and programmed a custom UV session. Tanners would never burn, and burning was the cause of skin cancer. Heck, the best way to get vitamin D is with UV light, and vitamin D keeps you from getting cancer. Despite the logic, the government put a 10 percent tax on indoor tanning under the guise of protecting health, while the true reason was to collect money, just like everything else in the world.

Each Tanator Turbo cost sixty thousand dollars, and Aaron had purchased five units. His two spray tan units cost forty-eight thousand each, and while they generated revenue, it was not enough to make his overall tanning service profitable.

Jolene's new house would be awesome to live in, but how could he enjoy it with all the money issues? But then again, summer was near, and the girls would wear bikinis in the pool.

The front door dinged. Jolene walked through the gym back to the office and sat down in Aaron's lap, almost causing his desk chair to tip over backward. Aaron stood up with Jolene in his massive arms and carried her to a chair, tossing her in like a rag doll.

"Hey, watch it, you big ape."

Aaron went back to his desk chair. "Don't mess with the Lord of the Jungle."

"I'll get you a bunch of bananas."

"Just peel your clothes off instead."

Jolene growled. "Finish your paperwork and let's go."

Aaron put his hands behind his head and sighed. "I'm balancing the books here, Jolene, and it's not a pretty picture."

"We'll be fine."

"The numbers don't lie. I have to make payments on those beds out there that look like spaceships, and we don't have enough tanners coming in."

Jolene crossed her arms. "My ex-husband has more money. I know it. He can be a clever guy, but I have a plan."

"You have a court judgment."

"Maybe so, but it ain't over yet, baby. He's still going to pay."

◊　◊　◊

Tuesday Afternoon
Harwood Heights, Illinois

Brady took a chair at Sherry's desk. "How are the executions going?"

"The terminations? Brutal. They call me the Firefly because I fly into fire people. I really just drive down there, but whatever."

"Hang in there."

"I've drank so much wine lately that I need to find an AA meeting. What can I do for you?"

"Can I ask you a question in extreme confidence?"

She pointed over his shoulder. "Close the door."

Brady got up and swung the door. Lexi appeared as the door closed in her face. Brady reopened the door.

"That was rude." She carried in an armload of folders and took Brady's chair, arranging them on Sherry's desk.

Sherry held up her index finger at Brady. "Don't go away."

Lexi finished and crossed her legs.

"Lexi, can you please give us a minute?" Sherry asked. "We're in the middle of something."

"You can talk in front of me. Why would a guy like Brady have secrets?"

"Please."

Lexi huffed and left.

Brady closed the door. "So you'll keep what I say in the vault?"

"Of course, part of my job is counseling. Go ahead and talk."

"How can I get myself fired and still get unemployment?"

Sherry put her elbows on her desk. "Believe it or not, that's not the first time I've been asked that question. Sorry, but I can't help you."

"Another question then. Where do you store the noncompete agreements?"

"That's strike two."

Brady rubbed his chin. "Last question, how do I murder Spencer and make it look like an accident?"

Sherry sat up. "Ah, finally something I can help you with."

They both laughed.

The door sprang open. Lexi walked in with a box and dropped it in Brady's lap. She pointed at the shipping label. "Next time you order something, spell your own name right, Bradley Wyman." She smacked Brady's shoulder and left without closing the door.

"What's up with you two?" Sherry asked. "Do I detect some tension? The good kind of tension?"

Brady chuckled. "Every time I ask her out, she shoots me down."

"At least you're back in the game. She's a healthy girl. Keep trying."

"I will, but I have other games to play."

◇ ◇ ◇

Wednesday Afternoon
Seward, Kentucky

Vijay gave Jen an errand she didn't want—locate Kacey. She couldn't find him on the second or third floor, and then Rich said he liked to eat lunch in the basement. Weird. She headed down the stairs, thinking maybe Kacey catches rats for lunch. Rich should have been the one to find him—a girl shouldn't have to wander around in Spiderville. At the bottom of the stairs, she let her heals click on the linoleum to announce her arrival—for Kacey, not the spiders. She clicked down a cinder block hallway, around the boiler room to the file storage area. The lights were on. She clicked her way in.

Kacey sat in a chair with a sandwich in his hand, staring at the wall. Jen ruled out asking if it was rat meat. As he sat, his head moved around slightly, seemingly unaware of her presence.

She stopped ten feet away. "Uh… Hi, Kacey."

Kacey tossed the sandwich in the air and spun away to the left. He lost traction in the grit and fell face forward on the concrete.

Jen put her hands to her face. "Oh my gosh! Are you okay?" She took a few steps in his direction.

Kacey pushed himself up, leapt to his feet, and glared at Jen. He glanced down at his sandwich, dismantled on the floor, then returned his eyes to Jen.

Jen stepped back. "Vijay is looking for you. I am *so* sorry to surprise you, Kacey."

Kacey stepped toward Jen. "I will join him after cleaning up the remains of my lunch."

"Okay." She turned and strode toward the stairs. Over her shoulder she said, "Sorry about your lunch."

Jen picked up speed down the hallway.

Chapter 6

Wednesday Evening
Chicago, Illinois

Brady opened the box delivered to Bradley Wyman in the back seat of his car, parked in front of the coffee shop on Lawrence Avenue. He took out the used laptop, set it on his knees, and powered it up with the cigarette adaptor. By having the machine shipped to the office to the name Bradley Wyman, the authorities could not track it to him, and because it was used, the CPU serial wouldn't be connected to him.

The coffee shop Wi-Fi required no password, so he accessed the Dark Web using the Tor browser, and found the site, Newyu.onion to purchase a new identity. Each time he took another step toward leaving town, his belly stirred with excitement, but then hopes of freedom drifted to the faces of his daughters.

When he paid with a Bitcoin, New-Yu informed he would receive a package at his office. He said a quick prayer, and then wondered what God thought about the Dark Web.

◊　◊　◊

Thursday Afternoon
Seward, Kentucky

Kacey could inhabit his body like a normal person. He just had to let his office walls contain him, allowing for a sense of self-awareness. As he felt the box shape around him, he considered how he continued to spook his coworkers. They were to blame, of course, by sneaking up on him, but regardless, he needed to be more careful and lay low before executing his plan.

Rich tapped on his door. "Hi, Kacey. Busy?"

Kacey manufactured a smile. "How can I help you, Rich?"

"I wanted to talk to you about Vijay and Jen. Can I sit?"

Kacey motioned to a chair.

"They feel bad about upsetting you. Why don't we all go out after work for beverages? Call it team building. What do you say?"

Kacey knew he had to say yes. "What a great idea, Rich. I accept."

"Awesome." Rich went to the door. "I'll set it up."

◊　◊　◊

After work, Kacey drove his Sonata at the end of a four-car caravan headed toward Lewisburg. Rich's jeep led the way, followed by Vijay's Lexus and Jen's Honda. Rich turned into Bigelow's Bar, a square brick building with neon beer signs. They parked in a row and walked in together. Vijay found a booth, and Kacey slid into the aisle seat after Vijay. Rich sat near the window with Jen on the aisle.

Kacey had worked with these people for years. They normally tolerated his eccentricities, but lately, there was tension as his focus on coworker relationships lapsed. The social gathering tonight offered an opportunity to repair the comradery.

Vijay ordered a pitcher of Heineken and a snack platter. The group settled into work chatter. Kacey joined in, speaking comfortably. The discussion turned to the future.

"You guys are going to be fine," Rich said. "I'll probably get canned when we go to the cloud."

"We'll still have hardware," Vijay said. "Thin clients will replace computers, but not all at once. The routers will stay the same, and then there's the bane of our existence—printers." He drank down his first beer and poured another.

Jen tipped her beer back, and Rich downed his. Kacey sipped. He relied on self-control for interactions like tonight, but the way the others were drinking was interesting, possibly drinking alcohol to lower their fear of him?

Jen let out a manly burp. "Kacey…were you in cyber warfare in the Army?"

Kacey set down his beer and thought of a response. "No."

"Oh, I assumed that's where you learned your stuff."

"I learned to kill in the Army. Afterward, I went to Kentucky Tech on the GI Bill."

The table grew quiet for a moment. The waitress brought another picture and filled their glasses. The snack platter arrived.

Rich stuck a mozzarella stick in his mouth. "Learned to kill, awesome… I should have joined the military to fly them jets. You should see me on Xbox."

"I'm a Halo freak," Vijay said. "Sometimes I wonder if I could really kill someone. Kacey doesn't have to wonder."

"Guys, Kacey probably saw some serious shit over there," Jen said. "It wasn't a game."

Kacey understood the prompt to speak. "Actually, Jen, I found combat to be like a game. By stepping back from my emotions and allowing my training to take over, my killing efficiency improved dramatically. My unit operated in mostly urban environments, so I developed patterns, killing around corners. By the end of my tour, I rose to the rank of sergeant major, which meant I could organize assaults, but I remained the head of the spear. My unit would follow me, covering my flank."

The three stared. He looked at each of their eyes before they picked up their glasses and drank in unison. Kacey took a sip.

"So you're Rambo…," Rich said. "That is so awesome." He held his fist across the table. Kacey looked at it for a few seconds and then bumped.

Laughter came from the table across the aisle. Four large men wearing reflective vests drank shots of whiskey. One of the men counted down, and then they raced through three shots each. The winner held up his arms while the others applauded.

Vijay drank down another half glass. "It's good to hang out with you guys. We've been through a lot together."

Rich took hold of Vijay's glass. "Better slow down, boss. You're getting sentimental."

Jen said, "I feel the same—"

Shouting and clapping came from the other table. Jen looked over. One of them said, "Hey, baby, why don't you come sit at a man's table. You don't belong with the nerd squad." He belched.

"Thanks for the lovely invitation. I have to decline."

"Anyway, we came here to talk things out. Vijay? You and Jen feel lousy about upsetting Kacey." Rich nodded at Vijay.

"That's right. Kacey, I would never eavesdrop—"

"Hey, sexy? You've given enough charity to the geeks. Come over here."

"Knock it off," Jen said. "My coworkers and I are bonding. Give me a break."

"I'm trying to give you a break. Come sit in my lap."

Jen chuckled and shook her head. "Go on, Vijay…"

Kacey glanced at the other table. The four men would become more unreasonable with the more shots they drank. The best thing would be to find another place. "Let's get a box for the snacks and sit in the park."

"They don't serve beer in the park," Rich said. "In fact, I found out as a teenager to not bring your own beer there either."

A straw wrapper floated from the other table and landed in the marinara sauce. The four men burst out laughing. A wadded-up napkin bounced off Kacey's head.

"If not the park, then we should find another tavern for our discussion."

"They're harmless," Rich said. "Drink your beer."

Vijay continued. "As I was saying, Kacey, the other day was a huge misunderstanding."

Kacey held up his hand. "I understand completely. A marriage breakup is an interesting topic to gossip about. You couldn't help but listen."

"No, that's not what—"

"At least let us buy you a real drink, baby, not that fancy German piss-water."

Jen got out of the booth. The three of them tried to stop her, but she batted away their hands. "Give me a sec." She approached the other table, picked up a shot glass full of whiskey, and tossed it back and then banged the empty glass back down on the table. "Thanks for the drink. Now please let us talk. We have things to discuss. I'm sure you understand."

"You got it, baby doll. Guess we know who has a pair in your group."

The guys laughed.

Jen sat back down and washed down the whisky with beer. "Please continue."

"Jen, you're my hero." Vijay turned to Kacey. "I had just walked down to your office the other day when I heard you on the phone with your lawyer talking about getting a divorce. All I could do was stop and wait for you to hang up. I wasn't listening."

Kacey arched an eyebrow and sipped some beer. "Rich, can you enlighten Vijay on his comment?"

"Vijay, man. How would you know he was talking about getting a divorce if you weren't listening?"

Jen giggled. "He's right. You're busted, dude."

The guy from the other table said, "It ain't right to listen in on a guy's private phone call, bro, especially when he's talking to his lawyer. It's a violation of… Help me out, girl."

"Lawyer-client privilege?"

"That's it. Bro?"

Kacey looked over.

"We can help you file a grievance. We do it all the time."

"Thanks, but like I said, my supervisor is not immune to human curiosity. I will excuse his behavior for the sake of peace in the workplace."

The guys at the other table nodded their heads. "Well said… Here's to peace in the workplace."

The man clinked glasses with his guys.

Jen raised her glass and clinked with Rich and Kacey. Vijay looked down at the table.

Rich said, "Come on, boss, be a good sport."

Vijay looked up with a goofy smile and clinked glasses, saving Kacey for last. "You're something else, man."

◊   ◊   ◊

They stumbled out of Bigelow's Bar close to midnight. Kacey had finished a second beer and remained sober. He and Rich helped Vijay out to the parking lot, still carrying a glass of beer.

Rich looked down. "Oh, man. Vijay copped a Bigelow's glass."

"It's an open container," Kacey said. "And Vijay is not fit to drive. I will need to—" Kacey was pushed from behind, causing Vijay to lose balance and fall to his knees. Rich grabbed under his armpits to keep him from going facedown.

Kacey spun around to face two young men, probably teenagers, holding knives and dressed like gangster wannabes. One waved his knife in Kacey's face. "Fool. Give up your wallet." Kacey reached slowly into his back pocket.

Jen backed away. The other young man walked toward her. "Where are you going, sweetie pie." Rich watched with his hands up.

Kacey waited with his hand behind him, not moving. The first young man waved his knife again. Kacey slowly brought out his wallet and held it out in front of him. When the guy glanced down to take it, Kacey grabbed his wrist and twisted. The knife fell to the ground. Kacey dropped the wallet and shot his fist into the guy's face.

The other guy moved toward Jen. Kacey leaped toward him, spun, and kicked his feet out from under him, sending him to the pavement. He screamed and rolled over with the knife stuck in his own shoulder.

Rich, Vijay, and Jen looked at each other. Red and blue lights flashed on their bodies. A spotlight lit up the area. "Nobody move!" Car doors shut. Two policemen walked from behind the spotlight with their guns drawn. "What's going on here?" The three shot their hands in the air.

"The two men on the ground attempted to rob us with knives," Kacey said. "I neutralized them. One needs medical attention."

"Did you stab him?"

"No, Officer. As my coworkers will testify, he stabbed himself when he fell."

Vijay brought down the glass of beer he was holding over his head. "I'll drink to that. Here's to Kacey."

The officer motioned to his partner to cuff the first guy still lying on his back, out cold, and then used a mic from his shoulder to call for an ambulance. Then he instructed Rich, Jen, and Kacey to go inside the bar to wait. "We need to sort out what happened here. We'll be in to talk in a few minutes."

Vijay stayed on his knees. "What about me?"

"You're going to the station for open container."

"Bullshit."

"Want to add public drunkenness?"

Vijay shook his head.

◊　◊　◊

By two twelve in the morning, Kacey, Jen, and Rich met in the public area of the police station. Kacey looked out into the parking lot and noticed Mrs. Lambert walking up the sidewalk to the police station.

She entered from the foyer. "Mr. Farrell, were you included in the hijinks tonight?"

The look on her face told him to be cautious. "I was present during the altercation. How were you notified?"

"Vijay called me. He sounded quite inebriated. I will arrange for his bail."

Jen came over. "We asked about that. He can't leave while he's still drunk."

Mrs. Lambert breathed out through her nose. "This is inappropriate behavior for members of the IT department. We expect you to uphold a respectable public image. Tomorrow, you will each meet with me concerning this event, but for now, go home and sleep it off." She turned and pushed the glass door open, banging it against the wall.

◇　◇　◇

Kacey arrived at corporate before 8:00 a.m. and requested permission to wait in Mrs. Lambert's sitting room. She arrived at 7:55 a.m.

"Come right in."

He followed her in, sat in front of her desk, and set down his briefcase. The case fell flat to the floor, and when he set it upright, the gun inside made a thud sound as it slid to the bottom.

"Mr. Farrell. Thank you for taking me seriously about the incident last night. I am very disturbed. What do you have to say for yourself?"

Kacey did not speak for a moment as he fought to remain calm. "My coworkers and I met at a drinking establishment. Afterward, two young criminals attempted to rob us. I used my military training to defuse the situation. Your feelings concerning the matter are irrelevant."

Mrs. Lambert's head jerked up after the last sentence. "It would be wise for you to show me respect, Mr. Farrell. As your superior, my feelings are indeed relevant. Four employees getting drunk and engaging in knife fights in the middle of the night is not the type of behavior Winslow-Carnac will tolerate. And this after a physical altercation with your wife."

"My wife agreed to drop charges in exchange for a speedy divorce."

"Details aside, I will not tolerate any more incidents with you, Mr. Farrell."

Kacey glanced down at his briefcase, but if he was to draw a gun in the workplace, he needed a good reason. "Will my employment continue?"

She turned her chair to look out the window. With her back to him, she did not respond for several minutes.

Kacey pulled the briefcase up on his lap and put his thumb on the latch.

"Mr. Farrell, consider this your final warning. Now please leave my office."

Kacey went to leave with the briefcase unopened. On his way out the door, Mrs. Lambert stopped him. "Before returning to work, please drive to Lewisburg and collect your coworker from the drunk tank."

◊   ◊   ◊

Friday Night
Evanston, Illinois

At his padded leather bar, Winston Haynesworth poured himself a scotch as his daughter Serena walked into the library. "Now, Father, what have I told you about drinking with your new medication?"

He took a sip. "And let me repeat my response. If I can't have a drink of scotch, then fuck the meds. I'll go ahead and die."

"I've changed my mind. Have a drink."

Winston savored the scotch. "It's Friday night. Will you be going on a date with your new boyfriend?"

"Yes, he can't get enough of me. I have to slap his hands when we're alone."

"Serena, please. Try to make things work this time. You're not getting any younger, and it would be nice to have little ones in the house again. What's your new beau's name?"

"Brady Witek. A handsome fellow recently divorced. His ex-wife has custody of their four daughters."

He set down his glass to pour another. "Four girls, you say? I desperately want you to have the experience of raising a child."

"No doubt he will pursue me, but will he behave himself? You know my track record."

"Let's not discuss that now. The latest scoundrel, Ricardo, settled with us."

"He was a boy in a man's body, just like the others. Immature little shits. They just want to play around."

"Try for a better outcome this time. A fellow with four daughters sounds down-to-earth, not like the men you meet in the night clubs."

"Brady is decent, but a little hot to trot. Divorced guys are like that, you know. They're used to getting it all the time."

Winston shook his head and tipped back another drink.

◊   ◊   ◊

Friday Night
Roger's Park Neighborhood
Chicago, Illinois

As Brady walked toward Cindy's building, his eyes passed over cars parked in the street, causing a flicker of memory to dance in his head.

Cindy didn't buzz him up this time. She met him at the front door as he walked up. "Hi there, handsome. Looking for a good time?"

"I am, but none of the ladies on Mannheim Street were affordable."

She smacked his arm and walked with him down the sidewalk.

He asked, "Did you have interviews today?"

"I canceled. I just wasn't up for another interrogation."

Brady got quiet. They walked for a while in silence.

"I'll get something soon, don't worry about it."

"Remember, I have to make payments on Jolene's student loan, and my rent just went up. It's going to be hard to help you out."

"I understand, but the jobs I'm applying for won't pay any more than what I get from the state."

A red car with tinted windows rolled past, causing Brady to think. Did he know anyone with a red sports car like that? When they arrived at Repita Pita, Brady opened the door for Cindy, and the red sports car parked across the street.

Brady and Cindy ordered their usual and brought trays to their usual table. Brady filled his pita. "Sorry I can't take you to a nicer place."

Cindy chewed before answering. "We're not your typical Romeo and Juliet."

Brady stared across the street and set down his pita.

"What is it, Brady? You look like you've seen a ghost."

"See that Alpha Romeo across the street? I think I know that person."

"That car followed us over here."

"Uh-huh." It had to be Serena. Maybe if they took their time eating, she would get bored and leave.

Cindy asked, "Why don't you go ask your friend to join us?"

"That is not a good idea."

Cindy shrugged.

When they finished eating, Brady cleared the table and took the trays with garbage to the bin by the window. He watched the red car pull out into traffic.

Brady frowned. *Doesn't look like I've seen the last of Serena Haynesworth.*

◊ ◊ ◊

Monday Morning
Harwood Heights, Illinois

Several blocks away from the office, a yellow Corvette filled Brady's rearview mirror, so he hit his brakes, causing Spencer to fishtail. Brady stepped on the accelerator to get to the parking lot first, but Spencer passed him on the left. The Trailblazer belched out blue smoke and fell behind. Spencer whipped into the lot flying past the last open space near the entrance. Brady drove in, turned the wheel hard, and hit the gas, sending the Trailblazer into a screeching doughnut. He spun around and rolled right into the space.

Spencer backed up and saluted him with his middle finger. Mark Seivers stood near the front door, shaking his head. Inside, Mark chatted with Lexi at the reception desk.

Brady joined them. "Good morning."

"Where did you learn to drive like that?" Mark pointed out the window. "Look, Spencer had to park in the street."

Lexi asked, "Do boys ever grow up to be men these days?"

Brady said, "Clearly, the answer is no."

"We're going to have a meeting in the lunchroom at nine," Mark said. "Both of you need to be there, and please inform Spencer when he gets in, okay?"

"Got it boss." Lexi reached under the desk and brought out a small cardboard box. "This came for you, Brady."

Brady took the box. "Thanks."

He followed Mark up the stairs. In his office, Brady locked the door behind him, cut open the box, and removed the wadded paper. His new identity had arrived. The driver's license looked perfect, but too bad he couldn't pick out the name. Eugene Pierre Brinkman sounded a little odd, but he could go by Gene. He pulled out more documents, including a certified birth certificate, passport, and credit card. New-Yu really came through. He would recommend them to all his criminal friends.

He tossed the identity documents back in the box and slid it under the desk when the door handle jiggled. "Hang on."

Spencer spoke through the door. "You can't jerk off in the office, it's against company policy."

"Okay, but just a second, I need to put your picture away." Brady turned the lock.

Spencer barged in. "You're a sick man. Don't ask me about the meeting—I have no idea."

"Wasn't going to ask. Maybe you're being promoted to janitor."

"Sure, asshole. I'm here because I want to know if Bigham is getting the job done. I'm getting a bad vibe from Mark."

"We're working as fast as we can, now let me check my e-mail before the meeting."

Spencer went out the door, turned up the thermostat, and went to his office. Brady turned on the fan on top of the wall.

◊   ◊   ◊

Brady arrived in the lunchroom a few minutes before nine. Employees got coffee from a machine before sitting down. Mark strolled in and allowed everyone to settle. Brady looked around for Spencer and found a chair on the other side of the room.

Lexi sat down next to him. "What do you think? Are we going to lose our jobs?"

"Not right in the middle of the merger, but if we do, then we'll get unemployment."

"I barely get by as it is. I may have to go to dinner with you to keep from starving."

Brady gave her a look. She arched her brows.

Mark went up on the stage and raised his voice. "Hello, everyone, we need to discuss a very serious matter today, and it directly affects our future with the company. As you know, we made a deal to buy out one of our rivals, Jenkin's Container."

Mark stepped down from the stage and walked closer to the crowd. "I need to be brutally honest with you. The deal was made to save the company from bankruptcy." He looked around the crowd. "I can see this fact is not a secret. Yes, revenues have been down for some time, but please remain positive. We have every intention on keeping the company running far into the future."

The crowd murmured and nodded approval.

"Unfortunately, that was the good news."

The murmuring grew louder.

Lexi leaned over. "Here it comes."

"We must address our cash shortfall. Our operating costs are too high, and the process of merging has its own costs. Therefore, we must make cuts."

The murmurs grew louder.

Mark held up his hands. "We are going to face this together. Instead of cutting staff, the burden will be shared. All salaries, including mine, will be cut by twenty-five percent. Once the benefits of the merger are fully realized and revenues increase, we will bring salaries back up, starting with the lowest-paid employees first."

Employees grew more excited. Several people stood.

"Vacation days will be cut in half, and we will only cover twenty-five percent of your health care payments."

The last statement effectively ended the meeting. Employees got up from the chairs and crowded toward Mark while some headed for the exits. Questions about paying bills and mortgages were shouted. Mark waved his hands and asked everyone to calm down.

Brady strolled toward the exit, leaving Lexi still sitting with her mouth hanging open. He was anxious to go through his new identity kit again. *Could come in handy real soon.*

◊   ◊   ◊

Monday Lunchtime
Seward, Kentucky

The Winslow-Carnac building was built years ago in a secluded area chosen by Marvin Winslow for the serenity of the woods, just a short drive from Lewisburg. Kacey had accepted Winslow-Carnac's job offer partly based on the environment.

The stone wall he often gazed at led down the south side of the building. A patio area on the north side had picnic tables for outdoor lunches, and the highway ran north/south in front of the building on the west side. Across the highway, a dense forest lay between Kacey's office and Bea's house a mile away. Behind the building to the east, a small strip of lawn lay before deep woods.

After Kacey finished looping camera footage, he went out the back door of the building, across the strip of lawn, and crunched through the trees for twenty minutes heading east, arriving in a clearing with the ruins of an old house and a dilapidated garage. Traffic noises came through the growth on the far side of the clearing. Walking around the house, he entered the garage and concluded it would serve his purpose in the plan.

He checked his watch and made his way back toward the corporate building, unseen from this distance. Sounds would not travel through the woods from this distance either, very good.

Arriving behind the building, he went in the back door and up to his office to reactivate the camera, but instead, he found Jen and Rich sitting in front of his desk. "How may I help you?"

Jen turned. "We wanted to eat lunch with you, but you disappeared."

Rich said, "You weren't in your spot down in the basement."

Kacey sat down behind the desk. "Did you look for me on the patio?" They shook their heads. "Then that's where I was."

"I found some strange macros on the accounting server," Jen said. "Can you take a look at them?"

Kacey flinched. "I've been working on security customizations. You must have found them."

"Oh, okay. If I read the code correctly, they reset wire transfer locations. Why would our system need to reroute money like that?"

"Well, Jen…we're talking about millions of dollars each year. If routing was compromised, our funds could be stolen, so I plan to implement an extra layer of security and route transfers through a secure proxy."

"Sounds good to me. Kacey Farrell, protecting the company's money and saving damsels in tavern parking lots. What can't you do?"

"Get along with the boss, that's what," Rich said. "Lambert is still pissed. She got on me again this morning, saying I must've been the one to take us to a bar."

"You were the one."

"Yeah, but Kacey put a guy in the hospital."

"There was little choice."

"I agree, and thanks again, but Lambert sees things differently. We better keep our heads down for a while."

Kacey nodded. "Agreed, and thank you Jen for keeping your eyes open. There's no need to worry about the scripting."

Jen and Rich left.

Kacey slumped in his chair.

Chapter 7

In his apartment, Kacey slid pictures of an older couple into the frames. He would soon leave to shop for a motorcycle. Bea knocked on his door. When he opened, she handed him a box. "Special delivery for John Wilson."

"Thank you, Bea. Come in."

She felt her way to the table.

Kacey sat down, remembering his gun dismantled on a towel near the sink. "I'm glad you're here—we need to chat. I will soon leave my job at the supermarket and be at home more often. Also, I intend to sell my car and purchase a motorcycle."

"Oh, my. Big changes on the way. But you're too young to retire and collect Social Security."

"Correct. My goal is to take a different direction in life, one with less pressure. I'm not built for constant interaction with people."

Bea considered for a moment. "When I was a young woman, back in prehistoric times, I worked in a dime store. Back then, customers could be crude and demanding. Nowadays, I can only imagine. People use the f-word in every day conversation these days."

"That they do."

"I'm glad to hear you'll try to improve your life, John."

"Thank you, Bea, and I'm glad to have found a nice place to live."

◊　◊　◊

Wednesday Evening
Harwood Heights, Illinois

Brady now had to work on Saturday's and worked past 5:00 p.m. on most weekdays. He checked his watch as he walked out to his Trailblazer—7:38 p.m. Spencer's Corvette was long gone. Brady climbed behind the wheel and checked his face in the rearview mirror, finding dark circles under his eyes. And the girls would be over this weekend. No rest for the weary. He put his Bluetooth in his ear and dialed Paul's number before putting the Trailblazer in reverse.

Paul answered. "What up, my friend?"

"Feel like hanging out? We can stuff ourselves with tacos and watch the Sox."

"I like the offer, but I'm visiting at the hospital this evening. Why does your voice sound so sad?"

"They cut my pay twenty-five percent. Don't forget my rent went up, and then there's the payments on the student loan. I'm about to drown."

"You have the checks in the bank."

"What do I do when they're gone?"

Paul breathed out. "I don't know what to tell you, man. Life has you by the balls. You'll have to find a better job."

"No doubt, but the economy sucks."

"Brady, you need to exercise your faith, my friend. Ask Jesus to lead you to the right place. Let's pray about it, what do you say?"

"I'm driving on Lawrence, hang on." Brady pulled into a Walgreen's parking lot. "Let's do it."

Paul prayed. "Lord, please lead Brady in the right direction. Allow him to be a part of your plan, so his life can glorify you. Amen."

"Amen. I feel better, thanks man."

"Great. I need to go. Hang in there."

"You too, later." He pulled out of the lot and headed home. At least the traffic had lightened up by this time of the evening. He got to his building in good time.

When he put on his signal to turn left, the color red caught his eye. Sure enough, a red Alpha Romeo parked across the street from his building. He turned off the blinker, accelerated, and turned left at the next corner, but no parking spots were open on either side. He stopped at the next sign and looked left—the Alpha Romeo headed his way. He stepped on the gas creating a cloud of blue smoke. In his rearview mirror, the red car turned the corner gaining on him.

Why did all the crazy people he knew have fast cars?

The Trailblazer could not outrun Serena's sports car, and he couldn't afford a ticket, so he slowed down and looked for the first spot available. When he saw one, he slammed on his brakes, causing Serena to screech to a stop behind him. He angled into the spot like a true Chicagoan, missing the front of Serena's car by inches. When he put the transmission in park, Serena pulled close to the side of the Trailblazer. Brady climbed over to the passenger seat and got out with his briefcase. Horns honked behind Serena. She punched the accelerator and squealed away, turning left at the next sign.

If she got her spot back in front of his building, he couldn't go in, so instead, he headed to Cindy's place to let Serena wait. He wanted to see Cindy anyway.

He strolled fast down the sidewalk looking over his shoulder, crossed the street, and went down the block to Cindy's building. At the front door, a lady came out, so he avoided the buzzer and headed up the stairs to Cindy's hallway. He tapped on Cindy's door and waited. A minute went by, and no one opened. She had to be there on a Wednesday evening, so he tapped again and waited. Finally, he tried the handle. The door was unlocked, so he went in.

His mouth dropped open.

A man's bare ass moved up and down on the sofa with Cindy's legs in the air on each side. Brady backed away, trying to leave unnoticed.

"Hi, Uncle Brady." Lane walked in from the bedroom.

Cindy's head came forward, and the guy looked over his shoulder. Brady froze.

"Shit." Cindy pushed the guy off, swung her legs around, and cupped her breasts. "What are you doing here?"

Brady pulled the door closed and took off for the stairs. Cindy called out through the door as he raced down the stairs and out into the courtyard, sliding to a stop when he realized he didn't know where to go. But he knew he couldn't stay here, so he ran down the street toward his building, despite seeing the red car parked across the street.

Serena better not get in the way, or she may get footprints on her forehead.

He swerved into his building's courtyard running full stride. A car door opened behind him. He fished out his keys and unlocked the front door, pulling it closed behind him.

Serena jogged toward the door. "How mature, Brady. Come out here and talk to me like an adult. Why haven't you called?"

Brady headed up the stairs.

◊　◊　◊

Friday Afternoon
Harwood Heights, Illinois

Another text from Cindy appeared on Brady's phone, but he didn't need to read, knowing it would be another request to call her. The beeping noises disturbed his concentration, but he couldn't silence the phone because he had to take tech support calls. He groaned and picked up the phone. The text said, "Just give me five minutes. I want to explain."

Brady typed back. "No more texts. I have to work." He didn't want to give her false hope, and he couldn't get the image out of his head. She'd never been a real thing anyway, just out for his money. He was done with Cindy.

Brady checked his watch, 3:37 p.m. *Screw the merger.* He wanted to make a stop before picking up the girls. Brady saved his work, shut down his computer, and grabbed his briefcase. He headed for the stairs, hoping no one was around to stop him. He made it to the foyer.

Lexi looked up from the reception desk. "Where are you going? I thought you were busy saving the company."

He slid up to the counter. "If anyone asks, tell them I have a family matter."

"You haven't told anyone you're leaving?"

"No. After the pay cut, I'm twenty-five percent less responsible."

"Fair enough."

◊　◊　◊

McHenry County, Illinois

In the gravel lot up ahead, Brady could see the RV was still parked there. He coasted to a stop right in front of the vehicle. He got out to look around with his hands on his hips. More RVs were available, but this one felt like the right one.

An older fellow came out of the office trailer carrying a pad of paper. "Looking for a home on wheels?"

Brady shook his hand. "I'm Gene. I have my eye on this one here. Can I take a look inside?"

"You surely can, young man, and call me Hank. If you like what you see, the keys are in it. We'll go on a driving date, you and I."

Brady went to the cab and climbed in. The dash and controls were simple and utilitarian. The seats had weave covers. A CB radio hung under the dash. Between the seats in the back of the cab, a vinyl curtain covered a passage to the living area. He went through and stood up. Down the left side were cabinets, a kitchen sink, and a small stove. A kitchen table occupied the front right with a cushioned bench in the middle of the right side, leaving space to move around. The toilet was behind a door in the back left. The sleeping loft over the cab had screened windows for ventilation.

He opened cabinets, inspected plumbing, and climbed into the sleeping area. The RV may be used but well taken care of, and it was clean.

Hank climbed in the back door. "It ain't the prettiest old girl, but she's clean and in good repair with plenty of life left. Want to take a spin?"

"Do I need a special driver's license?"

"No, this ain't no commercial vehicle. Like I said, the keys are in it. Saddle up."

Brady drove on the highway and then in Crystal Lake. Hank gave instructions. The trick was to center the back end by looking in the mirrors and then pick a gauge on the dashboard to keep on the center line. When he'd had enough, he rolled into the lot, backed into the space, and turned off the motor.

"Now, we can make you a deal on this old girl today," Hank said. "She's been waiting for someone like you to love her for her personality, not her looks. But I have three other units with a little more pizzazz. Care to check them out?"

Brady sat for a moment with his hands on the wheel. He could read all the dials in the dash. The chair fit his rear end. It was plain looking, and he wanted to blend in. "No, Hank, this one feels right."

The price on the windshield said eight thousand, requiring him to cash one of the checks in the deposit box. Hank crossed his arms. "It's a good price. We've marked it down to move her."

Brady sighed. "I'm close, but I need some time to think about it, and I would need a favor as part of the deal."

"Sure, name it."

"I would need to leave it here for a week or two before I take possession."

"No problem, Gene. We have extra space out back."

Brady climbed out of the cab with a sick feeling of doubt in his stomach. He'd prayed for direction before finding the RV, but were his own foolish ideas guiding him? He could always sell the RV again or, maybe, take the girls on a trip. Maybe he could live in it and lose the apartment.

Hank walked around the front to stand with him. "I'll tell you what, Gene, since you're a nice fellow, I'll put a Sold sign on this baby for a few days." He took a card from his pocket. "Call me when you decide."

Brady put the card in his wallet. "Thanks, Hank, you're a prince."

◇   ◇   ◇

Brady drove the Trailblazer out of the lot and headed to the mall in Crystal Lake. Jolene stayed in her car and popped the trunk from inside. Brady helped carry the girl's bags to the Trailblazer.

Crissy rode up front. Britney sat behind him, leaning where she could not be seen in the rearview mirror. Laurie entertained them with her story about a classmate that laughed so hard Kool-Aid came out of her nose.

As he drove back by the gravel lot, Crissy pointed over. "Look, Daddy. That truck is also a house. Why don't we get one of those?"

Brady glanced down at her. The Trailblazer tilted as the tires slipped off the edge of the road. As he eased back into the lane, he wondered if God had just spoken.

"The car went off the road," Laurie said. "What happened?"

"It was Crissy's fault," Brady said. "She wasn't watching the road."

"Daddy!"

"You have to pay attention, Crissy, or you will never get your truck driver's license."

"Then I'll drive helicopters instead."

Everyone giggled, even Britney.

Brady shook his head. "Okay, but how about a house with a propeller on top. Then if we vacation in Florida, you could fly us all down while we sleep."

"I will do it. And then we will fly to Gilligan's Island for a coconut cream pie."

"Awesome. You're a genius."

◊　◊　◊

Friday Evening
Roger's Park Neighborhood
Chicago, Illinois

Paul and Brady talked on the couch after dinner while the girls cleaned up the kitchen.

"I've been thinking about it," Brady said. "You're a single guy. Why did I have to go out with Serena?"

"Because I didn't want that crazy woman following me around."

Brady hit Paul in the head with a couch pillow. Ashley giggled from the kitchen.

"Hey, man, we can have a pillow fight. But then again, you have four girls on your team. I surrender."

Brady sat back and put his feet on the ottoman. "I'll accept your surrender if you agree to get Serena off my back."

"It's the least I can do, and I am always willing to do the least."

Brady put down his feet and sat up. "I just wonder…" He went to the front alcove, pulled open the curtain, and peered down to the street. He turned back to Paul, smiling. "Looks like you can get it done right now, my friend."

Paul sat up. "She's parked outside?"

"She is, and this is the perfect time. You can confront her in the act of stalking. Now, get down there."

Paul went to the window. "No shit… Have your phone ready to call 911."

"Hah. Don't worry, we'll back you up."

Paul grabbed the front of Brady's T-shirt. "Seriously, this is a bad deal. Her old man gives a ton of money to the church."

"What did you say about Jesus being the ultimate crapola detector?"

Paul shook his head. "I hate it when people listen to me." He went out through the kitchen door.

Brady noticed the girls had gathered in the living room to listen, so he motioned them over to the alcove. They all got down on their knees to look down at the street. The red Alpha Romeo sat parked under a street light in plain view.

"You have an actual woman stalking you?" Britney asked. "She must be nuts."

Brady reached over and pinched the side of her stomach. She contorted. "Don't do that."

Crissy asked, "Do you think she would like some leftovers from dinner?"

Ashley asked, "You want to invite a psycho to dinner?"

Laurie giggled. "Sure, and then we'll send Crissy home with her."

Crissy said, "No. Stop it."

"There's Paul," Brady said. "Let's watch."

As Paul walked down the sidewalk toward the car, the driver's window rolled up. Paul sped up waving, and the window rolled back down. He put his hands on the door and bent down to talk. After a minute, a hand came out of the window and slapped Paul in the face.

The girls laughed. Ashley and Laurie put their hands over their mouths. Brady laughed.

"I told you she was nuts." Britney looked down and contorted, expecting a pinch.

The car's lights came on. Paul ambled over to the sidewalk, rubbing his face. Serena sped away down the street, screeching her tires. Paul headed back. Brady went to the couch. The girls went to the kitchen to wait for Paul. When he opened the door, they all shouted questions at the same time.

Paul held up his hands. "Hold on. Hold on. Let me sit down, and I'll tell you what happened." He led the girls into the living room and sat down on the couch. The girls gathered in front of him. "Okay. When I asked her what she was doing here, she said she was waiting for a friend to see a movie. Then I told her I knew she was watching your poppa's apartment. She didn't like what I said and slapped my face."

Crissy asked, "Did it hurt?"

"It felt like this." Paul gave Brady a light slap in the face.

The girls laughed.

"No, it was harder than that," Britney said. "Do it again."

◊　◊　◊

Sunday Afternoon
Seward, Kentucky

Kacey stuck on a fake mustache and beard on his face in front of the bathroom mirror. They looked real enough, and they better look real after what he paid. Across the hall, he went into the workshop and unlocked a metal box to retrieve his new John Wilson driver's license from Get-Your-Man. It had a motorcycle endorsement, as requested. He wouldn't need the credit cards. Instead, he opened another lockbox and took out stacks of fifties and twenties. He put on a cabbie cap and a vintage jacket from Goodwill and headed down the inside stairs where Bea worked in the kitchen. He wished her well and got in the car.

He drove around the bend to the main highway and turned right to go to the corporate building. Five minutes later, his Uber driver picked him up in a silver Prius and drove him to a residential neighborhood in Lewisburg where Kacey had closed a deal the day before.

A blue Yamaha enduro motorcycle waited for him in the drive. The owner handed him the title after Kacey counted out the cash. He mounted up and kick started, sitting high on the knobby tires. After turning his cabbie cap backward, he used first gear to leave the driveway. In the street, he shifted from second gear to third, getting comfortable with the bike. Soon, he got the rhythm of the clutch and tried the main road. The gas gauge showed the tank half full, so he stopped for a fill-up before riding across town to a sporting goods store to purchase a helmet and riding gloves.

Back on the bike, he navigated rural roads leading to the old house in the clearing. Knowing it would be difficult to locate from the road, he'd made another visit from the building on Friday to hang a red rag in the bushes. On the same visit, he'd cleared a pathway through the undergrowth. A car followed him as he approached, so Kacey pulled to the shoulder to let it pass. When the coast was clear, he rode to the red rag and through the pathway into the clearing, stopping in front of the garage. He rolled in the motorcycle backward to face out for a quicker getaway and hid his helmet and gloves in a moldy wooden crate. Next, he yanked down on the garage door—it barely moved. He hung from the handle swinging his legs until it dropped, and then stacked bricks and loose boards up against the door, mixing in some fallen branches. Someone could come steal the motorcycle before the getaway, but he had to take the risk.

He headed toward the corporate building on foot, checking his watch when he arrived at the strip of lawn. This time, he ran a script to loop camera footage for several hours to hide his activity. He headed down the south side between the building and the stone wall, stopping to observe a utility door halfway. At the front corner of the building, he peered around to the front. Winslow-Carnac should be mostly deserted on the weekend. Finding no one around, he peeled off the fake beard and mustache, put them in a plastic bag, and strolled out to his car. He checked his face in the rearview mirror before driving out to the highway.

◊   ◊   ◊

Sunday Evening
Crystal Lake, Illinois

No one talked in the Trailblazer on the way back to Crystal Lake because of an incident the night before. As they passed the sales lot, Brady noticed his RV had been taken off the line. He'd called Hank in the afternoon and told him he would take it.

Two weeks should be enough time to clear out the apartment, get Bigham up to speed on the merger, and prepare the RV to leave town. According to the internet, Wal-Mart allowed RVs to park overnight. He would have a toilet, so he wouldn't have to wiz in a jar, and he could shower in truck stops, but probably not every day. *Better add cologne to the list.*

Crissy sat up front. "Are you okay, Daddy?"

"I'm okay." He refused to think about the incident that occurred last night. Sunday morning had been strained, and then he'd kept the girls involved in church activities all day. For the first time as a parent, he didn't know how to deal with a situation, and as a result, he'd called Hank and bought the RV. Call it the straw that broke the camel's back.

Laurie and Ashley looked back at him in the rearview mirror with wide eyes. Britney sat behind him leaning out of sight. Brady asked, "Have you girls heard bad things about me?"

"Momma said you were a bad man," Laurie said.

Crissy said, "Aaron said you were mean to Momma, and if you're mean to us, we should tell."

"Shut up, both of you," Britney said.

Crissy looked over her shoulder. Brady could see Laurie's lower lip stick out. Ashley elbowed Britney. "You're the one that needs to shut up."

"Everyone close their mouths," Brady said. "We'll meet your mom in five minutes. No one talks till then."

They rolled along in silence. Brady started to turn on the radio and decided against it. A few minutes later, he turned into the mall and drove across empty spaces. Jolene stood outside her car.

Brady parked four spaces away. "You know how much I love you, girls. No matter what happens, that will always be true."

Britney jumped out of the car. The other three girls said they loved him in monotone voices. The Trailblazer bounced as Britney tried to open the rear hatch. Brady hit the button, and she swung it open and took her bag to the other car. The other girls took their time moving to the other car. Jolene loaded them up and walked toward Brady's car. Brady put the Trailblazer in gear when he noticed, and Jolene sped up to stand in front of the hood. He put the transmission in reverse.

Jolene smacked the hood. "Get out here and talk to me like a man!"

Brady locked the doors and kept his foot on the brake, staring back at Jolene. He pretty much knew what was coming, and he might as well get it over with. He put the transmission in park, got out and stood with his hands behind his back.

Jolene crossed her arms and tilted her hips. "I want ninety thousand dollars. The settlement doesn't matter now."

"How could you do that, Jolene? She's your daughter."

Jolene sighed. "Welcome to the big leagues, Brady."

"What does that mean?"

"It means women can play hardball too."

"I can't believe I married you."

"Yeah, well listen up, church guy. You're the one who changed, not me."

"We were doing fine."

"When you got religious, you stopped trying to get ahead, and your family deserved better. I want great things for the girls."

Brady gazed at the oil stains in the parking lot. "And your price for greatness is ninety thousand dollars."

"I know you have it. You invested in the stock market, and your favorite aunt died. We just couldn't track it down."

Brady stayed quiet.

"You have two weeks to turn it over, or you know what's coming." She gave him one last glare before heading to her car.

Brady raised his voice. "Ain't going to happen, Jolene. Talk to Britney tonight."

It occurred to him that he'd planned to leave in two weeks, and then Jolene gave him the same deadline. Did God just speak again? He got back in the Trailblazer and drove straight to the Walmart in Crystal Lake to begin purchasing supplies.

◊　◊　◊

Wednesday Evening
McHenry County, Illinois

The Uber driver pulled his white Prius into the gravel lot, and Brady got out in front of Hank's office trailer. Hank greeted him inside. The walls of Hank's office were plywood, and the room smelled like wood, oil, and tobacco. Pictures of trucks and RVs were tacked on the walls. Brady sat down in an ancient metal chair in front of an ancient metal desk.

Hank ground out a cigar in his ashtray. "You won't turn me in, will you, Mr. Brinkman?"

"Never. I intend to become a scofflaw myself."

Hank tilted his head. "I hope you don't mind me asking, but are you feeling okay, Gene? You look very sad tonight."

"I'm okay. And thanks for getting plates on the RV."

"My pleasure." Hank leaned forward on the desk. "You're not the first customer of mine to have that look on his face, the look of a man about to run away from his troubles. Of course, buying an RV is a strong clue."

Brady looked into Hank's eyes. "I guess it's a bit obvious."

"Don't worry, I won't cause you any trouble. Years ago, I went over the road in an 18-wheeler to get away from my problems. The road is a lonely place, but it can give you time to heal."

"I'm not a criminal."

Hank chuckled. "Of course not. You're not the type. Too damn polite."

Brady chuckled. "You may be in the wrong profession, Hank."

"Maybe. You probably mean I should get one of those couches and listen to people's problems, right?"

"Exactly."

"Maybe I will someday. But for now, let's go out back and get the old girl rolling. I'll give you some pointers, and I'll even show you how to drain the shitter."

Brady stood up. "Great."

◊　◊　◊

Thursday Afternoon
Seward, Kentucky

Kacey sat at his office desk, going over the plan in his mind.

First quarter ended soon, and a week from Monday, Winslow-Carnac would wire money to their venders, most of which were in China. Fortunately for Kacey's plan, vendors were forgiving when the payments were a bit late, and as long as the money came in a reasonable amount of time, they stayed quiet. He didn't need much time with the big distraction in the plan. Forty-eight hours would be enough time to move money around the world before converting to bitcoin for the cool down period.

One of his final tasks was to reroute messaging. The accounting program sent an announcement e-mail when wiring money. Vendors only replied when something went wrong, and in this case, they would not get the money.

Vijay was a concern—he might be goofy, but he knew his stuff. The big distraction had to neutralize him and the rest of the staff, and it would. Office workers were not equipped for the stress of combat.

He felt under the desk and verified the 9 mm Glock was still taped underneath.

◇   ◇   ◇

Sunday Afternoon
Chicago, Illinois

Paul and Brady sat down with coffees in a restaurant a block away from the church.

Paul said, "Spill it."

Brady sipped and set his down to cool off. "I cannot tell you something."

"Then we're done. Finish your drink."

"The reason I cannot tell you something is because there's two sides to the story, and I can only tell you one side, but then you would be suspicious of me."

"So we really are here for you to *not* tell me something."

"Right, but I believe God has given me direction. A couple of things happened. They were coincidences, but they felt like signs. You know what I mean?"

"Tell me more about what happened."

"There was a troubling incident that caused me to make a decision. Then a person told me to do something that coincided for when I planned to do something else. Another person pointed at something that I had purchased without knowing I did."

Paul held his forehead. "Yikes! You just scrambled my brains, but let me stop you right there. God doesn't do parlor tricks. Coincidences happen. The Bible should guide you."

"The things that happened felt like signs."

"Don't be looking for answers in the tea leaves because you don't know who's arranging them. Last week, I dealt with a church member who would put his Bible on his picnic table and let the wind blow open a page."

Brady sighed. "Okay, but the Bible is sometimes hard to apply to real life. Things have gotten crazy."

Paul folded his hands on the table. "And you're sure you can't tell me?"

Brady nodded.

"Okay, my friend, we'll turn things over to God, and then we'll have faith in the outcome."

"Thanks, Paul."

Paul nodded. "Just so you know, the correct outcome is to serve God and his glory, not necessarily where you just get out of trouble."

"Got it."

Chapter 8

The RV parked facing a chain-link fence in a self-storage lot in Lincolnwood in the early hours. The Trailblazer was parked behind to transfer supplies.

Each night after work, Brady traveled from his apartment to Niles to the RV, taking unneeded items from his apartment to Goodwill, purchasing supplies at Walmart, and stopping at the RV before returning to the apartment.

In his late thirties, he couldn't keep up the pace like he used to.

The bed over the cab beckoned, and he thought about giving it a test run, but instead, he turned off the lights, locked up the vehicle and got in the Trailblazer after deciding to keep up appearances and be at work on time in the morning.

Mark and Spencer had chewed his ass for leaving early on Friday. Spencer suggested something bad would happen to him if the merger didn't proceed, and Mark hadn't corrected him. He could take down both of those jerks if he needed to, but if he wanted to get out of town without a problem, they couldn't get a hint of his plan.

Leaving town would ruin his life. He had no illusions about it. He'd lose custody of the girls, and the court would file a warrant after he missed child support payments. Fitzgibbons would file a complaint for jumping rent after he'd been forced to sign a new contract. Brady Witek would become a scoundrel.

But Eugene Brinkman would escape the consequences.

Brady went home to bed and fell asleep in seconds.

◊   ◊   ◊

Wednesday Midmorning
Harwood Heights, Illinois

Brady's fingers flew around the keyboard, typing up a guide for the merger so Bigham could take over. He planned to call Bigham in the afternoon and go through the guide, explaining the guide to be insurance if something bad happened. Maybe the guy would be suspicious and put two and two together, but he didn't want to leave a disaster behind.

Knuckles tapped on his door, and Bigham walked in.

Brady spun in his chair. "What the hell are you doing here?"

Bigham shook Brady's hand. "I wanted to talk to you in person, and then I'm going to talk to Mark Seivers."

"You're quitting?"

"Let's have lunch and talk." He looked back at the hallway.

"Fine, but I want Sherry to come with us, okay?"

"Good idea. Bring Sherry. I'll meet you at that place across the street."

◊   ◊   ◊

Brady and Sherry found Bigham sitting at a table in Ernie's. They ordered food before talking.

"You showed up here without notice," Brady said. "What's going on?"

Bigham looked around the restaurant and then turned to Brady. "You're right, I'm leaving the job." He turned to Sherry. "I'm sure you'd agree it's the right move for me."

Sherry looked down at the placemat.

"Don't say anything, and don't worry about me, I start a new job next week."

"You're not giving notice?" Brady asked. "Shit, man."

"Yeah, sorry for sticking it to you, but tough shit for Polyglomerate. I know I'll get canned when the time is right."

Sherry said, "I can't blame you, but Brady is going to suffer."

"And that's why I'm here now, to tell you in person. Also, I found out a few things, and you guys need to watch your backs."

"Keep going."

"The merger happened for reasons you don't know about. Your boss and his sidekick, Spencer Moss, are degenerate gamblers. They lost company money on the riverboats and had to borrow from the Outfit. Now the Outfit plans to launder money through Polyglomerate Container."

Sherry gasped.

Brady sat up straight. "I thought the walls in the system were there to keep Jenkin's management in the dark."

"That's what you're supposed to think."

"How do you know about the money laundering?"

Bigham checked the room again. "I talked to old man Jenkins. With Polyglomerate nearly bankrupt, they needed the merger to make things work. Jenkins could either agree to sell or get fitted for cement shoes."

Brady and Sherry stared at each other.

Bigham noticed someone walking toward the table and jerked his head around. The waitress set down their plates. He continued when she left. "I'm not stupid. Blowing a whistle would get my head blown off."

Sherry didn't touch her food. "Bigham, I'm very grateful you told us, but you better be careful."

"I intend to look Seivers in the eye when I tell him I'm leaving. He'll be relieved to not have to fire me later."

"No, man." Brady shook his head. "That's a mistake. Stay away from those guys. Get back in your car, and get the hell out of here. If they found out you drove all the way up here to quit, they'll be suspicious. Go back to Indiana and quit like a weasel."

Bigham sat for a moment. "Damn it, Witek, you're right. I better get the hell out of here." He took a bite from his fish taco and then another.

"Call Spencer when you quit. I'll give you some nasty names to call him."

◇　◇　◇

Wednesday Afternoon
Evanston, Illinois

The stick turned blue, and Serena's eyes grew wide. She got off the toilet and wrapped the stick in toilet paper so no one would see it in the garbage. She turned the box inside out and jammed it into the bottom of the trash. She paused and then pulled out the plastic bag and took it down to the blue garbage bin in the garage.

Her father would disown her. She would lose her inheritance, and soon she'd be living on the street. Stupid internet hookup site. Her future was ruined.

She searched for Clarice the housekeeper, her only friend and confidant, and found her napping in the servant's quarters. Clarice wanted to know what the emergency was, but Serena clammed up. If she told her about the pregnancy, she would have to count on her to be quiet. No, she better think things through. She told Clarice never mind, went out to the Alpha Romeo, and drove away.

Her mind raced. There must be an abortion clinic around. Her problem could go away fast. But then again, father was a deacon at the church, and if he found out she killed a baby, she would definitely be thrown out in the street. She was damned either way.

Europe. She would fly to the chalet in Switzerland to miss winter in Chicago. No, father loved to ski, and the staff at the chalet didn't like her.

Why not just have the baby? Her life was going nowhere, and father would love to have a little one in the house. There had to be a way.

She glanced around the road. Where was she going at this very minute? Without thinking, she drove toward Brady Witek's apartment. Sweet Brady, a real gentleman. If she could only spend more time with the big lug, he would fall in love with her. She made the turns and pulled the car over in front of his building.

She needed to have sex with Brady Witek, and it needed to be very soon—so he would believe the baby was his. She would explain to her father how she had sinned with Brady, but they would get married. The plan would fix everything and even bring happiness. Can't get much better than that.

Only now, she had to figure out a way to get into Brady's bed. As she gazed up at his bedroom window, it came to her: She would literally get into Brady's bed.

She pulled away from the curb to drive back home and research how to break into an apartment building.

◊　◊　◊

Friday Morning
Harwood Heights, Illinois

After the final night of prep work, Brady had everything ready. The utilities were scheduled for shut off. Bank accounts were closed. Loose ends were tied. Only one item remained on the agenda.

He parked in the Trailblazer half a block from the office, planning to make the most of the last drive to work. While he waited, he opened a plastic jar of antacids and shook out a few.

Doubt burned in his gut. Sometime tomorrow, he would leave his whole universe behind. Maybe guilt would overwhelm, driving him to find a way back before the end of the weekend, somehow to carry on, despite the wretched conditions. But the fact still remained that the sum of his obligations was greater than his earnings, and in due time, his hidden reserve would run out, along with any hope. His job searches suggested a lateral move for about the same money.

A warm tingling sensation spread across his face when he recalled Jolene's threat of blackmail. By now she'd know she failed, but what she'd done shocked him, using his own children against him, and they were too young to know how to deal with the situation. The best way to avoid damage to them was for him to go away, even if it broke his heart.

He couldn't stay at this job, not with the Outfit involved. And he couldn't just quit either and tell the judge he'd heard mobsters ran the place.

As the lot filled up across the street, Brady started the motor and put the Trailblazer in gear. The timing had to be just right. As he watched the side mirror, a yellow Corvette appeared. Brady gunned the motor. At the last second, he shot out into the street. The Corvette went into a skid, spinning in the street, —coming to a stop facing the opposite direction. Brady fishtailed into lot and took the last parking space. Mission accomplished.

As Brady strutted to the building, Spencer blasted his horn and waved his fist as he drove by, looking for a place to park in the street.

Inside, Lexi worked on paperwork at the reception. Brady strolled up and set down his bag. "I'm going to give you one last chance. I'll take you to dinner tonight after work. Yes or no?"

Lexi didn't look up. "Brady… Brady… Brady… Dear boy. The tough guy approach doesn't work with me. Sorry, but I'm busy."

◊　◊　◊

Friday Afternoon
Harwood Heights, Illinois

The text message was typed. His finger hovered over Send. Then he pressed. He'd just informed Jolene he would not be picking up the girls tonight, and it was the last minute. No doubt she'd be calling her lawyer in a few minutes. He had to wait to the last minute, or she would contact the court. Sending the text seemed to seal the deal.

He would leave, despite the fact Mark called for another meeting a few minutes ago. When he got to Seiver's office, Spencer paced back and forth in front of the desk. Brady sat down and stretched his feet out in the way. Spencer kicked his leg and took the other chair.

Mark crossed his arms at the desk. "Bigham resigned effective immediately. It's time for you two to step it up, even if we're on schedule. We're going to stay on schedule, get ready to work some serious hours, starting right now. You can leave at eight, and we'll be here all day tomorrow."

Brady stood.

"Mr. Witek? Do you have something to add?"

It would feel so good to tell off the boss right then, but he needed to leave without complications, so he shook his head. "I have to pick up the girls."

"Make arrangements. Pick them up late."

Brady paused but left. Spencer followed and went to his office.

Brady's phone vibrated with an incoming text, no doubt from Jolene. In his office, he brought up the internet to screw around on for three hours, and then he would leave.

◊　◊　◊

Friday Night
Roger's Park Neighborhood
Chicago, Illinois

Serena waited in her car across the street from Brady's building, checking around for Pastor Paul. She couldn't let him see the fuzzy handcuffs, edible panties, or the rubber penis in her play kit. He would be suspicious just to see her in a spandex outfit.

Instead of her Alpha Romeo, she sat in her father's black Bentley. She needed to park by the building to spot Brady coming home without being recognized. But he hadn't shown up yet, and it was almost nine. Maybe he'd spotted her and sneaked in. She watched for light in his apartment window.

Ahead, in the intersection, a white Trailblazer pulled up with its turn signal on. She ducked down as Brady drove past leaving a trail of blue smoke. She sat up to watch him look for a parking spot in the mirror.

She tingled with anticipation. Maybe the perverts on the internet were right about rape fantasies: It was exciting to stalk a victim. She would let Brady victimize her if he was into it.

She ducked down again when he walked up the sidewalk and into the courtyard. In a few minutes, light appeared through the curtains in his apartment. When they went out, she would make her move—pick a couple of locks, strip nude, and then slip into bed with the father of her baby, or so he would believe. Not just the perfect crime, but some hot fun as well.

At 10:00 p.m., Cindy used her key for Brady's building and went up the stairs. After numerous attempts, she could not get ahold of him, and he never seemed to be home. But tonight, she saw the Trailblazer in the street and decided to try again. She had to clear things up with Brady. Sure, she was fooling around with Brett, but she needed Brady's support, and she would let him have her tonight to get it back.

His apartment door was open a crack when she arrived. Strange. She gave the door a push to swing it open, and the light from the hallway illuminated a bare butt. Brady didn't have a huge rear end with cellulite damage.

The person with the butt turned around. She was a woman with frizzy hair wearing hooker makeup and completely naked.

"Who the hell are you?" Cindy asked.

The woman covered her boobs with one hand and between her legs with the other. Something fell on the floor. "Me? No one. Leave now, please."

Cindy looked down as a rubber penis rolled up to her feet.

A clunk noise came from the bedroom. Brady came out wearing nothing but briefs, holding a shoe as a weapon. "Cindy?" He turned to Serena. "Psycho woman?"

Serena thrust out her boobs. "I don't know who this skinny girl is, Brady, but she can't give you what I can."

◇　◇　◇

Brady rubbed his eyes. Serena stood by the living room naked, wearing hooker makeup. Cindy stood in the doorway wearing a tank top and tight shorts. Was this one of those dreams?

Serena came at him with a lusty look on her face. Cindy charged in and grabbed Serena around the waist. Serena put her arm around Cindy's neck. Brady dropped the shoe and tried to break them up. He pulled at Cindy's waist, but Serena had her arm tightly around her neck. They all spun around. The back of Cindy's hand smacked Brady in the balls. He went down. The two women fell over and rolled on the kitchen floor. Brady got up on one knee, groaning. Serena ripped off Cindy's tank top.

Mrs. Fitzgibbons appeared in the doorway wearing a robe with curlers in her hair. She held a flashlight on the pile of skin on the kitchen floor and then on Brady holding his groin. "People, please. Keep the door closed for this type of activity." She pulled the door shut.

Cindy and Serena stopped wrestling in the darkness. Brady limped to the living room and switched on a lamp. Cindy pushed Serena away and covered her boobs with her hands. Serena pushed up off the floor, sticking her butt in the air. Brady cringed.

Serena pointed at Brady. "Was this great fun for you, Casanova? You've got so many women chasing you that fights break out in your apartment?"

"Get out of here before I call the cops."

Serena frowned. "Fine. But you'll never know what you're missing." She cupped her boobs.

Brady pointed at the pile of her clothing.

Cindy found her ripped tank top and hung it on her shoulders, covering herself as best as she could.

Serena pulled on her spandex, slipped into sandals and picked up her bag.

"Don't forget your penis."

She snatched it off the floor and stormed out.

Cindy shuffled toward Brady, still holding his groin. He put up his hand. "Enough. Please go home."

"Who was that gross woman?"

"Cindy, why are you even here?"

"You won't answer my calls. You're never home. Please talk to me so we can work things out."

"You'll have to wait for a better time."

"You're right." She gathered her shirt to her chest and left.

◊   ◊   ◊

Aaron cracked his knuckles in the passenger seat while Jolene drove. It was after 11:00 p.m. when they circled the block a third time looking for a parking place near Brady's building. Finally, a taxi pulled away from the curb, and Jolene made a U-turn to take the spot.

Aaron said, "Run it by me again."

Jolene sighed. "Tell him to come up with the ninety thousand dollars, or we're going to the cops anyway, and he knows why."

"He does?"

"Let me worry about the why."

"Got it." He pulled the door handle.

Jolene grabbed his arm. "And make him pay for not picking up the girls. Hurt him a little, okay?"

Aaron patted his bicep. "Time to fire the guns."

Jolene grinned.

He went to the front of Brady's building and pushed all the buttons. A few voices mixed together from the speaker, and then the door buzzed. He snatched it open. Up the stairs, he found the door for Brady's apartment. Aaron breathed in and out, getting himself psyched up.

"Showtime." He rapped on the door with his knuckles and waited.

He made fists and focused his eyes on the doorframe. When the door opened, he would reach in and grab the shithead by the neck.

He rapped again. No sounds came from the other side of the door. The doorframe looked old, so he took a few steps back and lunged at the door. It splintered. He put his fingers through the crack and broke the door open the rest of the way.

Witek wouldn't stay quiet now, so Aaron charged into the apartment, flipped on lights and opened doors. He checked the kitchen and bathroom. The guy didn't appear to be home. He wasn't in any of the closets. Aaron looked around—something was off—the kitchen had no table and chairs. The living room only had a sofa. The bedrooms were mostly empty. He opened a dresser drawer—no clothes. The closets were empty. The kitchen cabinets were empty. He left the apartment and went back down to Jolene's car. "Let's get out of here."

Jolene sped away from the curb and headed for the expressway. "So what happened? Did you knock him around?"

Aaron shook his head. "No, babe. He wasn't there."

"Then what took you so long?"

"I checked out the place. You're not going to like this, but it doesn't look like he's coming back."

"What do you mean?"

"The guy moved out. There's big stuff still in there, but the rest of the place is empty."

Aaron turned toward the windshield. He didn't like the look on Jolene's face.

◊　◊　◊

Saturday Morning
Lincolnwood, Illinois

Brady got a great night's sleep in the RV with a cool breeze coming in through the window, until the city morning sounds woke him up. When he first opened his eyes, he had to think for a minute where he was, and then the events of last night came back to him.

His sore testicles were another reminder, and his shoulder was sore from falling out of bed.

He'd come to the RV last night to sleep after Mrs. Fitzgibbons got a good look inside the apartment, possibly noticing how empty it was. He dropped down to the floor and went to the bathroom, time to test the toilet. After relieving himself and getting dressed, he climbed out and went to the Trailblazer. He would miss the old thing, but its time had come. He would drive to the used car lot, sell it, and then Uber back to the RV.

And then, onward to the open road.

Spencer rang his phone. He turned it off and started the motor. "Sorry, Spencer, there's no Brady Witek here. You must have called Gene Brinkman by mistake."

Later in the afternoon, Brady got out of the Uber car and walked across the storage lot to the RV. Fluffy white clouds floated across the blue sky with the temperature around seventy. Go sit in a stuffy office today with Spencer and Mark? The chances were between zero and none. It was time to venture.

As Brady ambled up to the plain old RV, he realized it needed a name. "Plain Jane" was too obvious. No cute traveling names like "Rolling Thunder." "Serena" would work because it had a big rear end, but then no. He rubbed his chin. How about "Libby," short for "Liberated?" Nah. The paint was mostly white. How about "Ghost?" That would work because he planned to vanish. He patted the fender. "If you want to be called 'Ghost,' don't honk your horn." He waited. "Then, it's settled." He stretched out his arms and breathed.

Brady climbed in the Ghost and buckled up. With sunglasses on, he started the engine and backed up. The sensor at the exit activated the gate when he pulled up, and he realized he didn't know which way to turn. The lake was to the left, so he took a right and headed west toward the expressway.

It just felt right to head for the mountains. At least it sounded good. Heading for the mountains made a good beer commercial. Camping in the mountains with a cold beer, how could you go wrong with that?

Brady pulled over and stuck his new GPS on the windshield with a suction cup. He made the destination Colorado and pushed the Go button. A British female voice told him to drive ahead, and he obeyed, conceding the GPS girl would be the only female giving him orders for a while.

Through the city traffic, he came to a low viaduct, but the RV went right under. He should have known ahead of time, but then screw it. The ramp for the expressway came up on the right, so he pushed down the accelerator to merge into the flow of traffic. The motor rumbled under the hood.

He was on his way.

He knew he shouldn't, but he turned on his phone. It chimed away with missed texts. Hah! When he got hungry, he would find a place to eat, and he would amuse himself by reading the angry text messages.

Or whatever, he didn't have to do anything he didn't want to do. He was free and easy.

Chapter 9

Sunday Evening
Seward, Kentucky

The plan was still a go after Kacey risked wiring a dollar to a vendor and the money had gone to his account. If the vendor had received the transfer, even for a dollar, they may have inquired about it, but the coding worked. A bogus notification arrived in his e-mail announcing the payment. Kacey closed his connection, shut down his computer in the storage room, and headed to his apartment.

His phone rang. He staggered after reading the identity of the caller. "Hello. Agent Bessing."

Verna Bessing spoke in a warm voice. "Kacey Farrell, how good to hear your voice. Are you well?"

"Very well, and you?"

"Still after the bad guys. That's not why I called you, Kacey. The FBI just wants you to know we're thinking about you."

Kacey measured his response. If she knew something, he would have been in custody by now. "My wife and I will divorce, but there is no need for concern."

"Well, your wife is concerned, and that's why I'm making this courtesy call. You've been a good boy for many years, but then a red flag went up for domestic violence."

"I have cooperated with the authorities. Charges were dropped. I intend to act honorably and end the marriage without a dispute."

Verna chuckled. "You always say the right things, Kacey. But I believe there's more going on inside that killer mind of yours. The military psychiatrists explained how you'd be a handful someday. Where are you staying?"

Kacey stumbled. "Where… With an acquaintance. His marriage is also ending, so he let me stay on the couch in his apartment." The answer didn't sound right.

"Okay. That's why we don't have a current address for you. Give me your friend's address, if you would."

"I cannot remain at this location. Tomorrow, I must find a motel room."

"Okay… Please text your new address to me when possible."

"Yes, ma'am."

"And Kacey?"

"Yes, ma'am?"

"Like I said from the start, we're here to help you."

Kacey breathed. He needed human feeling in his voice. "Agent Bessing, other than a disturbance with my spouse, I have lived a calm, normal lifestyle here in Kentucky. My workplace is stable, and my private life is quiet. It has been idyllic to work and live in a forested area."

"That had not occurred to me. Tall trees instead of desert sand. Very encouraging. I'll check on you again." She hung up.

He set down the phone and replayed the call in his head. Bessing gave no clue, even a hint, that she knew about his plan. She truly must have called because of the domestic disturbance, especially if Billie contacted her.

After undressing in the bedroom, he sat in the chair gazing at the wall for a time in the living room, stepping away from the anxiety remaining from the phone call. A good night's sleep was required for a successful day tomorrow, and when he could detect no emotion, he got in bed, pulled up the covers, and drifted off.

◊　◊　◊

Monday Morning
Seward, Kentucky

Kacey drove his Sonata to his old house, parked at the curb, and left the keys in the mailbox. An Uber driver pulled up to drive him to the office. While in the back seat, he jammed his cell phone in the seat cushion with the sound off.

At the corporate building, he wore a backpack through the foyer, up the stairs, and into his office. No one spoke to him. The money transfers were set for today. The scripts were active. The new e-mail account would collect notifications, and when enough money filled his bank account, he would execute phase two: the disturbance.

A quiver occurred in his stomach, and his throat tightened. Verna Bessing entered his thoughts. He stepped into the hallway and let his eyes roam over the cinder block wall. The feeling of separation took him away from anxiety. He went back to his desk.

Vijay strode in without knocking. "Jen just told me how you're running scripts to send money transfers through a proxy? Why didn't you tell me about it?"

Kacey stood. "Hello, Vijay. Good morning."

"What about these scripts?"

Kacey motioned to a chair. "Please sit."

"Quit stalling, Kacey. Tell me what's going on."

Kacey shrugged. "It's like Jen said. I felt another layer of security was necessary these days."

"And you set it up without telling me?"

"No, Vijay. I only tested them. You were to be told after I knew they worked. Why would I bother you before?"

"You and I need to go to Lambert's office. You made changes to the server without telling me. This is serious."

"Okay, I'll join you. But I'm only interested in better security. If you want to take credit, please do so."

"Knock off the excuses and follow me." Vijay walked out.

Kacey considered the 9 mm pistol under his desk before following.

Vijay called from down the hallway. "Get moving. Let's go."

◊　◊　◊

"This sounds harmless to me," Lambert said. "If Kacey wants to improve our cyber security, why not let him?"

"Because he made changes to the system without telling me."

"I'm guilty, ma'am." Kacey nodded. "To fill my day, I look for ways to improve the system. It was wrong of me to keep things from Vijay, and I am very sorry."

Vijay sighed.

Lambert asked, "Does your new system work?"

"It does. It's not complicated, just a new way to route sensitive transfers."

"Yeah, whatever." Vijay frowned. "We may use it, I don't know. For now, it needs to be removed."

Lambert waved. "Then off you go."

Kacey and Vijay left together. Vijay sped away without speaking. Kacey ran back to his office. Vijay would go after the scripts, and he had to get to them first. Back in his office, Kacey changed the directory of the scripts and pointed the accounting system to a new directory called "cache." If Jen had told Vijay were to look, he would now find an empty directory.

The e-mail account showed two transfers were completed. If he could keep the scripts running, he would soon be a millionaire.

Kacey strode to Vijay's office near the server room. Inside, Vijay focused on his computer screen with Jen looking over his shoulder.

Jen turned. "You deleted the scripting?"

"Yes, as instructed."

Vijay turned in his chair. "But I needed to look at them."

Kacey shook his head. "Sorry, they're gone."

"What? Do you have backups?"

"No. You rattled me. All my work was on the server."

"Was it included with the online backup?"

"I never added the directory to the list."

Vijay sat back. Jen crossed her arms.

"I will recreate the scripting from my notes."

Vijay just stared. Jen didn't move.

Kacey excused himself and left.

◇   ◇   ◇

Lunchtime came and went. Kacey ate a sandwich at his desk. No one else had visited his office. No memorandums arrived, no calls came from accounting—all good signs while his secret bank account continued to fill. But as the minutes ticked away, his anxiety grew, causing physical discomfort. He stayed close to himself for now, planning to head to the basement to first sit in front of the wall, and then make the final preparations.

As he went for another bite of the sandwich, Mrs. Lambert walked in. Kacey flinched.

"Sorry to startle you, Mr. Farrell, but I need to speak with you."

Kacey dropped the sandwich and stood.

"Your supervisor, Vijay, returned to my office and advised that he no longer wished to have you on his team. After your unauthorized security measures and other recent incidents, I have decided to end your employment at Winslow-Carnac. You have until the end of the day to clear out your personal belongings."

Kacey's lungs seized. Pressure bulged behind his eyes.

"Please remain calm, Mr. Farrell. You will receive a generous severance check, and we will not dispute unemployment payments."

He put his hands behind his back to conceal the shaking. His face became hot. He tried to speak. "How? Why? You can't."

Before he lost it completely, he closed his eyes and followed the afterimages on his retinas. Memories from the war entered his thoughts as his eyes floated around the shapes. He fought a spinning sensation until a calmness settled in. His face cooled, and he opened his eyes.

Mrs. Lambert stared with a shaken expression. "There you are. I was afraid you had a stroke. Should I call for medical assistance, Mr. Farrell?"

"That will not be necessary, Mrs. Lambert. I will begin to clear out my personal effects as requested. Thank you for my employment. I found the stable environment suited for my temperament."

Lambert took a deep breath. "Yes, well, I will arrange for a letter of recommendation. We will say you resigned. Thank you for making this easy, Mr. Farrell."

Kacey nodded. Lambert left. He dropped to the chair and typed on the keyboard to open a command prompt, after changing to the correct directory, he typed the word "engage" and added a hyphen and the number 15. Fifteen minutes should be enough time. He pressed enter, ripped the pistol down from under the desk and slid it into the back of his pants. He unlocked a cabinet. Inside, a large UPS battery sat fully charged next to a black rectangle device for blocking cell phone transmissions. He switched it on. Everyone in or around the building just lost their signal. Land lines would go down in three minutes.

He grabbed the backpack and went down flights of stairs to the basement. Several employees passed by. One looked at his phone with a frown. When he arrived in the open area near the wall, something felt wrong.

Light bulbs had been replaced. Why now? Off to the right, an area was darker with bulbs missing. Kacey went over and noticed new wiring along the top of the wall leading to a camera on top of a row of shelving, aimed at his chair.

Kacey glanced at his watch. Eight minutes left.

The camera could not be explained. Vijay must have started collecting evidence to get rid of him by recording strange behavior. He took out the pistol, blasted the camera off the shelf, and then sat in the chair to gaze at the wall. His eyes traveled around the familiar surface, drifting to each imperfection. The camera on the shelf was not going to be a factor, even if they'd seen him raise the pistol. Time was almost up for Vijay and Winslow-Carnac.

Getting up from the chair, he pulled out parts for an AR15 rifle from his backpack, along with a black overcoat and ski mask. He dropped ammo clips into coat pockets and then assembled the gun. Right when he glanced at his watch, the fire alarm whaled. Emergency lights came on, and sprinklers activated.

He pulled on the ski mask and raced up the stairs to the foyer. Freddy ran in front of him. Kacey aimed and fired. Freddy dove to the ground as a window across the foyer shattered. Women screamed and threw files in the air. Kacey charged up the stairs to the second floor. In the hallway, Vijay and Jen slid to a stop on the wet floor. They put their hands up, Kacey fired over their heads, and they dropped to the floor. He squeezed off two rounds into the wall and jumped over them, heading to Vijay's office.

Inside, he located Vijay's workstation computer and laptop and shot them to pieces. He ran to Jen and Rich's workstations in a room nearby. Rich leaped up, saw Kacey, and dropped. Kacey fired into the wall. Rich crawled on the floor like a dog scrambling away. He shot their computers and checked his watch; three minutes had passed. His own workstation would be shredding data on the hard drive.

The bosses were next.

He went up the stairs and around to the corporate suites. Jill was gone as planned. He wanted everyone to exit the building when the sirens sounded. Around the corner and down the hall, Mrs. Lambert splashed in the water running from her office. Kacey put on the brakes to keep from sliding into her. She gasped when he raised the gun, and then he fired a shot into the wall next to her. She grabbed her chest and slid down the wall as sprinkler water cascaded down from the ceiling.

He went from office to office, firing shots into computers, wide-screen televisions, and scotch bottles. The water cooler took a bullet, so did the microwave oven and refrigerator in the executive lunchroom. On the way back, he went into Lambert's office and blasted her desk. Back in the hallway, he jammed another clip into the gun. Lambert hadn't moved from the wall.

The siren went quiet on schedule. The sprinklers stopped. He planned them to stop so he could hear. The building became quiet, except for the sound of dripping water.

He splashed down to the second floor and around to the server room. His former coworkers were now gone. He checked his watch, eight minutes, too early. The scripting on the servers needed ten, so he went to his office to look out the window. No flashing lights yet, but people ran to their cars. Some sped out of the lot while others hid.

He fired a shot through his office window. After the glass fell away, he could hear screaming. People out in the open vanished behind cars.

Two minutes were up, and Kacey ran back to the server room knowing the scripts on the hard drives would be finished. He shot up the hard disk array for the main server and then the reporting server. Next, he destroyed the camera hard drives. He killed the file server and then shot the voice over IP machine.

With the servers dead, it was time to go. He went to the stairwell and made his way to the ground floor, careful not to slip in the water. He circled to the south side and found the service door leading outside to the rock wall. He resisted the urge to give it one last gaze as faint police sirens came from the highway out front. He ran east toward the back of the building through the narrow gap between the building and the wall.

At the back corner, Kacey collided with Freddy, chest to chest, bouncing away from each other to their backs.

Kacey recovered, jumped to his feet as Freddy charged swinging his night stick. Kacey ducked too late and took a blow to his head. Freddy took hold of the AR15 to wrestle it away. They jerked with the gun, back and forth. Kacey pulled in on the weapon and broke Freddy's nose with his forehead. Freddy stumbled away, still on his feet.

Freddy had to be neutralized, or he would inform the police of his escape route. Kacey took out his pistol and aimed at Freddy's head. Freddy turned to run. Kacey sprinted forward and clubbed him in the back of the head. Freddy went down, out cold. Good enough.

Kacey went to the trees and made his way through as the sirens grew louder. They faded the farther he made it through the trees. In ten minutes, he arrived at the old house and found the motorcycle where he'd left it. He dismantled the gun, took off the coat and ski mask and loaded up the backpack. He put the helmet on and started up the bike. A lump on his head pressed into the side of the helmet.

He drove to the bushes beside the road and got off the bike, setting the kick stand to observe the road. Three police cars raced by from the south. Once they were out of site, he drove out to the road and accelerated slowly to keep the noise down. When he was down the road a few miles, he got up to the speed limit. No cars passed him on the way. He took a turn for another road that would take him to the woods south of Bea's house.

He passed houses on the way, but with no people in the yards. He made his last turn down a dirt road where he needed to stand on the foot pegs because of the dips, the bike bucking like a horse beneath him. The road disappeared at a clearing with an old foundation.

Kacey slowed the bike near the shack he would use to hide the bike. No paint remained on any of the boards, dark with decay. The roof had collapsed decades ago, and the remainder of the walls leaned in like an A-frame. He pushed boards around to create a crevice to hide the motorcycle and then used a loose board to prop sections of wall to create space. He rolled the bike inside, tossed in the back-pack, and covered them with boards. He backed up and inspected. The motorcycle was hidden, but he had to cover up the tracks, so he collected pine needles for the job.

Bea's house was a two-mile hike to the north, but as Kacey strolled in the direction, something felt wrong. Directions to his body were not being followed. His vision blurred, and then the woods seemed to spin to the point he held himself up with a pine tree. Normal consciousness returned. Pain coursed through his head.

The bump on his head stuck out like a rounded-off horn. Kacey grimaced, thinking how people described it as having their bell rung. How accurate.

He trudged over to a fallen tree to sit. Two miles would be difficult to walk in this condition—he could pass out and be found by a stranger.

Tracking dogs shouldn't be a problem after he fled on motorcycle. His cell phone would lead authorities on a wild goose chase in the Uber car. Freddy may direct authorities to the woods behind corporate, but only after he woke up, and he may not remember the encounter.

The sound of a helicopter came from an unknown direction and grew louder. Kacey located a clump of bushes and crawled under as the helicopter flew over. When the sound grew faint, he went back to the old shack, retrieved his back pack, and climbed over fallen boards to the rear of the structure. He found a sturdy wide board to lie flat and lean more against the back wall to create a shelter. He crawled in to rest using the backpack for a pillow and the coat as a blanket.

You were not supposed to sleep with a head injury, but he would have to take his chances. As he fell unconscious, the helicopter passed overhead for another sweep.

◊　◊　◊

Monday Afternoon
Seward, Kentucky

Responders at Winslow-Carnac quickly discovered radio and cell communication were blocked, leading to more chaos. Employees had either sped away in their cars or remained hiding, shaking with fear. By the time Sherriff Millard arrived from Lewisburg, he found the three Seward Police officers in a state of panic, believing the loss of communication meant terrorism.

Millard took the bullhorn from the trunk of his cruiser and called out to the building several times, asking for those involved inside to make contact. He had Winslow-Carnac employees brought to the side of a fire engine and got his men to calm them down. A nice-looking female named Jen seemed collected enough to speak.

Millard spoke in a gentle tone. "Ma'am, what happened here today?"

"A man wearing a ski mask and a long black coat went around shooting at employees with a scary-looking machine gun."

Millard felt his stomach tighten. "How many victims did you see?"

"He missed, and then we ran out here."

"But how many gunshot victims did you see?"

"Everyone ran out as fast as they could. Some got in their cars and raced away. A shot came through the second story window, and then we all ducked behind cars."

Millard frowned. "Ma'am, please calm down. I want to know how many gunshot victims you saw lying on the ground."

"Well." Jen paused to think. "I guess I didn't see any. There were holes in the walls and broken glass, but nobody seemed to be shot."

Deputy Kline ran around the end of the fire engine. "Boss, we found a casualty behind the structure. It's the security guard."

"Gunshot?"

"No, he received a blow in the back of the head. He's still too groggy to talk, so we took him to an ambulance."

Millard rubbed his chin. "Okay, Kline. Have someone kill the power to the building. Maybe we'll get our radios back."

A loud bang sounded right next to Millard. Jen screamed. Millard drew his pistol and turned. A Seward patrol car sat with its back bumper smashed into his cruiser's front grill.

Millard raised his voice. "People, we all must stay professional. Remember your training." He turned and surveyed the area. "Cooper, get over here." Cooper ran up. "Get in your car. Drive down the road until your radio starts working. Contact the state police, and confirm SWAT is coming. Go."

Millard went into the cab of the fire engine and peered at the building with binoculars. The windows were reflective, so he couldn't see anything but the shattered window. Nothing moved inside.

Without radio coordination, he wouldn't go in there. They never had anything like this happen in Central Kentucky, and he sure as hell wouldn't try an incursion until he knew what they were up against.

The sound of a truck engine came from the entrance, along with the screech of brakes. Millard climbed out of the cab when a black truck with SWAT written on the side pulled up. The team spilled out and took cover. One man approached Millard. "I'm Commander Phelps. What's the situation?"

Millard ran down everything he knew. Phelps tried his radio, and it didn't work.

"So you can't confirm any more casualties?"

"That's right."

Commander Phelps walked to the front of the fire engine and surveyed the scene. He waved one of his men over and spoke in his ear. The man gathered the rest of the team, leading them north to the tree line where they melted in.

Phelps came back to Millard. "I'm sending my team into the building. Based on the circumstances, we'll strike quickly."

"Aren't you worried about a trap? What if the place is set to blow?"

"My men know the risks."

Millard went around to the back of the truck to watch black figures enter the side of the building over the patio.

◊ ◊ ◊

Monday Night
Seward, Kentucky

Kacey woke in a state of confusion, lying on boards in the dark, believing a building had collapsed. He felt around and found the rifle and then felt the knot on his head, pulsating with pain. He pushed the boards away and stood up, swaying on his feet. The site of the old shack brought back his memory. Before climbing out, he unzipped his trousers, relieved himself on the back wall, and took out an LED flashlight to climb out over the boards. Confidence returned as he stood on the ground.

Raindrops rustled the leaves, stirring up the scent of pine. A rumble of thunder came from the west. Kacey lit up his watch. It was 10:11 p.m. After a few awkward steps to the north, he went to the nearest tree to steady himself from the head injury. He needed to step back from himself, or he wouldn't make it. Time to improvise—he put the flashlight in his mouth and aimed it at the tree bark, steadying himself with both hands, allowing his eyes to wander.

The conscious part of his mind separated from his bodily functions, and he ordered himself to move forward at a slow pace, focusing on each step through the trees. Halfway home, the rain came down steady, soaking Kacey's clothing. The cold rain seemed to calm his head and maybe reduced the swelling.

Up ahead, Bea's house finally came into view with a faint glow coming from the kitchen window. Bea always left a light on for his benefit. Before going inside, he hid in the bushes for surveillance.

Ten minutes passed, and nothing moved. If the police were hiding, waiting for him to show, then he was caught. No way could he get to the motorcycle in time.

He made his way carefully around to the back of the house and shined the light on the steps. He'd made black marks on the steps where he could step and not make a noise. On the way up, a step in the middle cracked, but he continued up and let himself in. In the bathroom, he undressed and hung wet clothing on the shower rod. He took a washcloth to the kitchen and wrapped ice cubes to place on his head. Finally, he turned off all the lights and went to bed.

From the night stand drawer, he took out a smartphone and opened a camera app. A night-vision shot of Bea's yard appeared. No police cars were parked out front. He turned on a metal box and plugged in an earpiece. An alarm would sound in the earpiece if a laser beam was interrupted across the drive.

Kacey laid back on the pillow, placing the ice pack on his throbbing head. He closed his eyes and tried to rest his rattled brain before attempting to move the money.

◊　◊　◊

A beep sounded in his ear. The clock on the nightstand read 3:37 a.m. He snatched the phone from the nightstand and forced his eyes to focus. A deer walked from the driveway into the front yard. He set the phone down. *The laser alarm worked.*

He laid back on the soggy pillowcase. The ice cubes had melted. Once again, he drifted off.

The beep sounded in his ear again. He sat up too quickly and held his head—time for some aspirin. As he went to the kitchen to find the bottle, weak morning light came in through the windows. A car door shut outside.

He dashed back to the bedroom and checked the phone app—a patrol car sat out front. Two police officers were walking to the front door. Kacey straightened the bedcovers and flipped the pillow over. He turned off the phone and laser unit, set them both in the bottom drawer of the dresser and covered them with clothing. He went to the bathroom, took yesterday's clothing off the shower rod, and put them in the hamper. He went to the workroom and shut the door, noticing footsteps on the stairs.

◇ ◇ ◇

Bea led the two deputies up the stairs. The one named Cooper stayed on the second floor to search while Kline continued with her to the third floor. He tried to take her arm several times, and she insisted she could make it up the stairs by herself. "I really don't think my renter is here now, Deputy. My hearing is still very good, and other then a crack and a few groans from the old house, I've heard nothing."

Kline walked down the hallway to the apartment door. "For your safety, I'd still like to check the place out."

"Don't you need permission from the tenant to go in?"

"You're the owner… You said it was okay."

Bea unlocked the door with her key. Kline went in and searched every room before returning to the hall. "What about this door here?"

Bea unlocked. "He uses this room for an office. His name is John Wilson, and he's fifty-seven years old. He can't be the man you're looking for."

Kline went in. A computer table sat in the corner. An old Persian rug was spread across the floor. On a dresser, several picture frames displayed a middle-aged couple.

"Is this John Wilson in the pictures?" Then Kline remembered Bea was blind. "Sorry, there are several pictures of a middle-aged couple."

"It must be John and his deceased wife."

Kline glanced around. "Okay, I'll join Cooper and check the lower levels. Please call 911 if you see…if you encounter Kacey Farrell."

"I certainly will, Officer."

They left the room and went down the stairs.

◇ ◇ ◇

In the workroom, the Persian rug bulged up at one end and fell to the floor as Kacey pushed opened the hatch underneath. He breathed in fresh air and climbed out. Back in the apartment, he found the aspirin bottle in the kitchen. According to his watch, the police had left forty-five minutes ago. He went back through the room and down the steps in back, avoiding squeaks by stepping on the black marks. He strode across the lawn and headed south with renewed energy. His head still hurt, but not enough to hinder the march the two miles back to the motorcycle.

Once there, he pulled out the backpack and hid it deeper in the fallen boards. The motorcycle started right up. He weaved through the trees back to Bea's house and pulled into the barn across from the house.

Bea came out the front door. "Mr. Wilson, is that you?"

Kacey walked over. "It's me, Bea. I have my new motorcycle now. I hope I didn't startle you."

"No, John. But there was an incident in the area. A man in the corporate building on the highway fired gunshots at employees. The police were here a short time ago and searched the house."

"That explains all the activity. Was my apartment searched?"

"Yes. The officer wanted to rule you out as the suspect. He saw the pictures of you and your deceased wife. I told him you weren't the one, but he insisted."

"It's okay. I believe we're safe here, but I'll keep watch. Try not to worry, Bea."

"Thank you, John. The officer said the man did not actually shoot anyone, but an older woman died of a heart attack. We are to consider him dangerous."

Kacey didn't move. He would now be wanted for felony murder.

"John, are you there?"

"I'm here, Bea. I need to attend to some financial matters on my computer. Please excuse me."

Kacey headed upstairs.

Chapter 10

Tuesday Afternoon
Harwood Heights, Illinois

Sydney Brandenburg entered the foyer of Polyglomerate Container and walked up to the front desk. The attractive receptionist asked, "How may I help you?"

"I'm an attorney, and I wish to speak with Mark Seivers."

The secretary took his name and got on the phone. She hung up. "I'm sorry, but Mr. Seivers is busy now. I can make an appointment."

"Please tell him I am here regarding Brady Witek."

The secretary seemed surprised to hear the name. She called again and set the phone down. "He'll see you now on the third floor."

Sydney took the stairs and found the office. Inside, Mark Seivers stood and shook his hand. They sat down.

"Has something happened to Brady? We can't get ahold of him."

Sydney set his briefcase on the desk and opened the lid. "Brady Witek is alive and well. He sent me here to conclude his employment with your company." Sydney handed Seivers a paper. "Here is his letter of resignation."

Seivers took the paper, glanced at it, and then wadded it up and threw it at the wall. "That piece of shit can't leave. We're in the middle of a critical merger, and he's the only one that knows what to do."

"Mr. Witek anticipated your reaction." Sydney took out a manila envelope full of documents and placed it on the desk. "Everything you need to know about your systems is right here. You will notice the top page includes logins and passwords for every function. Also, he printed out configuration pages for every app. You now have a complete catalogue of his knowledge and can start working right where he left off."

Seivers took out the documents and leafed through. "I'll sue Witek's balls off if we can't access anything."

"Mr. Witek is aware of the laws concerning software access when an employee leaves the job. You have everything you need."

Seivers leaned back in his chair. "Let me talk to him."

"My job is to wrap things up for him."

Mark sat forward and opened his desk drawer. He poured scotch into a glass, lifting his eyebrow at Sydney.

"No, thank you, Mr. Seivers. One last thing, Mr. Witek wishes to express his regret at leaving on short notice and says your company will continue to run well with an outstanding computer technician like Spenser Moss."

Seivers chuckled. "Yeah, well, tell him 'Fuck you too.'"

◊ ◊ ◊

Thursday Afternoon
Lewisburg, Kentucky

The meeting took place in the Lewisburg Police Station conference room. Sherriff Millard sat at the head of the table. Deputy Kline took a chair to the right. Commander Phelps sat at the other end. An officer strode in, introducing himself as Lieutenant Jameson from the State Police. Billie Farrell arrived with a man in an expensive suit who introduced himself has Mike Lowen, Billie's attorney. They all settled.

Millard glanced around the table. "First, I want to thank Mrs. Farrell for cooperating with the search for her husband."

Billie nodded.

"The purpose of this meeting is to get all departments on the same—"

The door opened, and a broad-shouldered woman walked in wearing a pantsuit. "I hope you haven't forgotten about the FBI, Sherriff Millard."

"This is a state matter, Agent Bessing. No state lines were crossed."

Bessing took a chair. "The FBI gets involved when it wants to. Don't worry, you can take the press."

Millard frowned. "Kline, give us an update on the search."

"All we know is Farrell escaped through the woods behind the building. Dogs traced him out to an old garage, and then the scent went cold, but we found motorcycle tracks. Searches of houses in the area turned up nothing. No residents in the area spotted him. We scared an Uber driver half to death when we traced Farrell's phone to his back seat."

The door opened again. An older gentleman, well-dressed but with dark circles under his eyes, came in. He introduced himself as Frank Whiteside, president of Winslow-Carnac.

Millard motioned for him to sit. "Our condolences for Geraldine Lambert."

Whiteside nodded. "Thank you. I'm here to explain some background."

"Please, go ahead."

"Just prior to the shootings, Lambert fired Farrell for taking liberties with the server. I approved his termination."

"Definitely goes to motive," Millard said. "Phelps, what did you find on the premises?"

"We found a large jamming device in Farrell's office, plugged into a battery. He really screwed us up with that thing. Our radios wouldn't work until we turned it off. As far as the attack goes, he didn't actually shoot anyone, so we assume he meant only to frighten employees. Upstairs in the executive suites, he shot the shit out of everything, including toilets in the fancy washroom. Then, he blasted the servers."

Bessing raised her hand. "Mr. Whiteside, you said Farrell tampered with the servers before you fired him. Can you describe the tampering?"

"He said he was testing a new security feature for wire transfers."

"Are any funds missing?"

"We can hardly check. Farrell shot the hell out of our servers. Our IT department is trying to put us back together again."

"Have you checked your bank accounts?"

Whiteside shook his head. "We haven't. We would have to call the bank."

Millard asked, "Agent Bessing, just what interest does the FBI have in this case?"

Verna held her hands together and looked down at the table. She looked up. "Kacey Farrell has been under our watch since his discharge from the Army. Exit evaluations suggested his condition could someday be a problem."

"What condition?"

Billie Farrell spoke up. "Kacey has depersonalization disorder. Some call it derealization syndrome. It's hard to describe, but basically, he feels disconnected from himself, like he's outside his body. He described it to me as being an observer of himself. Most people have a hard time with the condition, but Kacey figured out how to use it to his benefit in the Army." She looked over at Bessing.

Bessing took papers out of a file. "This report says the Army knew of his condition, but kept him active because of his effectiveness in combat situations. Now this is the critical part—he could control the disorder through meditation, allowing it to occur during times of stress, and thus allowing himself to function in combat without the burden of emotion."

Millard asked, "So because of this condition, this guy was a super soldier?"

"His file is classified. All I can say is, Kacey Farrell was the go to guy in urban warfare. They sent him into town alone to clear out the unfriendlies. A comment was left in his file about how his uniform was still dry afterward. He didn't even work up a sweat."

Phelps shook his head. "And we let this guy return to civilization? How are regular cops supposed to deal with him?"

"We can handle ourselves," Lieutenant Jameson said. "Most of my guys are ex-military."

Billie said, "If you find him, please don't kill him."

"We always use lethal force as a last resort," Millard said. "Mrs. Farrell, why did your husband do what he did? Why snap now?"

Billie looked around at the faces at the table. "It started when he hit me a few weeks ago. I'd done my best to live with him for years, but when he got physical, that was the last straw. We decided to divorce, and Mr. Whiteside just said he was fired from his job. That's why Kacey snapped. The quiet, stable life he'd settled into was ending, and he can't deal with big changes. It's hard enough for him to function in society, but starting all over again would be overwhelming."

Millard asked, "But you said he could control his condition and operate without stress."

"Stepping away from stress does not mean you have people skills. He has to think about what to say and how to act all day long. It's a hard way to live."

Bessing spoke up. "Regardless of why he did what he did, we have a dangerous man on the loose. I was assigned to keep an eye on Farrell. In fact, I spoke with him on the phone the night before the incident. He gave me no indication of his plans. Now my orders are to apprehend Mr. Farrell to avoid further incidents."

Jameson said, "Fine, if we find the guy, we'll call you. You can dodge the bullets."

"Actually, that is exactly what I want. Don't engage him. I'll be glad to deal with him myself." She turned to Whiteside. "But first, I'll work with you to find out how much money he stole from your business."

Whiteside's eyes grew wide.

◊　◊　◊

Friday Afternoon
Evanston, Illinois

Serena Haynesworth wept softly in her father's library. She got up and paced around the edge of the room, near the bookshelves.

Each time she passed the crystal scotch decanter, she cried some more, knowing she couldn't drink while pregnant.

A door meant to look like part of the shelving opened, and Winston walked in. "Hello, kitten. What do you need to speak with me about?"

Serena motioned to the high-back leather chairs by the fireplace. Winston sat down, Serena poured him a generous scotch and set it on the table between the chairs.

"What do you need to say that requires me to drink this much scotch?"

Serena sighed. "Father, what I have to tell you should be seen as a blessed event, not one to scorn. We live in modern times now."

Winston set his scotch down with a bang. "How could you let this happen, Serena? Birth control is a modern convenience as well."

Serena's mouth opened. *Father's mind was still razor sharp.* "Yes… But there's more I need to tell you."

Winston drank down the scotch. "Turns out, I need a refill." He got up and went to the liquor cart. "Continue speaking."

"On the date the other night, the one with the church member, he got frisky and had his way with me. He was so attracted to me he couldn't help himself, and now…"

The scotch glass bounced on the floor and rolled by Serena's feet. Serena turned to see her father's red face.

"He took advantage of my daughter? I'll have him neutered with a rusty hacksaw. And then I'll break the pastor's knees, the one who set up the date."

Serena got up and took her father by the arm to lead him back to his chair. "Father, I forbid you from harming Brady, and leave the pastor alone. All I want to do is to marry the father of my child. You will finally have the grandchild you always wanted."

"You want me to make a son out of the man who accosted my daughter?"

Serena turn away. This wasn't how she wanted it to go. She had to fix it. "I have to admit, my loneliness caused me to succumb to his advances. To say he forced me would be an overstatement."

Winston looked in her eyes. He gazed down at her belly and then drank scotch. "I understand, Serena… Your luck with men has been abysmal. If this man wishes to make an honest woman of you, then I will tolerate him. It's true that I want to hear the patter of little feet in this house again."

Serena sat in her father's lap and put her cheek against his. "Thank you, Father. Soon, we'll all get what we want."

◊   ◊   ◊

Friday Evening
Crystal Lake, Illinois

Aaron stepped out in the hallway, heard screaming girl voices, and jumped back into the bedroom as Laurie and Crissy tore past. Ashley stuck her head out of her room and laughed. Aaron looked both ways and tried again. The girls loved the new house, no doubt, and they each had their own room. The upstairs had three bathrooms, which was still barely enough. They planned to use the movie room tonight for the first time after swimming in the pool. The place was awesome.

He found Jolene downstairs, surrounded by stainless steel in the massive kitchen. After a week of moving in, everything was put away. She had pizzas cooking in the oven. Aaron fixed himself a drink from the liquor cabinet. "Need a drink, babe?"

Jolene walked over and grabbed his rear end.

"Hey now…let's eat dinner before we have dessert."

She walked away and sat down at the table. "We finally got the house of our dreams, and that prick Brady takes off."

Aaron sat across from her at the table. "Listen, this place is awesome. I love being a dad to your girls. We're going to make this work. Count on it."

Jolene's frown became a grin. "That's what I want to hear, but we have to find Brady and keep the fifteen hundred coming in."

"You didn't get the money this month?"

"No…I called where he works, and they said he quit. His landlord is pissed. That slut, Cindy, doesn't know where he is. Let's face it, he left town."

"Let me ask around. Maybe someone can help us. Meanwhile, you need to get more hours at work. We'll burn through my cash in no time."

◇　◇　◇

Arizona

Joe clinked beer bottles with Brady as they sat around a campfire in the desert. Motorcycles were parked all around, many with packs strapped on the back. People slept on sleeping bags uncovered in the warm desert air.

The Ghost was parked in a line of RVs, owned by travelers who like to stay off the beaten path. Brady met Joe in Colorado, and when his group headed south, he decided to tag along. The mountains were fun, but he wanted to keep moving.

"Joe, what is it you do again?"

"I contract out as a software engineer. My current deadline is in a few weeks. I'm customizing an interface for a medical company."

"No kidding? I'm a coder. It never occurred to me I could work anywhere."

Joe threw back the rest of his beer and got a new one for himself and Brady. "You've discovered the calling, the calling of the road. We don't worry about mortgages or light bills out here. And we never get stuck in one place. If someone needs a job done and I don't feel like doing it, I turn it down. We're talking about real freedom here."

"You're right about leaving my bills behind, but I'm actually on the run."

"You may need to elaborate."

"I decided to leave town when there wasn't enough of me to go around."

"As good a reason as any. How long do you plan to live out here?"

"I have no set plans, but I may head north. There's a lodge in Wisconsin run by a friend. I need to find a way to get back into my children's lives, but I have no idea how."

"That does complicate things, but you see the Bradford's over there? They parked their rig next to yours. They have three kids and stay on the road. Jeanie homeschools and the kids test in the upper percentile."

Brady clinked his bottle with Joe's again. "It can't be a mistake meeting you out here, Joe. You have the answers. Do you believe in God?"

"Sure, I do. I've accepted Christ as my savior. Out here, you find plenty of occasions to do His work. We help people out all the time. How about you?"

"I've turned my life over, and I want to live the simple life, just like you."

"Excellent. You can hang with us as long as you want. We're heading down to the boarder tomorrow."

"The border of Mexico?" Brady shook his head. "I'm going to have to decline."

"Suit yourself."

"I fed my sandwich to a coyote a couple of hours ago. That was cool."

Joe chuckled. "May you have many more adventures, my friend."

◊   ◊   ◊

Monday Morning
Crystal Lake, Illinois

Doreen Angelo giggled as Aaron smoothed tanning lotion on her butt. He moved around front, and she began to purr.

Sue from the front counter tapped on the door to the tanning room. "Get out here, Aaron. Jolene just walked in."

Aaron dropped the bottle and left Mrs. Angelo standing naked. He wiped his hands on a towel, put an innocent look on his face, and told Sue to have Jolene meet him in his office. He waited for a moment and went in. "Babe, what are you doing here?"

"They laid me off at the school. Budget cuts."

"You can't lose your job now."

Jolene looked out the office window. "I'll work here. Fire the bimbo at the front counter."

Aaron shook his head. "No can do. She's certified as a trainer and certified for tanning."

"I didn't just get here, you know."

"What do you mean?"

"I saw you go back to the tanning rooms with that blond. You had a silly grin on your face."

Aaron went around and sat behind his desk. "Don't start with that crap. The gym is about bodies. We get friendly with the clients, but nothing naughty happens."

Jolene came around and shoved Aaron's shoulder, causing him to roll away in his chair.

"Jolene, get ahold of yourself."

She put her purse over her shoulder and went out to her car.

◊   ◊   ◊

Tuesday Afternoon
Chicago, Illinois

Winston Haynesworth walked into a deserted warehouse on Forty-Seventh Street near Pulaski. Grit and glass crunched under his feet. Hoisting equipment dangled from steel girders overhead. Ancient brick columns held them up. He looked around the empty building, noticed a light in a row of offices, and walked toward it. He couldn't see through the dusty windows, so he opened the thick wooden door. A man turned as if startled. "Did Sal send you?"

A lightbulb dangled from the ceiling. The place hadn't been occupied in years. Haynesworth shook the man's hand and introduced himself. "I'm Winston Haynesworth. I thought Sal sent you."

"I'm Mark Seivers. There must be some sort of a mix-up."

The door creaked. A large man with a bald head entered wearing a long gray coat and polished shoes. "I would be the man you're both looking for. My name is Gavin." He approached and shook hands.

"I don't understand." Haynesworth asked, "Why does this guy need to be here?"

"It's an unusual situation. Sal sent me to clarify a few things. Both of you made a request for our help concerning the same fellow, Brady Witek."

"I'm here because Witek impregnated my daughter and disappeared. He needs to be found and taught a lesson."

Gavin turned to Seivers.

"Brady Witek is my most talented IT tech at Polyglomerate Container. He disappeared, and now, I have a mess. My dipshit IT manager is lost. The first two contractors fucked things up. I need Witek back."

Gavin scratched his nose. "Of course, I am aware of the merger deal. Wasn't there a tech working for Jenkins?"

"He found another job before Brady left."

Gavin paced down to the end of the office and back. "You both want the guy brought back to town, but for different reasons, so we have a conflict. If we teach Mr. Witek a lesson for violating Mr. Haynesworth's daughter, he would not be in good condition to complete the merger."

Haynesworth stepped away, attempting to pace.

Gavin stopped him. "Sorry, Mr. Haynesworth, but there's nothing to consider here. Sal's interests in Polyglomerate are a priority. I hope you understand."

Haynesworth sighed. "My daughter, Serena, says she has feelings for the guy. Just bring him back and make him understand his responsibilities."

"Are we talking about a shotgun wedding?"

"Something like that, but I don't see a long-term relationship with this guy."

Gavin turned to Seivers. "Is there a possibility Witek left town because he discovered Sal's involvement?"

"I don't know. It's possible… Maybe he was afraid Haynesworth would castrate him."

Gavin nodded. "Regardless, we need to find Witek." He turned back to Haynesworth. "Seiver's gets Witek first, and then we'll deliver him to you. You okay with that?"

Haynesworth nodded.

Gavin headed for the door, holding it open for the other two. "Pleasure doing business with you guys."

◊　◊　◊

Kansas

Brady drove east through the rolling terrain of Kansas. A sign advertised a place to stop and eat with a picture of a camper, meaning he could park the Ghost. He pulled in, rolled around to a gravel lot in back, and found an open spot in a line of RVs with water and electrical hookups. Farther back, the place had a facility to empty the toilet. After paying inside, he came back and got hooked up. A skinny young man appeared as he went to climb in the back door.

"Hello, mister, I was wondering if you could help me. My car broke down a few days ago, and I need a few bucks to get it fixed. The fuel pump went out."

He looked like a drug addict with sores on his face and shabby clothing. Brady slipped a twenty out of his pocket and gave it to the guy so he would go away.

"Hey," came voice from behind Brady. "Don't be giving money away like that. He'll be shooting it in his arm in two minutes."

Brady turned around to find a black fellow wearing a floppy hat. "I was trying to get rid of the guy."

The man walked up. "I'm Jonah." He shook Brady's hand. "Go in and pay for food, or complain to the manager about panhandlers. Handing out cash to addicts just adds to the problem."

"Got it. Call me Gene. Need some company for dinner tonight, Jonah?"

Jonah's frown became a grin. "Sounds nice. Let me clean up and I'll join you." He entered an RV three down from the Ghost.

Brady went in to freshen up, changing his clothes and combing his hair. As he climbed back out and locked up, footsteps in the gravel came from the side of the RV.

The skinny fellow carried a pipe, leading another guy and a girl, each holding knives. "Hello again, sir. Sorry to be ungrateful, but we want the rest of your money."

Brady put his hands up and stepped back. He reached behind and took out his wallet.

"Nice, but open up your ride. We want to look around."

Brady tore cash out of the wallet and tossed it on the ground before he turned and ran.

"Hey!" Gravel rustled behind him.

He ran past the backs of campers, one with the back door partially open. When he passed, Jonah swung the door with all his might. *Bang!* He nailed the skinny fellow. Jonah climbed down with a baseball bat. The other two held up their knives. Jonah walked toward them, pointing the end of the bat in their faces.

"Collect this piece of garbage if you know what's good for you."

They put the knives away and pulled the skinny guy up by his armpits. He bled from his nose and mouth. Brady followed them to his RV to make sure they didn't cut his tires. The skinny guy's legs started to work, and the three ran away, disappearing into the lot.

Brady came back to Jonah. "So are you hungry?"

"Famished."

"Then I insist on buying you a steak with all the trimmings."

Jonah bowed. "Okay, since you insist."

◇　◇　◇

It would be hard to sleep in the gravel lot knowing a band of skinny bandits could exact revenge, so after a nice dinner with Jonah, Brady drove on, pulling into a rest area late in the evening, finding a spot with the big trucks. He used the facilities and struck up a conversation with several truckers smoking on the sidewalk. At midnight, he retired to the Ghost. He put on a pair of shorts and a T-shirt and climbed into the loft over the cab. Truck engines purred along with the crickets. A cool breeze drifted in through the screened windows. He read in a novel before switching off the light, lying peacefully. Life on the road had drawn the stress out of him.

He chuckled to himself, replaying some of his adventures in his head. Several days ago, he'd met a prostitute. She came up to the driver's window and asked to use his CB radio. He had no idea it was really a solicitation. Prostitutes didn't come right out and offer sex for money; instead, they asked to use the radio. When he agreed to let her use it, she climbed in the passenger side of the cab and took her top off. When he told her to keep her clothes on and just use the radio, she looked at him like he was an idiot, but it turned out okay. He talked to her, discovering her name was Tammy. He didn't preach but encouraged her to find a better life. Then she'd put on her top and left, wishing him well.

Colorado had been great. He'd rode a horse in the mountains with a church group. The horse in front of him had a gas problem. His horse walked the cliffs without fear.

But for the first time in decades, he was alone. He reached over to the side of the mattress, pulled out his old cell phone, and powered it up, not worrying about giving away his whereabouts—he took the sim card out days ago. He looked through the texts still in storage.

Spencer's last messages went from the ridiculous to the sublime, filled with hateful warnings. Jolene's cold threats were frightening. The girls sent nothing, as expected. Paul had sent a few thoughtful messages, wishing him well.

Brady took out the burner phone from Walmart and typed in Paul's number.

"Hello, this is Pastor Lemon."

"Hey, brother. You still up?"

"Brady! Wow, man. You really left. Do you have any idea the trouble you caused?"

Brady swung his legs over the edge of the loft and sat up. "Trouble? No, what happened?"

"For starters, everyone called me looking for you. Cindy cried on the phone for an hour. Jolene threatened my life if I didn't tell her where you were. Your boss Spencer called. You were right about that guy. What an asshole."

"I didn't figure they'd call you. Sorry, man."

"How did your landlord get my number? Did you really have a wild threesome on the kitchen floor the night before you left?"

"What? No! Serena snuck into my apartment. Don't laugh, but I think she was going to rape me. Cindy happened to show up, and they got into a wrestling match. None of us had a lot of clothes on."

"How can you leave a life as interesting as that?"

"I'm enjoying the peace." Brady got quiet. "What about the girls?"

"They called me a few times, except for Britney. They aren't allowed to call your cell, but I think you have it turned off anyway."

"I truly regret leaving them, but it's complicated."

"Brady, you made the decision to leave. You left so many responsibilities."

"So I'm on my own."

"I'm still here for you, Brady. Always will be. Just keep turning to God, and you'll find your way."

"Okay, man. Tell the girls I love them. Please explain that I just had to get away from my problems."

"I'll tell them."

"Thanks, Paul. I'll call you again."

◊   ◊   ◊

Missouri

Brady woke up in a Missouri truck stop, planning to rent a shower room. He put on sweats and packed a duffel bag with soap, shaving kit, and fresh undershorts and climbed into the driver's seat to let the sun wake his brain up before going in. A guy in his twenties walked by with a grin on his face.

He stopped when he noticed Brady. "Hey, buddy. You have to come see this. A truck driver won the lottery, and he's giving money away."

Brady got out of the cab. "Good for him."

"Come on, I'll show you where he is."

"I'm not going to take the guy's money."

"Come on, he's drunk. You'll get a laugh."

The fellow headed through the parked trucks, and Brady, still not quite awake, decided to follow just to see something interesting.

Behind a line of parked trucks, two men gathered around a truck driver kneeled down in front of three red cups turned upside down on the ground. He covered a dice with the center cup and then moved the cups around and around.

When they walked up, one of the men, an older guy, leaned to Brady. "He won the lottery and celebrated all night. Now he's letting guys try to win some of the money. Just watch."

The guy stopped moving the cups and looked up at the other man with bloodshot eyes. The man put a stack of bills in front of one of the cups. The man on his knees lifted the cup, exposing the dice. "Winner… Holy crap, you guys are good at this." He pulled out a wad of bills and counted them out.

The older guy said to Brady, "Go ahead. Try to win some money. Why not? He's celebrating."

Brady took out four twenties. The guy moved the cups around and around for a while and then stopped. Brady set the money next to the left cup. The guy picked up the cup, and no dice.

Brady looked around at the four guys and smacked himself in the forehead. "I can't believe I just fell for that."

The "lottery winner" grabbed the money, stacked up the cups, and the four guys headed in different directions, disappearing into the rumbling trucks. Brady remained standing there with his mouth open. *Those guys should be on Broadway.*

He started toward the truck stop to take his shower with a grin on his face, considering how getting hustled by professional con artists was worth eighty dollars.

◊　◊　◊

Friday Afternoon
Seward, Kentucky

Agent Bessing thought Downtown Seward looked very modern for a small town, likely developed with tax money collected from Winslow-Carnac. She parked in front of a glass municipal building. Inside, a woman in her sixties wearing jeans and a plaid shirt came out from behind the front desk to greet her. Her name was Alice Delmont, Mayor of Seward.

Bessing shook her hand. "Nice to meet you, Mayor Delmont."

"Come back to my office." She led Bessing back. "Anything new on Kacey Farrell?"

Bessing took out her notepad. "I'm afraid there is. Farrell routed payment money to his own account, stealing a large sum of money, but that's not the worst of it: He erased online backups before he shot up the server room. Looks like the company will never recover their data."

"If the servers are down, then how do you know he stole money?"

"Whiteside called the vendors after checking the bank accounts. The money was transferred, but the vendors never received payments."

Mayor Delmont sat back. "How much are we talkin' about?"

Bessing reached back and swung the door shut. "I cannot give out facts of the case, but if you guessed over seventeen million dollars, you'd be in the ballpark."

The mayor smacked the desktop. "Doggies! How could they let this happen?"

"Farrell had administrative rights, and the IT staff was a bit naive."

The mayor shook her head. "So how do they fix things?"

"I was over there yesterday asking questions. I heard a few disturbing sentences, like 'no way to recover' and 'call clients for information.' Mayor, you have to prepare your town for the demise of Winslow-Carnac."

"Is there no hope?"

"They never had tape backups stored off-site. What are they going to tell their customers? Who wants to do business with them now? Their competition may have to buy them out."

"Then all the employees living in Seward will move away. We're screwed, blued, and tattooed."

Bessing remained silent. There was nothing to say.

"When will you catch Mr. Farrell? I'd like some time alone with him."

"We have no leads. Farrell vanished into thin air, maybe on a motorcycle. We've pulled footage from camera systems on all possible routes out of town and found nothing. If he hid the bike and got into a car, we don't know what the car looks like."

"Okay, Agent Bessing. Thanks for giving me the straight-up truth. Can I talk to a group of town leaders about this?"

"Go ahead." Bessing stood up to leave. "You have a nice little town here. I hope it survives."

Chapter 11

Stationed out of Louisville, Bessing could have driven home for the weekend, but she stayed in a hotel room in Lewisburg. Officers continued the manhunt with only a cold trail through the woods as a lead. Bessing decided to get in her car and drive the area, looking for anything that might be a lead.

White-collar criminals didn't normally shoot their way out of the crime scene, making FBI profiling resources practically useless. Embezzlement happened behind the scenes with crafty suspects trying to lie their way out or by leaving town in the dead of night. Many got greedy and continued to steal, leading to their arrest.

Kacey Farrell shot up the place to cover his crime, and so far, it had worked. The company hadn't even considered theft at first, giving Farrell plenty of time to hide the money. The forensic team tracing the money found nothing but dead ends. They think transfers headed to Tonga, and that was as far as they'd gotten.

The night before on the phone, Farrell had convinced her he lived a normal life. The split with his wife had actually made him seem more normal. The field office didn't place the blame on her for the incident, but her career would suffer. *I need to find that creepy son of a bitch.*

She found herself driving down the highway toward Winslow-Carnac. *Someone could get lost in woods like these.* The idea struck her. What if Farrell hadn't actually gone on the run but had stayed close by, hiding somewhere in this wooded area? The police had searched all the homes in the vicinity, but Farrell would have planned for that.

A road came up on the right, leading off into more woods. She braked and took the turn. The road headed west for a mile or so and turned south. Every so often, a driveway connected to the road, and Bessing slowed to take a look. Some homes were built amongst the trunks of tall trees, resting under a canopy. Others sat in a clearing with the drive cut through dense vegetation.

At the end of the road, a driveway curved away into the trees. She sat in the road idling for a minute and then drove down the drive, her tires crackling in the gravel. The drive opened to a yard with a large white farm house and several barns. When she pulled up near the house, an old woman came down the steps to greet her tapping a white cane.

The woman approached her open window. "How may I help you?"

Bessing got out. "Hello, dear. I'm Agent Bessing with the FBI. Please, don't be alarmed. I'm just following up on the Winslow-Carnac shooting."

"Hello, Agent Bessing, I'm Bea Herman."

"The Winslow-Carnac building is almost directly east of your house. I understand you couldn't see anything on the day in question, but maybe you heard something or noticed something unusual."

"I'm afraid not, but my renter, Mr. Wilson, hasn't spoken to police. Come inside, and I'll fetch him for you."

"That would be great." Verna followed Bea up the steps and into the kitchen.

Bea went to the coffee maker and pulled out the decanter. "I know how law enforcement loves their coffee."

"Please. Black is fine."

Creaking noises came from the upstairs.

Bea poured a cup and set down the decanter. "I'll be right back with Mr. Wilson." She went up the stairs leaving Bessing in the kitchen.

Bessing felt guilty sipping coffee while the blind woman climbed the stairs. Bea's footsteps continued for a while; floors creaked in the distance. A door shut, and then another. The footsteps came back down.

After a few minutes, Bea walked into the kitchen. "I don't understand it. I thought for sure Mr. Wilson was here today. He doesn't seem to be in his apartment. Can you look over at the barn to see if his motorcycle is parked there?"

"Motorcycle?" Verna's set down her coffee and gripped her pistol. "Mrs. Herman, do I have your permission to search the house?"

"Well, yes, but—"

"Please stay here in the kitchen. I just want to have a look for myself."

Bea handed over her keys, and Verna started up the stairs. The creaky staircase would announce her approach, so she stepped more quickly and stopped on the second-floor landing to listen. Hearing nothing, she climbed to the third floor. A hallway led across to the other side of the house with doors on both sides. She tried the one on the right. It was unlocked. She followed her pistol in, ready to engage. Farrell would be ready. She looked in the shower, closets, and under the bed. She put her hand on the blankets. They felt a bit warm, but she couldn't be sure.

Across the hall, the door was locked. She tried keys until it unlocked and pushed it open. The room was vacant with only a few items of furniture. A dresser had pictures of a middle-aged couple arranged on the top. The man was definitely not Kacey Farrell. Bessing exhaled and holster her gun.

She walked over a Persian rug to the door in back and stepped out on the landing. External stairs led down to the backyard. She went down to the second-floor landing where the door was locked. As she sorted keys, a black mark on a step caught her eye. There were black marks on every step. She looked underneath one of the steps and found nothing. Maybe they marked where the step squeaked, but the step didn't squeak when she stepped on the mark. *That's it.*

Bessing took her gun out and climbed the stairs, using the black marks to hide her approach. Kacey Farrell was in the house. She stepped lightly across the landing, went in the back door, and tried to understand what she was seeing.

The far end of the Persian rug swung up from the floor knocking the gun free from her hand. She stumbled backward through the door and hit the railing. It broke. She tipped back, then lunged forward as she fell, grabbing hold of the vertical beam, dangling over the side.

Kacey Farrell stepped out on the landing, holding her gun. "Good afternoon, Agent Bessing. Nice to see you again."

"Help me up, Kacey. Don't be stupid."

Kacey bent down and clubbed her fingers with the butt of the gun. She let go with one hand, still dangling from the other.

"If you don't break your neck when you fall, please don't follow me." He clubbed her remaining fingers, and Verna dropped.

◊　◊　◊

In the yard below, the agent lay spread-eagle on her back, out cold. Kacey allowed himself to think. First, he should find Bea.

He strode to the stairs and slid down the railings to the first floor. Bea had her back toward him, dialing the phone on the kitchen counter. She heard him approach and turned.

"Agent Bessing, was there an accident? I heard a calamity upstairs."

Kacey snatched the phone off the counter and ripped out the wire. "Bea, I want you to take a seat at the kitchen table. If you do as I say, everything will be okay."

"John, can you tell me what's going on?

"Soon enough. Now sit down and be quiet."

Bea took a seat at the table. Kacey went out the front door to the back corner of the house. The agent hadn't moved. He crouched down beside her, checking her pockets while keeping an eye on her face. He pulled out a cell phone, ammunition, and a set of handcuffs. He felt her ankles and found a small revolver in a leg holster which he put in his pocket. The agent's chest moved up and down, and she had a pulse, but how long would she be out? Her neck didn't look broken. She may have landed flat.

He picked her up by her armpits, ducked down, and put her over his shoulder. He carried her around to the front of the house and called for Bea to hold open the front door. In the living room, he set the agent in Bea's reclining chair and pushed it to the bottom of the staircase. He secured her arm to the bottom post using the handcuffs.

Bea said, "Mr. Wilson, please tell me what's happening."

"Stay at the table, dear. Everything will be fine."

Kacey went upstairs, booted his computer to an emergency partition, and gave a command to shred the contents of the main partition. By the time authorities arrived, the computer would be useless. He raised the hatch covered by the Persian rug and grabbed his go-bag.

Back on the stairs, he heard voices. They silenced as he got to the second floor. He stepped down on the side of the staircase away from the agent and into the center of the room. "Agent Bessing, I'm happy you survived your unfortunate fall."

Bessing opened her eyes and tugged at the handcuff. "You're not a cop killer, Kacey. Do you plan to change that?"

Kacey rubbed his chin and glanced at Bea, quivering at the kitchen table. "I'm not the monster you think I am. Agent Bessing, you are a credit to law enforcement. Somehow, you found me. When I leave, I will place your service pistol in your car to keep you out of trouble with your commander. No ammunition, of course."

"How nice of you. Let's consider your situation—"

Kacey held up his hand. "Let's not. You have an obligation to convince me to surrender, and consider the attempt made. Now, I'll make you a deal."

"Go ahead."

"Sit quietly, both of you, and I will exit. No one will be harmed. Obviously, I need a bit of a head start for a successful getaway, so I'll need to do a few chores before I leave."

"The Lambert lady died, and you stole seventeen million dollars. You can't get a big-enough head start."

"I could shoot you."

Bea whimpered.

Bessing kept her eyes on Kacey and yanked at the handcuffs. "This stair railing was built to last. Just go."

Kacey nodded. He set the go-bag by the door. "Bea, stay seated at the table. I consider you my dear friend. Please continue to behave."

A sound came from Bea's throat.

Kacey went out the front door and opened Bessing's car door. He unscrewed each side of the radio and yanked it out. He cut the valve stems on the tires and then went to the back of the house to toss the radio into the woods, followed by the keys. He removed the battery from the agent's cell phone and through it and the phone in the woods. Next, he went up to the middle landing and cut the phone wire.

What had he forgotten? Bea had no vehicle, being blind. She had no cell. The women would try to find help right away. They're only option would be for Agent Bessing to break through the thick wooden post, or for Bea to go to the neighbors for help.

Kacey went back inside and found Bea's white cane leaning by the doorway. He picked it up and his go-bag. "Thank you, Bea, for taking care of me. Goodbye."

He went out to the car, emptied the bullets out of the gun, and set it in the front seat. In the barn, he threw the cane and bullets into the loft. The motorcycle waited on its kick stand. He strapped on the bag, started the engine, and rode south through the trees. After two miles, Kacey skidded to a stop by the ruined shack to retrieve his own pistol and the AR15. Using the motorcycle's mirror, he smeared glue on his face and stuck on the fake beard and mustache. He put on his helmet and sped south to the road, turned left, and headed east toward Richards, Kentucky, a forty-minute trip. If a police car pursued, he could go off-road almost anywhere.

Along the highway, he passed a state police car moving fast. Kacey tracked in the mirror—it kept going. At some point, police could pursue, and leaving Agent Bessing alive would work in his favor. She would describe his special skills, causing them to use caution.

Forty minutes later, the downtown area of Richards came into view with a motorcycle shop on the right. Kacey pulled in and dealt with a salesman, who had a mechanic inspect the bike. They negotiated for a price and made a deal. Kacey signed over the title.

The motorcycle was in the name of Brian West, his new identity. He walked half a mile to Enterprise car rental. After presenting his new documentation and credit card, he was taken to a white Chevrolet Malibu. He put his bag in the trunk and climbed in.

Brian West looked nothing like clean shaven Kacey Farrell, and the new identity materials had worked like a dream. No cop cars raced by. The open road was in front of him.

Kacey drove out of the parking lot and on to the road. He'd always wanted to visit Chicago, a heavily populated area where Brian West would disappear into the masses.

◊   ◊   ◊

Monday Morning
Wisconsin

Brady always had a possible destination in the back of his mind when he left town, and he couldn't keep blowing money on the road forever. Eventually, he needed a place to land.

To the best of his recollection, he'd never mentioned his uncle's friend to anyone. Ryland Kromer owned a lodge in Wisconsin and he'd last seen Kromer years ago at his uncle's funeral. Kromer had told Brady to visit him at the lodge someday, but Brady never had the opportunity until now. Located up north in Frost, Wisconsin, it may be a nice place to hide out for a while.

He didn't want to travel near the Chicago area, so he crossed into Wisconsin near Galena and stayed the night in Madison. From there, it took several hours to drive up north to Frost with the forest growing thicker the farther he went. Deer stood on the side of the road watching the Ghost rolling by. The temperature dropped into the comfortable seventies, nice for summer.

Another RV led him into the city of Frost. Store fronts lined the street, some with old dates set in stone. North of town, Brimm Lake hosted fishing vacationers. Shops sold tackle and boating supplies.

Past the quaint downtown and up on the hill to the right, the Moose and Bear Lodge was located. Brady drove in the gravel underneath a carved sign featuring a Moose and a Bear glaring at each other, preparing to rumble. The rugged lodge was built with logs and stone, jutting out from the hill. Stone walls at the bottom receded up the hill. The main entrance was at the top of the hill. Rows of hotel room buildings were built across on the top of the hill to the right. Behind them, cabins were for rent. Tall pine trees stuck up between the buildings.

Brady surveyed the area. RVs parked by utility poles in the far back area, meaning he could stay the night. He parked next to the main lodge and went in. A young girl came up to the counter. "Come to stay with us?"

"Yes, and I was wondering if Ryland Kromer is around."

Behind the counter, a chair squeaked inside an office door. A silver-haired woman walked to the counter. "I'm sorry, sir, but Mr. Kromer passed away three years ago."

"Oh, I hadn't heard. Too bad, he was a nice fellow. Are you his widow?"

"No. I'm Sylvia Banner. I bought the place after Mr. Kromer passed. Been running it ever since."

"Okay, I'd still like to stay. My RV is outside."

Sylvia turned to the girl. "Lisa, set him up." She went back in the office.

Lisa smiled at Brady. "Your name."

He paused.

"Did you forget your name?"

"Sorry, I'm Gene Brinkman." He took out his wallet.

◊   ◊   ◊

Monday Evening
Frost, Wisconsin

Brady needed to walk after driving for so long. *No wonder truck drivers were tubby.* He walked down to the Pine Cone Café and pinched his own midsection before going in—he was able to grab more stomach then when he left, so he ordered a salad for dinner. It was good, but when the waitress asked if he wanted to try the pecan pie, he gave in to temptation.

The door jingled. Sylvia Banner came in. The waitress sat her down next to Brady's table. "Hello, Ms. Banner. I didn't introduce myself before, I'm Gene."

She nodded. "How do you like our little town?"

"It's very nice. In fact, I'd planned to stay for a while. I thought Mr. Kromer could need some help at the lodge."

Sylvia set down her menu. "What's your skill set?"

"Well, I'm a computer guy, but I'm handy enough. Worked in construction when I was a kid. Tended bar."

"And you plan to stay in the RV?"

"Yep."

"Maybe we could work something out. You could be on call for maintenance, make minimum wage, plus free RV hookup."

"Could I use a bathroom with a shower?"

"The men's locker room would work." She pointed to the other side of her table. "Why don't you sit over here?"

Brady brought his pie dish and coffee over to Sylvia's table. "Sounds like this could work out. If you feel comfortable, I could do some accounting work."

"Sounds like a dream come true. A handsome young man shows up and offers to solve all my problems. Can you start tomorrow?"

"I don't see why not."

She stared at him for a minute. "So what's the story? Are you on the lamb?"

Brady had a bite of pie near his mouth. He lowered it. "You mean, like a criminal on the run?"

She stared at him.

"I'm not a criminal."

"But you are on the run?"

Brady thought of what to say. "I'm looking for a new life."

Sylvia tilted her head. "The same reason I bought the lodge."

Brady waited.

"Eat your pie, Gene. Come to the office tomorrow morning, and I'll get you started."

◇　◇　◇

Tuesday Morning
Harwood Heights, Illinois

Mark's desk phone buzzed at Polyglomerate Container. He pushed a button and listened.

Lexi said, "Mr. Seivers, a big bald guy just came in. He didn't stop when I told him to wait."

"It's all right, Lexi." He moved a horse racing form into his drawer.

Gavin Ricci walked in. "Hope you're not busy."

Mark stood up.

"Sit down and call the aging hipster in here." Gavin took a seat.

Mark called Spencer and told him to get over here. They heard him talking loudly in the hallway before arriving. When he saw Gavin, his eyes got big.

Gavin pointed at the other chair. "Sit."

Spencer sat. His shirt front was unbuttoned halfway down with several gold chains around his neck.

Gavin asked, "Is this your idea of business casual?"

"I like to be stylin' when I can."

"Sure thing. You might as well look like a clown. You're no good with computers."

Spencer turned to Mark. Mark cleared his throat. "Spencer, why don't you stay quiet and listen to our friend."

Gavin nodded. "Thank you, Mark."

"What about you, tough guy?" Spencer said. "You were supposed to find Witek."

Mark put his hands flat on the desk. Gavin nodded. "Fair enough. I'm willing to take constructive criticism. Brady Witek has eluded me, which is why I'm here today. I need something to go on, or I'll be forced to lean on a church minister, and I really don't want to resort to those measures. Please give me information I can use."

The room got quiet.

Mark said, "We have no idea where he went."

"His cell phone made it out west for a while," Gavin said. "Other than that, his name doesn't come up anywhere. He must have gotten a new identity, or maybe he's just using cash all the time."

Spencer said, "The little prick isn't that smart."

"If we can't complete the merger, we'll have to keep running the companies separately," Mark said. "We currently have temps manually collating between servers."

"Which means Sal can't wash his money yet." Gavin glared at Spencer. "Give me your car keys."

Spencer gaped at Gavin with his mouth open.

"You heard me, douche' bag."

"The fuck I will."

Gavin stood up. Mark and Spencer stood up. Gavin held out his hand.

Spencer didn't move. Gavin took a step toward him, and Spencer dug his keys out of his pocket and held them out. Gavin snatched the keys and then yanked the gold chains off Spencer's neck, holding them up in his fist.

Mark tried to speak, but Spencer's face turned bright red. His body tensed and he swung his fist a Gavin's head. Gavin ducked and shot his fist into Spencer's nose, causing him to stumble backward, holding his nose.

Gavin jammed the chains in his pocket and dangled the keys. "Consider this a down payment on the money we're losing." He nodded at Mark. "Try to jumpstart this hippie's brain while I find Witek. Got it?"

"Understood."

Gavin left.

Spencer pinched his nostrils shut to stop the bleeding.

◊　◊　◊

Monday Night
Crystal Lake, Illinois

"What do you mean cancel the reservations?" Jolene's eyes bulged.

Aaron winched. She had that vicious look on her face again. "I'm using my savings to pay the bills, Jolene. We can't be eating out at fancy restaurants. There's sandwich stuff in the fridge."

Jolene crossed her arms. "We are not going to eat baloney sandwiches for dinner."

Aaron turned. The four girls came down the stairs dressed up for dinner. All the money he spent on these females lately… "Fine, get in the car. But things can't go on like this."

Jolene sighed and went behind Aaron to massage his shoulders. "I'll get back to work soon. We're going to be fine. This is our lifestyle now."

Aaron thought about showing her his bank account, but he didn't want more trouble. "If that low-life husband of yours kept up his payments, we'd be fine."

She squeezed his shoulders. "Can't you find him?"

"No, but if he turns up, I'll take care of him."

The girls passed through the kitchen and out into the garage. Jolene followed.

Aaron got himself moving, trying to remember which credit card would work tonight.

◊   ◊   ◊

Tuesday Morning
Frost, Wisconsin

Brady got to the lodge early in the morning, hoping to create a good impression and eager to get started. After years of sitting at a desk, followed by sitting in a RV for weeks, he hoped he could perform manual labor. He waited in the lobby near the huge rock fireplace. The fire was out in the morning. Maybe he would be assigned to get it going.

The walls of the lodge were made of stone and logs. An open ceiling stretched overhead, supported by wooden beams. Rustic light fixtures hung down from chains, lit with old-fashioned filament bulbs. The place had the right atmosphere for a rustic lodge, but it had a worn feeling. The freshness was gone, even though it looked clean. The moose and deer heads on the wall were appropriate, but they didn't look happy to be there.

Brady slapped his own cheek. He needed to stay positive. He'd done as Paul suggested and prayed for direction. He felt like he was there at the lodge for a reason.

Sylvia showed up at seven forty-five, noticing Brady in the lobby. "Gene, you're here. Great. Come on back to the office."

He went around the counter to the office, reminding himself he was now "Gene." The office was also rustic with two bare log columns supporting the wooden ceiling. Four desks—two in the front and two in the back, faced forward except for the back right desk that faced the side wall with a computer. Sylvia's big wooden desk faced forward in the left rear area. Fish were mounted on the walls. The scary one must be a northern pike.

Sylvia waved him over to the computer desk. "Sit down and have a look."

Brady moved the mouse to awaken the machine. The old XP operating system came up. The desktop was covered with spreadsheet files. The Office program was well out of date. He looked at the system page—the resources were low. "Can I start up QuickBooks?"

"Go ahead."

He waited for it to open. "How do you back up your files?"

"Jose, head of maintenance, uses a USB drive. It's in the drawer there."

Brady pulled open the drawer.

Sylvia sat in a metal chair beside him. "Is it that bad?"

He shrugged. "What about your hotel software?"

Sylvia led him to the front counter to another computer running XP. Third-party software ran a point of sale system and kept track of the guests. An old phone switchboard sat next to it.

"Let's go back to the office."

They went back and sat.

"Here's the scoop," Brady said. "Your computers have been running for a very long time, and many PCs die in three or four years. The cool, dry air up here must have helped them out. Regardless, businesses don't normally run software locally anymore. They use the cloud and pay a monthly fee. Data is stored with the software company. If you had a fire or burglary right now, you better hope the flash drive survives, or you'll have nothing."

"A salesman recently told me the same thing. He could put in a complete hotel system, but we'd need to convert the old data."

"Well, look who you have sitting here—an expert at converting data."

Sylvia had a smirk on her face. "When things are too good to be true, they usually are. Let me see your driver's license."

Brady handed it over. Sylvia opened a laptop on her desk and booted. Brady waited as she worked away on the keyboard, feeling a sense of dread. This would be the first time his identity went through an examination. Sylvia did not describe what she was doing, but it had to be a background check. If it went bad, then he needed that license back so he could get the hell out of town.

Sylvia passed the license back to him. "Gene Brinkman, the computer doesn't have much to say about you. What's your birthday?"

Brady spit out Gene's birthday without hesitating or looking at the license. Sylvia watched closely.

"Where were you born?"

He spit out the town's name in New England. Sylvia continued to watch.

"Why does it say you worked at a leather goods factory in Milwaukee?"

"I ran the IT department for the plant."

Sylvia stared. "Okay, Gene, I'm not completely sold on you, but despite what my gut is telling me, I'll take a chance. You'll be paid minimum wage and stay in your RV for free, like we discussed. You'll work maintenance with Jose, and you'll be in charge of the computers. Agreed?"

"Is water and electricity included?"

Sylvia nodded.

Brady reached over and shook her hand. "Agreed."

"But understand this, Mr. Brinkman. I'm close friends with the mayor and the sheriff."

Lisa walked up to the desk. "The computer is frozen again."

Sylvia smiled and turned to Brady. Brady saluted and headed for the front desk.

◊　◊　◊

Brady met Jose midmorning and liked him. Even though he was just twenty-five years old, Brady would have no problem taking orders from him. Jose was the kind of fellow who just wanted to get the job done so he could go fishing. He lived in an old cabin in the woods behind the RV lot. The cabin had once been part of another camp, gone for many years. Raccoons and owls lived in the other two cabins.

Brady's first manual task was easy. Jose handed him earplugs and a gas-powered weed whacker, and he whacked weed around the cabins. The wooden fence out front looked shabby with growth, so Brady whacked some more.

In the afternoon, he helped Jose install a new toilet in one of the cabins. When they were finished, Jose instructed him to clock out on the POS computer to track his hours. Lisa entered him in as an employee and adjusted his hours for the day.

In the evening, Brady used a shower in the locker room. It wasn't modern, but it was clean, and the water stayed hot. Back in the RV, he sat at the table with his laptop, fooling around on the internet for fun. He accessed his new bank account at the Frost Bank and Loan. The Wi-Fi signal made it out to the RV.

A cool breeze drifted through the Ghost. Frogs sang in the woods, backed up by crickets.

Things were falling into place here at the lodge, but he needed to figure out meals. A grocery store had recently been built out by the town's residential area, but too far to walk. He needed fresh food to stay healthy, and he needed to drive the Ghost once in a while to keep it running, so during the trip, he would stop for supplies at the grocery store. The plan was to stay here at the lodge for a while, but he needed the Ghost to be ready to leave.

He climbed up to the loft looking forward to tomorrow.

Chapter 12

The next morning, Brady worked on the computers, getting an online backup started. Ten gigs of data needed to be uploaded. He used a free trial to get started. Eventually, files would backup continuously over the internet, and they could stop using the USB flash drive.

When he turned in his chair, there was a loud crack.

Lisa giggled at the closest desk. "Did you just break the chair?"

Brady squeezed his midsection. "Time to offload the extra ballast." He turned back to the screen, and the chair cracked and tipped sideways. Brady grabbed the desk to keep from falling. Lisa rushed over and grabbed the arm rest.

Brady got up. "Thanks for saving me." He really noticed Lisa for the first time. "How old are you anyway? You're surprisingly strong."

"I'm almost eighteen. Like, in eight more months."

"You seem older."

She smiled and shrugged. "Why don't I take you downstairs and find another chair?"

She led him out of the office to the front of the lodge. A large open room had windows with a view of Brimm Lake. The carpeting needed replacing. A table and chairs sat in the far corner.

Brady stopped. "What is this room?"

"It used to be a banquet hall. It isn't used much, but sometimes the guests have parties."

Along the wall separating the room from the lobby, she went down a staircase. At the bottom, she felt around for the light switch. A couple of bulbs lit up. They were in an old restaurant, cluttered with junk. He couldn't see very well, but the place looked awesome, like an old western tavern.

"Can you turn on more lights?"

Lisa flipped switches. An old wooden bar sat in front of a kitchen pass. All the walls were either brick or stone, with wooden planks on the floor. Tables and chairs looked like they sat where they were last used, but were now covered with clutter—doorknobs, bed-covers, screws, light fixtures, and boxes. One table had tube televisions. Broken bureaus sat in the aisles.

Lisa pulled out a chair with wheels. "This will probably work."

"Can I go in the kitchen?"

"Suit yourself."

He went into the kitchen and switched on a light. It was in decent shape. Stoves and machines were covered with tarps. A walk-in refrigerator had its door propped open to stay dry. Stainless steel surrounded him.

He came back out and found Lisa rolling the chair to the base of the stairs.

He asked, "Why isn't this place open?"

"Don't know. I've only worked here a year. Sylvia could tell you."

"It was closed when I bought the place." Sylvia's voice came from nearby.

Brady jumped. Lisa shrieked and held her chest. "Where did you come from?"

Sylvia stepped from the shadows near the stairs. "Sorry, I thought you saw me come down. Kromer closed it when the Captain's Table opened around the bend."

Brady came over to the two women. "Have you considered reopening it? Maybe we could partner in it."

Sylvia rubbed her chin. "Maybe we could."

◊ ◊ ◊

By late afternoon, Brady and Jose finished installing a new shower liner. The maid cleaned the room while they picked up tools. Jose sent him to the lodge to carry bags over for newly arrived guests. The room would be occupied right away. Brady came out of the unit after the young family went in and leaned his head back, cracking vertebra in his neck and upper back. He twisted sideways and made more popping sounds. Back in the office, he went to the computer desk and sat in the new chair. Sylvia came in and sat at her desk. Brady spun around.

"Gene, I just got back from the municipal building," Sylvia said. "I talked about you."

Brady sat quietly.

"Are you okay? You look spooked."

"I'm good. What's up?"

"Mayor Gould likes your idea to reopen the restaurant."

Brady tilted back. "Oh, nice. I went back down during lunch, and the place just needs to be cleaned up. There's plenty of dishes and silverware."

"Yes, but you noticed the door is boarded up."

"Jose and I can work on it. How long would it take to get a license?"

Sylvia winked. "Remember, I'm friends with the mayor. He'll get us a license, and we could open next week if we wanted too."

"I say let's do it. We'll be partners and put everything in writing."

"We should keep it simple, just a few things on the menu."

"And we should call the place Sylvia's."

Sylvia sat for a minute and then nodded. "Well, okay."

◊　◊　◊

Brady's mind stayed active while he drank a beer in the Ghost that evening. The restaurant could be a very good thing. He tingled with excitement. Sylvia had brought Jose in for a meeting that evening, and they talked about getting the restaurant running again. They needed a crew to clean and a repair service for the kitchen. A new sign and door had to be installed, and then the food.

A restaurant could be a risky venture, and the waitresses and cooks had to be paid regardless of revenue. Brady would need to put in thirty thousand dollars. But the Captain's Table had closed a year ago, and Frost had no burger pub. Plus, lodge had potential diners staying with them.

Brady pulled up a spreadsheet with his current finances. He had just over seventy thousand dollars, not much, all things considered, but plenty for a guy with a free place to stay. If the restaurant made any money at all, he would be set up nicely.

He'd seen businesses throw good money after bad, but he would get nowhere without risk. He just wished it wasn't happening so fast. He barely knew Sylvia.

Brady got up and climbed into the loft to retrieve his burner phone. He tapped in Paul's number and waited.

Paul answered. "Is this the weary traveler, bringing me tales of peril and adventure from the open road?"

"Avast, it is I. How are you, brother?"

"I'm living the life, however tame it may be. What trouble have you found lately?"

"Actually, quite a bit. I forgot to tell you, I met a nice prostitute."

"You remember what I do for a living, right?"

"I did not partake of her services. We just talked."

"Then no lectures are needed. What else?"

Brady described the encounter with the young drug addicts and the experience with the con men. "What about the girls? Talk to them lately?"

"They called, and I've given them encouragement. I said you left because of serious problems in your life, but you miss them like crazy."

"Thanks, man. I'll find a way to contact them. I can't risk it now."

"Ah, Brady. The three younger girls seem to think Britney is the reason you disappeared. They seem to be taking things so well. It's like they understand why you left."

Brady didn't respond.

"I finally got Britney on the phone."

"What did she say?"

"She said her mother made her be mean to you, and now you're scared of getting in trouble."

"Do you still trust me, Paul?"

"Of course, I do."

"Then leave it alone. Someday I'll explain a few things."

"Okay, I'll leave it alone. Where are you now?"

"In a little burg named Frost, Wisconsin. I met a guy who owned a lodge up here, but he died before I arrived."

"Was he clinging to life waiting for you?"

"No. He croaked three years ago. The current owner gave me a job, and I get to park for free, but there's an opportunity I want to get your advice on."

"Tell me."

"The place has a restaurant that's been closed for years. It's in decent shape, and the town can use a burger joint, but I would have to put in about half my money to get it going."

"You know I'm going to ask if you prayed about it."

"I have, but this door has to be opened with a big chunk of money."

"Are these Christian people you're doing business with?"

"I don't know."

"Find out before you sign anything. Be careful who you connect yourself with. You may have different values."

"I will, but why is it so hard to move forward on this type of thing?"

"You're still a new guy. Your faith isn't strong."

Brady thought about it. "Fair enough."

◊   ◊   ◊

Thursday Morning
Frost, Wisconsin

Sylvia and Jose were waiting for Brady when he walked into the office right before 8:00 a.m.

Sylvia said, "We want to talk about the restaurant."

"So you guys are anxious about it too?"

Jose said, "It could really help us out."

Brady sat at his computer desk. "Are you guys Christians?"

Sylvia looked at Jose. "Why, is that a problem?"

"To the contrary, I would be more comfortable partnering with people who have the same values as I do."

"We both go to the Methodist Church on Sunday," Jose said. "I'm an usher."

"I teach Sunday school," Sylvia said. "Fourth grade little rascals."

Brady nodded. "Then I'm in, what the hell—heck, I mean. We barely just met, but I have a good feeling."

"The place can open next week," Jose said. "We'll clear out the junk today and load it in my truck. We can store it in the two old cabins out back."

Sylvia said, "We'll hire some young people to work as waiters and have them start now on clean up."

Brady said, "We can use the old manual register for now."

Jose said, "We'll call in a service crew for the kitchen."

Brady said, "Let me find the food supplier."

"Do it, but we have two pieces of business to settle before we get started," Sylvia said. "First, we need to agree on the partnership, and then we need to discuss the menu."

Brady thought for a minute. "I saw an attorney's office down by the municipal building."

"Right. Jackson and Sons can draw up an agreement."

"For the menu, you're right, we definitely need to keep it simple and serve awesome burgers. The menu should be a single page. When we get the hang of things, then we do breakfast."

Sylvia and Jose nodded.

Jose stood up. "I think this is a good time to shake hands."

They got up and shook hands several times.

◊   ◊   ◊

Monday Morning
Chicago, Illinois

The alarm clock went off at 7:00 a.m. Pastor Paul swore at the machine and then asked for forgiveness for swearing. He'd forgotten to turn off the alarm on his day off, and after staring at the ceiling for twenty minutes, he got up knowing he couldn't go back to sleep.

He cleaned up, dressed, and fixed some eggs and toast for breakfast, thinking about what he would do with the day. A pastor's job was a lifestyle, committed to the people of the church, meaning he didn't have time for hobbies. Taking care of his people made for a full life, and even a pastor needed a day off once a week.

He didn't have many chores. The house belonged to the church, one block away, and the custodial staff kept it cleaned and well maintained. He used the living room and kitchen to entertain parishioners who needed counseling. He brought the youth group over all the time, playing games and ping pong in the basement. Occasionally, he hosted foster kids in the basement bedrooms, and during marriage problems, men would stay over until they worked things out.

He wasn't currently in a relationship, but God may eventually bring a lady around. No doubt he was a target at the church, constantly introduced to single women, but God had him in a single life for now, and that meant using his time for service. If and when he had a family, priorities would change.

He went out the back of the house to the garage and drove down the alley in his Kia SUV. His cell phone buzzed, so he stuck his Bluetooth in his ear. "Pastor Lemon."

"Tell me where Brady Witek is, or there's going to be trouble."

"Serena Haynesworth?"

"I'm pregnant with his baby, and you're the one who introduced us. How is that going to look to the congregation when they find out?"

Paul stopped the car. "Serena, you sound upset. Why don't you talk to me?"

"Cut the preacher bullshit and tell me where Brady is. No one has seen him for weeks, and you're his best friend."

Paul grimaced. "I'm not telling you shit, nutjob."

Serena laughed. "Very nice. The real Pastor Lemon appears."

"I'm sorry, Serena, but your tone can be aggravating, and I find it hard to believe Brady Witek had sex with you."

"Oh, he stuck it in me all right. I tried to hold him off, but he took what he wanted. Father is not happy. Would you like to talk to him?"

"No, this is between you and Brady."

"Father doesn't see it that way. You set up the date with the man who had his way with me. You're involved, Pastor foul mouth."

Paul's eyes became unfocused. "Do your worst, Serena." He ended the call, breathing in and out.

Brady and Serena? No way. What a mess. She must be lying. Or did Brady leave town because it was true? It just didn't sound right. Brady would have told him about it, and Brady wouldn't run away from something like this. *Or would he?* He was running away from his other children.

Paul shook his head, stopped, and shook it again. He wiped a tear from his eye with the back of his hand. The cell phone lay in the tray by the dashboard. He picked it up and called the number in the call log for Brady's burner phone. The message said it was turned off, so he sent a text for him to call as soon as possible about Serena Haynesworth.

He restarted the car and turned around to head back to his house. Inside the garage, he climbed out of the SUV and shut the door. A man wearing a ski mask came in the side door. Paul turned to run. A full-size SUV screeched up with the doors opening. Men jumped out wearing ski masks. A hand with a cloth went over his face from behind, soaked with a chemical. His vision went blurry before he blacked out.

Paul started to come around. A small hand felt his neck. He could hear young voices talking.

"I can feel the blood pumping in his neck."

A hand pressed in the middle of his chest. "Here, feel his chest. His heart's beating."

Paul rolled his head around and opened his eyes. Two young girls gasped and stepped back. He tried to speak. "Hi. I'm Passer Paul. Woo are you?"

The girl on the right said, "I'm Kim, and she's Leena. What happened to you?"

Paul looked around. He was in a building with old boxes. No lights were on. A musty smell hung in the air.

Kim said, "We heard you moaning."

"I only remember some guys grabbing me. Then I'm sitting here." He tried to get up, but something held him in the chair. His arms wouldn't come up.

"Pastor, you have tape around you."

He looked down at the duct tape around his midsection. "Help me girls."

Kim took a knife from her pocket. Paul sat still as she cut him loose. He got up and staggered. The girls got on either side to hold him up.

"Pastor, you should sit back down. I'll call 911 and get you some help."

"Good idea." Paul sat down. "You're in charge."

◊   ◊   ◊

At the hospital, two officers took his statement after the medical staff checked him out. He explained what happened as best as he could, including the phone call from Serena right before the abduction. They told him they would visit the Haynesworth home and question Serena and her father. When he was discharged, the policemen brought him home, having him wait in the car while they checked his place out.

The police said they weren't sure what to make of the incident. Paul hadn't been harmed, his wallet still had cash, and his cell phone was in his pocket. He'd been knocked out and left in the old building for no apparent reason.

Paul suggested Serena and her father were trying to scare him into telling them the location of his friend, but the police thought they would have smacked him around if that were the case.

When the police left, he realized his day off was almost over, so he went back to his bedroom and sat on the bed. The blanket made a crinkling noise. When he pulled it back, he found a note and unfolded it. He gasped. The paper had a picture of him kissing a girl with his eyes closed. His hand was on her breast. The "girl" sported a goatee. Below the picture was a message. "Keep out of it."

Paul ran to the kitchen to rub hand sanitizer on his face.

◇　◇　◇

Gavin waited in the office of the abandon warehouse after his crew gave him a rundown of the pastor's abduction. A handsome man in his sixties walked in and hugged Gavin, slapping him on the back.

"What do you have for me, boss?"

"Sit down, Gio." Gavin went behind a desk, dusted off the old chair and sat. He put papers on the desk. Gio dusted off a metal chair and sat in front of the desk.

Gavin slid over a photo. "We need this guy returned to town. His name is Brady Witek."

"Still breathing?"

"Yes, and unharmed. All his fingers need to work to finish one of Sal's new projects. Afterward? We're not sure yet, but we may use you again for that too."

"Where is Witek?"

"We traced his phone to Northern Wisconsin. The priest sent a text to Witek about the Haynesworth broad, so we know it's legit. The location is out in the boonies, so we're only sure about the cell tower, not which town. You'll need to look around a bit."

"Won't I stand out up there?"

"Work on your wardrobe."

"How much time do I got?"

"Get it done soon, but don't cause a ruckus, and try not to antagonize him. We need him to finish a sensitive project that only he can do."

"He'll travel first-class all the way."

"And, Gio? One more thing. The priest may try to warn Witek again."

"Did you give him the facts of life?"

"We sent him a message with a picture."

Gavin slid over a file with information on Brady and the cell tower location.

Gio stood up. "Better get right on it before he bolts."

Gavin nodded. "Do that."

◊ ◊ ◊

Later in the evening, Paul left his house and walked over to the church to find Senior Pastor Wells after he finished his Bible study class. They went into the sanctuary and sat in the back pew. Paul told him about the incident and gave him a copy of the police report. Wells was Paul's friend and ally, but Paul figured the police report would erase any doubt.

"This is very odd, Paul. And you think the Haynesworth's are behind it?"

Paul unfolded the other sheet of paper and handed it to Wells. "The police haven't seen this."

The senior pastor's eyes grew wide. He folded the paper and gave it back. "Okay, Paul. You did the right thing coming to me. The bottom of your paper says all you need to know. Keep out of it."

"That's why they set me up?"

"Haynesworth is a deacon. If you talk about Serena's illegitimate pregnancy, he'll be humiliated."

"Makes sense…"

"Let Brady Witek handle this himself and stay quiet. Consider that an order. For your own good."

"Got it."

◊ ◊ ◊

Tuesday Morning
Wisconsin

The drive through the country relaxed Gio. After Chicago traffic, he enjoyed actually driving at the posted speed limit, and there were more trees. The cows seemed relaxed. His Cadillac fit right in with the summer people—a lot of oldies came up here to fish. The deer needed to take better care—corpses lay on the side of the road every so often. Gio chuckled. They couldn't pin the bodies on him.

His phone led the way, but he had a paper map on the seat next to him to take notes while he looked for Witek. His phone had the guy's picture, but there was the rub. How could he walk around showing the picture without the locals getting suspicious? Up here was like another planet.

The road widened as Gio noticed a Farm and Fleet. Inside, he headed to the clothing department. He could turn himself into Old McDonald in this place, no problem, but first, he meandered up to the front entrance and spent an hour people-watching, checking out the latest styles. Overalls were surprisingly popular.

He went back to the clothing department and loaded up a cart with clothes. He tried on some items, including brown denim over-alls, and inspected himself in the mirror. He thought he could pull it off, but his hair was too stylish. He picked out a John Deere hat. After he made his purchases and loaded them in the car, he got roll-ing north again, planning to find a hotel in the city of Frost, and from there, snoop around the general area.

But he had to do some thinking on the way. Should he throw the guy in the trunk and get him back to Chicago in a single trip? While the boss said to go easy on him, how would he also keep him in line during the trip? Clubbing his head was out of the question. He needed another kind of leverage.

His phone made a ding-a-ling noise. He tapped to read a text from Gavin. A picture of a cute little girl appeared with a message underneath. "Witek's daughter."

Nice. The boss always knew what his guys needed.

◇　◇　◇

Tuesday Afternoon
Chicago, Illinois

Agent Bessing hung up the phone in the Chicago field office after updating her supervisor, calling him from the local Enterprise Car Rental where Brian West had returned his car. Good old-fashioned police work got her this far. Verna recognized Kacey's face in Richards Kentucky, despite the fake beard and mustache, but now he could be anywhere, and he probably wasn't named Brian West anymore.

She called Sherriff Millard in Kentucky to fill him in on the progress. "He dropped off his rental car at Enterprise and walked into an area with nine million people."

"I wish you luck. Shouldn't you take some time off?"

"Nothing's busted, so I'll take a pill and keep going."

"I've assigned patrols to stop by Bea Herman's house every day to make her feel safe. She's a tough old bird."

"Yes, and I think she actually misses Kacey Farrell."

"I think you're right. Good hunting, Agent Bessing."

"Roger that."

◊   ◊   ◊

Tuesday Afternoon
Burbank, Illinois

Kacey Farrell set down his grocery bag on the sidewalk and caught the Frisbee flying toward his head. A large black Labrador charged toward him. Kacey turned sideways and held the Frisbee out straight. The dog leaped, grabbed the Frisbee, and landed in the grass on a dead run.

A young Latino boy ran up to Kacey. "Hey, mister. How did you do that?" The dog ambled up and dropped the Frisbee at the kid's feet.

"I just reacted. Pretty slick, huh?" He held out his hand. "I'm Manny Kolinski, who are you?"

"Juan, and this is Bixby." He scratched the dog's head. "Do you want to try the trick again?"

"Can you ask Bixby if I can put my groceries away and change my shoes first?"

"I will, but he won't mind."

Kacey took his groceries into the building, climbing the stairs to the third floor and entering his apartment. He'd found a new razor for his bald head with a flexible blade advertised to not nick up his scalp.

Brian West had been replaced by Manfred Kolinsky, his last identity from Get-Your-Man, specifically obtained for Chicago, full of Polish people.

He put on tennis shoes and a T-shirt to throw the Frisbee around with his new friends.

Chapter 13

Wednesday Morning
Frost, Wisconsin

In the middle of the night, Gio covered up with an old quilt to keep warm. Nights were chilly, even in summer. The fact that he was pushing seventy didn't help. Wood trim, paintings set in the 1800s, and old-fashioned utensils decorated his room in The Dew Drop Inn of Frost, Wisconsin. How quaint.

In the morning, he put on his new overalls, a plaid shirt and the green John Deere hat and went out to the car. He decided to start his search in a little town called Castor a few miles away on the other side of the lake. The drive took him through the deep woods. Rolling into Castor, he noticed the similarity to Frost and headed toward a diner to chat up a waitress. A bell tinkled over the door. He found a stool at the counter, and a middle-aged woman, light on her feet, stepped up in front of him. Gio showed her the picture of Brady Witek on his phone and explained why he needed to find him—Witek had lapses of memory from an Army injury and hadn't been seen in a few days.

She gave the picture a close look and shook her head. Two men in the diner gave the picture a look and didn't recognize him. Gio decided to get breakfast and hang out at the counter for the morning, talking to customers as they came in.

◊   ◊   ◊

Wednesday Afternoon
Frost, Wisconsin

Brady inspected the restaurant with his arms crossed. The place looked pretty damn—darn good. The cleaning crew had the place so clean, you could eat off it, which was the point. The new glass door was so clean it looked invisible. The wood bar shined with a fresh coat of polish. Even the brick had been blasted clean. ACME Appliance Service had the kitchen 100 percent. A neon sign in cursive hung on the stone wall out front. All it said was Sylvia's.

The "keep it simple" approach had kept them on schedule. The walk-in fridge was full of food, and tomorrow night, they would have a test opening. Family and friends would eat free.

Last Monday, Jose introduced him to his cousin Ephram, an experienced short-order cook in Des Moines. He'd agreed to relocate to Frost.

Brady had discovered a dumbwaiter in the kitchen, but they couldn't find the opening upstairs. Jose used a paint scraper and jimmied boards loose, and there it was. This meant they could host dinner parties in the banquet hall and send food up.

A sizzling noise came from the kitchen. Brady headed back, drawn by the smell of meat on the grill and found Jose and Sylvia grilling burgers over the flames.

"Bad news, Gene," Sylvia said. "We had to cook up some of the hamburger patties for testing purposes, but we got lucky, it's dinnertime."

"Whew. Lucky how that worked out. But as partner, I insist on sharing the testing duties. Where are the French fries?"

Sylvia punched Jose's arm. "We forgot the French fries."

Brady dropped a basket of fries and tossed a hamburger patty on the grill. Condiments were ready in the prep station. Buns were ready to toast. He went back to the refrigerator, grabbed three bratwurst links, setting one on the grill and raising his eyebrow. Sylvia and Jose shrugged and nodded. Brady tossed the other two links on the grill.

◊   ◊   ◊

Wednesday Night
Frost, Wisconsin

Gio brought take out dinner in a bag back to the Dew Drop Inn and ate at the desk in the room. No luck today finding Brady Witek in Castor or Carol's Landing. That meant he would go to Gravelton next and then search Frost. Those were the only two towns remaining that accessed the cell tower.

They called Carol's Landing a town, but it was more of small gathering of houses. No one knew Witek. He'd search the smaller towns first considering how a man on the run would normally find an obscure place to hide. The logic was still valid, so he would scope out Gravelton first thing in the morning before Frost.

He pulled a greasy grilled ham-and-cheese sandwich from the paper bag and frowned. Rigors of the job…

◊　◊　◊

Thursday Evening
Frost, Wisconsin

Friends and family arrived at 7:00 p.m. and settled into tables. The two new employees, a teenage boy and girl, waited tables while Ephram cooked. Jose started to put on a white apron, but Brady snatched it away from him. Orders came in, and Ephram cooked.

After two hours, Sylvia discovered they would soon run out of mozzarella sticks, so she headed to the supermarket and bought a large bag full of sticks, thinking they might as well have enough on hand until the next truck. She paid and pushed the cart out the automatic doors. As she rolled across the white stripes in the walkway, a man in brown overalls wearing a John Deere hat approached from the handicap spots.

"Excuse me, ma'am. I was wondering if you may've seen this man around town. He suffered a head wound in the service, and we haven't been able to find him for a few days. His name is Brady Witek."

Sylvia walked over and looked at the phone. She paused. "No, I'm sorry. I hope he's okay."

◊   ◊   ◊

Gio thanked the lady, and she headed to her car. He slipped around to the Cadillac and got in. The lady had reacted when she saw the picture. He could see her climb into the driver's seat in his rearview mirror and followed when she drove out of her spot and headed to the exit. She headed back toward downtown Frost and went all the way through, turning right into the lodge. Gio slowed down to take a look. The Moose and Bear Lodge. A number of cars parked near a sign that said Sylvia's. Maybe he had just met Sylvia, or maybe a woman who really loved cheese sticks.

He found a place to turn around and drove back to the lodge, parking in the gravel to the west in front of a line of motel rooms. In his glove box, he took out binoculars and trained them on the restaurant. The place looked a little strange with a glass door on the side near the front, but the rest was all stone, like it was an underground hideaway or something.

People were leaving, laughing, and rubbing their bellies. The woman from the supermarket walked out several times, chatting with the customers. *She had to be Sylvia.* By nine thirty, most or all had left.

Sylvia came out with a Mexican fellow, chatting back and forth. Out walked another Mexican wearing a hair net and an apron, followed by a taller white guy wearing an apron with mustard and grease stains.

Gio looked at the picture on the phone and then trained his binoculars on the white guy's face. "Hello there, Brady Witek. I'm so happy to finally see you."

Gio sent a text to Gavin. "Found your pigeon."

◊   ◊   ◊

It was time for cleanup. They were still figuring things out, setting procedures, and came to realize another garbage dumpster was required near the back door of the restaurant. Until then, they would have to haul trash bags up the hill and behind the lodge.

Sylvia felt great about the trial run. People raved about the burgers, and no one complained about the simple menu. They planned to open for dinner tomorrow, but her excitement for the restaurant was tempered with her misgivings about her new partner. The guy at the supermarket had referred to Gene as Brady Witek. Gene admitted he left a previous life behind, but was he really a guy named Brady with a brain injury?

Sylvia headed back to her quarters in the lodge to clean up. She smelled like hamburgers and her skin felt greasy. After all that work, now was not the time to stir up trouble. She would confront Gene later. She didn't need to stress about it now. After all, they used Gene's money to get the restaurant going, not a normal practice for a con artist.

◊　◊　◊

Friday Afternoon
Frost, Wisconsin

Brady worked with Ephram in the kitchen learning how to cook. Ephram couldn't cover all the hours, and Brady could make more profit covering shifts. Sylvia walked into the kitchen as they were filling the dressing bins. She watched the entire process and then left.

Brady asked, "Why would she get nervous now?"

Ephram shrugged and looked at his watch. "It's four. Let's open the restaurant."

Brady unlocked the door and turned on the open sign. With Lisa handing out burger coupons to lodgers and Jose setting out a sign by the road, hungry people should show up. He noticed Sylvia staring. She glanced away and headed up the stairs. She'd kept away from him all day.

The door swung open and bumped him. A young couple with two kids came in. The waitress walked over and led them to a table. Brady went to the kitchen and brought out a tray of ice-waters. The bell over the door rang again, and a steady flow of customers continued past 10:00 p.m. Frost, Gravelton, and surrounding towns were drawn to the new place to eat out on Friday night. The young waitress collected healthy tips. Ephram kept the plates coming at the pass. Brady hustled to keep the tables cleared, trash bins emptied, and water glasses filled. Sylvia worked the bar area, serving burgers and beer. Jose washed dishes and backed up Ephram.

A sign in the front door listed closing time at 11:00 p.m., but Brady took the sign down at 10:50 p.m. A little before 1:00 a.m., the place emptied for the first time. Sylvia joined them in the kitchen during clean up. "Why did I wait so long to open this place up? The cash drawer is full of money."

"Now was the right time," Brady said. "Don't second-guess yourself."

"It took your energy and resources to get us going."

"When the time is right, the time is right. I need to take garbage up the hill."

He grabbed the tops of several bags in each hand and went to the rear side door. Sylvia held it open. As he went up the gravel slope, he heard Sylvia crunching in the gravel behind him. "We need to talk, Brady Witek."

He stopped and stood for a moment, bags dangling from his hands. He dropped the bags and turned around.

"Why did you lie to me?"

Brady looked her in the eye. "Like I told you, I'm trying to start over. I'm not a criminal, just a guy that couldn't handle his old life."

"Uh-huh. You signed papers in the attorney's office using a false identity. How are we going to fix that?"

Brady didn't know how to answer. "Wait a minute, how did you get my real name?"

"A guy at the supermarket was asking around for you. He had a picture of you on his phone."

"Shit, did you tell him where I am?"

"No, I covered for you."

"What did he look like?"

"A guy in his sixties wearing brown overalls and a green cap, he didn't look right in those clothes."

Brady rubbed his forehead. "I need to get out of here. I can't believe someone tracked me down."

She put her hands on her hips. "We have the restaurant open one night, and you're going to run away. What about your money?"

"We'll work something out. You guys can handle the place. All I've done so far is bus tables."

"Let's go downtown tomorrow and talk to the Sherriff. You need to be here."

Brady paused again. "I'll think about it, but right now, I'm going to take this trash up the hill and go hide in my RV. Keep an eye out for that guy." He picked up the bags.

"Hold it. The guy said you were an army vet with a head injury. You must have wandered off."

"Never been in the military."

She waved him off, and Brady headed up the hill.

◇   ◇   ◇

Saturday Morning
Frost, Wisconsin

Brady woke up in the loft with fingers that smelled like pickles. He remembered the guy looking for him and peered out the screens. Men walked around, but they looked like vacationers. Maybe one of them was trying to look like a vacationer.

He pulled out the burner phone and turned it on. It beeped with a text. Paul texted about Serena? Was she the one who sent someone to track him down? He rang Paul's number, but he didn't pick up.

Serena must have lost whatever marbles she had left. She would get twenty years in jail for kidnapping. Or maybe she sent the guy to tell him she loved him or some other crap like that. The guy would probably hand him a letter, or he would tell Serena where he was staying, and then she would come up here to Frost. He may never even see the guy at all. Serena will just show up in a few days and check into the lodge. Maybe Paul could warn the father what his daughter was up to and say Brady planned to get a restraining order.

Brady sat up. *That had to be it.* Serena hired a private investigator to find him, and he could use it to his advantage. He'd ask Sylvia to use her connections to obtain a restraining order and explain he used the name Gene Brinkman after she broke into his apartment with a rubber penis. He's terrified of her.

Brady got dressed, grabbed his shower bag, and walked down to the office to find Sylvia at her desk. "Good morning, Sylvia. You're right, when the time comes, we'll visit the Sherriff. I'm not going anywhere."

Sylvia shook her fists over her head. "Yes!"

After showering, Brady headed back to the RV to change into work clothes. He opened the back door and climbed in to find a man sitting at the table.

Brady started to climb back out of the RV, but the man put up his hand. "Please stay, Mr. Witek. We need to talk. Sorry for the intrusion."

Brady checked the guy out: a handsome man in his sixties with silver hair. He looked like an Outfit guy, and a dangerous one at that.

"Look, I know Haynesworth paid you, but you can save the speech," Brady said. "Tell Serena I'm not interested, or tell her I'm dead, whatever. Consider your job done."

"Please allow me to speak." The man motioned to a chair.

"I have an idea instead. Why don't you get the fuck out of my RV before I kick your ass." Brady walked down the aisle and found a chef's knife in the kitchen drawer.

The guy reached into his sport coat, pulled out a Glock pistol, and set it on the table in front of him. "Put the knife away and sit down, please. Or were you going to prepare a sandwich?"

"I'm going to prepare you for the morgue, asshole."

The man waited.

Brady figured the guy knew how to use the gun, so he put the knife back in the drawer and sat down on the bench.

"Call me Gio. I was sent to speak with you, but not by Winston Haynesworth. Quite frankly, Mr. Witek, you should stay away from Serena Haynesworth. She's a nutcase."

"She was a blind date."

"Okay, must have gone well. But I'm here on behalf of your employer, Polyglomerate Container. They need you to come back to work and finish the important merger you were working on."

Brady's tone grew sharp. "I left a pack of instructions. They can finish it themselves."

"Apparently, Spencer Moss, your supervisor, doesn't have the proper skills to complete the merger. Several consultants have tried and failed. Seems you set up everything yourself over the years, and only you know all the tweaks."

"Which is why I typed up the instructions. If they need more help, I'll answer questions on the phone."

"I'm here to bring you back to Harwood Heights to finish the job."

"No. Now get out of here."

Gio pulled out his phone and held it up so Brady could see a picture of his daughter, Crissy. "Is she your favorite?"

Gio set the phone down and took hold of the pistol. "I don't like the look on your face, Witek. Calm down."

"Listen, fucker. If you lay a finger on my family, I'll fire that gun up your asshole."

"We don't want to bother your family. Just come back and finish the job."

Brady stood up. "I'm calling the FBI, and then I'm going to hack into the Polyglomerate servers and erase everything. And then I may just burn the place down."

Gio chuckled. "You're more like a wise guy. Sit back down."

Brady crossed his arms. "Explain exactly what you want."

"We're a good six or seven hours away from Chicago. I checked the fuel gage on the dash. The tank is full. We'll take a nice ride together, you and me, back to Harwood Heights, and then you'll meet with my boss. He'll work something out with you."

"What if I don't?"

"My Cadillac is parked in the lot. You won't get to enjoy the scenery from the inside of my trunk, but let's head back in your RV. I'll have a guy come get the Caddy."

Brady went to the back of the Ghost and rested his head on the back door to weigh his options. If he contacted the FBI, they would have to protect the girls, possibly putting them into witness protection. He had to keep them out of this.

Brady walked back to the table. "Put the gun away unless you plan to use it."

Gio shrugged and put the gun in his coat pocket. "We'll need to leave immediately. You won't need to pack since you also live in your vehicle."

"Then let's go before I change my mind and fuck you up."

"Try not to let that cross your mind again, Witek. I've been doing this for a while. You'll be sorry."

Brady went to the back door. "I'm going out to uncouple the RV, and then I'll drive."

Gio waved bye-bye.

Outside, after he disconnected the supply lines for water and electric, he took a few steps into the trees and prayed out loud before climbing into the driver's seat. Gio came through the curtain with his gun swinging in his jacket in front of him. Brady fought the urge to grab it and squeeze the trigger.

With the engine running, Brady turned to Gio. "They're going to miss me at the lodge and call the police."

"I don't want you going in there. Call later."

Up ahead, Jose walked across the road between the lodge and the motel rooms.

"Get in back until we're out of here," Brady said. "If they see a gangster in the jump seat, they'll call the cops."

Gio chuckled. "Gangster, eh? You're a piece of work." He went back through the curtain.

Brady put the Ghost in gear and pulled down the gravel, waving at Jose as he passed. Near the lodge, Lisa came out and waved at him. At least they saw him drive away on his own.

He pulled out on the road, straightened out, and put the pedal down. A clunk noise came from the back. Gio grunted. In a few seconds, he came back through the curtain. "Very funny. Now, give me a smooth ride the rest of the way."

Brady smirked. "By the way, what do you mean my date with Serena must have gone well?"

"You don't know? You knocked the broad up, that's why."

The Ghost swerved off the asphalt. Brady eased the tires back on the road.

◊　◊　◊

Saturday
Evanston, Illinois

Winston Haynesworth set down his scotch and answered the phone.

"This is Gavin Ricci, Mr. Haynesworth. We found Brady Witek."

Winston grinned. "Excellent."

"Keep your daughter away from him, at least until he finishes with us. We don't want any interference. Got it?"

"Fine, but when you're done with him, you'll do as I say."

"We'll talk about it. Sal's interests come first."

"Keep me informed." He hung up and pushed a button on the table. Clarice appeared. "Get Serena." Clarice left.

Ten minutes later, Serena walked in. "What do you want?"

Winston sighed. "I just received word that Brady Witek has been located and will be brought back to town."

Serena put her hands to her face. "Oh, thank the stars. My man is coming back to me. Thank you, Father." She wrapped her arms around his neck from behind. Drink splashed out of his glass.

"Now, listen to me," Winston said. "You will refrain from contacting Witek until I give you permission. When he disappeared, he left behind many responsibilities, and he must not be disturbed. Do you understand?"

Serena rubbed her belly. "What wonderful news." She skipped out of the room like a schoolgirl.

Winston poured another drink. Maybe he shouldn't have told her about Witek.

◊　◊　◊

Brady and his new friend Gio drove down the tollway wearing seat belts, an important safety feature, especially for Gio; otherwise, he could get booted out of the vehicle by the driver. Gio kept quiet most of the way, checking the mirrors and staying aware of his surroundings. He texted several times. After a few hours, they stopped to urinate. Brady used the toilet. Gio went by the side of the road with Brady's keys in his pocket.

Brady felt a growing ache in his stomach. Instead of fading from everyone's memory, he would soon have to face all the messes he left behind.

He took the Tri-State and headed south, exiting for the drive east to Harwood Heights. The sight of the building made him angry. Was it too late to escape?

Gio said, "Drive this barge around back and park it."

It was Saturday, so the back of the building was clear. Brady nosed in the Ghost, keeping the windshield to the north away from the sun. He noticed a cover for an electric outlet and a water spigot, meaning he could stay right here behind the building. He put his forehead on the steering wheel.

"Come on, Witek. You can get gloomy later. We need to meet the fellas upstairs."

Brady jumped out, wishing he wore shabbier clothes and hadn't shaved. He'd rather look like a bum. Too bad he didn't stink.

Two new signs reserved parking for Mark Seivers and Spenser Moss. How nice. But a Volkswagen Beetle parked in Spencer's spot. Good, maybe someone else was screwing with him now.

Brady climbed the stairs behind Gio. When they got to Mark's office, Gio nodded for him to enter. Inside, Mark and Spencer were joined by some bald ape looking guy. Gio closed the door and didn't come in. Spencer bounced on his heels, smiling. The bald ape clicked his fingers and pointed to a chair. Spencer sat down.

Mark turned to Brady. "Mr. Witek, you forced us to take drastic action. You're the only one who can make sense of our systems."

Brady didn't respond.

"Please sit down." Mark and the ape sat down. Brady stayed standing.

The ape said, "Sit down, Witek."

Brady held up his middle finger. "Why don't you sit on this?"

The ape chuckled. "I'm starting to like this guy… Listen, my name is Gavin. Won't you please join us in sitting so we can get this over with?"

Brady smacked Spencer in the back of the head. Spencer's head lurched forward. "Hey! What the hell?" Brady sat down.

Gavin laughed. "No doubt about it, I like this guy."

Mark pointed. "Don't do that again, Brady."

Brady started to get up.

Gavin said, "Don't press your luck with me, Witek."

"So, Gavin, who are you? Why don't you go polish your head with car wax?"

"I'm an associate of Mr. Seivers, and that's all you need to know." Gavin sat forward in his chair. "Look, I know you were shown a picture of your daughter by my associate, and I regret that occurred. We don't want to involve your family. Please complete the outstanding project, and then you'll be free as a bird. How about it?"

"My lawyer gave you guys a packet with all the information needed to get the job done. Why is Spenser still around? Why was he even born?"

Spenser got up. Gavin stood, grabbed the back of Spencer's shirt and sat him back down.

"You container guys are a lively bunch," Gavin said. "But you have a point. From now on, Brady is the head of the computer department, and Spencer works for him. How does that sound?"

"Like I may have never left in the first place."

"I don't care who's in charge," Mark said. "Spenser can get you coffee for all I care."

"Yeah right. I'm not drinking coffee with his piss in it."

Gavin chuckled again. "Who knew I would enjoy this meeting so much?"

"Okay, then, here it is," Mark said. "Brady, complete the merger, and you can go. Nothing will happen to you. And I'll give you a ten-thousand-dollar severance. What do you say?"

Brady breathed in and out a few times. "Make it twenty thousand, in cash, and never contact me again."

Mark said, "I'm not going to negotiate—"

"We have a deal, Mr. Witek." Gavin pointed.

"I'll have to park my RV out back and hook up water and electric, but I'll come inside to take a shit."

"Done. Would you like to shake hands?"

"No. Go shake hands with your own dick."

Gavin chuckled. "This guy should be in charge of the entire operation."

◊   ◊   ◊

Saturday Evening
Harwood Heights, Illinois

Brady called the lodge from his burner phone in the Ghost.

Lisa answered, "Moose and Bear Lodge."

"Lisa, it's me, Gene."

"Where are you? We're worried sick. We had to open the restaurant without you."

"Something came up. I'll be gone for a while. Please don't worry about me."

There was a clonk and rustling sound. Sylvia came on the line. "Brady, where are you? What happened?"

"The guy with my picture showed up, but I'm all right."

"When are you coming back?

Brady thought about it. "I'm not sure. I'll keep in touch."

"Okay, Brady. I hope everything works out for you."

"Me too. Please pray for me."

Brady put the phone behind the mattress and wiped sweat off his forehead. He opened the windows, but a hot breeze came through with a garbage smell from the dumpster. Loud music played from the street on Saturday night. Car tires screeched and horns honked.

He lay in limbo, not even able to get started on the merger because they didn't trust him alone in the building. He put on his shoes and got out of the Ghost. The neighborhood was decent enough around here, so he would go for a walk, either to get tired enough to sleep, or to find a liquor store.

The liquor store sounded better. He walked around the building to begin the search.

Chapter 14

Sunday Noon
Harwood Heights, Illinois

When Brady awoke the next day, he faced a terrible decision: His bladder was full, he needed to puke, and his bowels were loose. He rolled over focusing, thinking about how to climb down without letting go of something.

He dropped down to the floor and stood for five minutes, concentrating to keep three different orifices closed. When the pressure eased, he shuffled like Frankenstein toward the toilet, pausing to take a large salad bowl out of the cupboard.

He had to stand for another five minutes in front of the toilet, and when the pressure subsided again, he yanked the door open, dropped his drawers, and sat while he vomited in the salad bowl.

He sat recovering in the tiny room for half an hour while the dry heaves came and went. Once stabilized, he got up and poured puke in the toilet and then cleaned himself up with a rag. A bottle of water from the fridge went down fast, but then he raced to the toilet to give it all back.

He took out another bottle and sipped. Now that he was pushing forty, he couldn't drink booze like this anymore. An empty fifth of Jack sat by the sink. He climbed back into the loft to rest a bit more, enjoying the empty feeling in his body. A few hours later, he recovered enough, so he climbed down to find some greasy food to eat. He could smell meat cooking somewhere in the neighborhood. He got out and followed his nose to Larry's Burger Haven around the block. He brought back a cheeseburger and fries and wolfed them down.

With nothing else to do, he decided to drive the Ghost over to the church and find Paul. He disconnected the extension cord and water hose from the building and drove to the church following the familiar path back to the neighborhood. The streets gave him fond memories mixed with regret as things would never be the same.

Brady parked the Ghost out on the edge of the lot taking up several spaces before going in looking for Paul. Paul came around the corner holding the hands of two little boys. "Brady? I can't believe my eyes. What are you doing here?"

"I came to see you, but I can wait for bathroom patrol."

Paul looked down. "Oh, right. We'll be done in a minute. Wait in my office."

Brady went to his office. Ten minutes later, Paul came in and walked straight behind the desk, not bothering to shake Brady's hand. Brady started to get up but then sat back down.

"This is awkward, Brady. Pastor Wells told me to stay away from you. Maybe you should leave before he sees us."

"You want me to leave? Listen, Paul, I planned to get back in touch with you on a regular basis."

Paul shook his head. "I know that." He stood up and went to the window. "You put me in a bad spot, man. I can't be involved in even the appearance of a scandal, and what you did was just not right."

Brady leaned forward. "She told you?"

"Yes, she did. It was awful with her yelling like that."

Brady felt tears coming to his eyes. This was the worst-case scenario. "I don't know what she told you, but stand by me, Paul. It truly wasn't my fault."

Paul sat down at his desk again. "Okay, Brady. But you have to take responsibility."

Brady looked Paul in the eyes. "I swear, nothing happened, Paul. No matter what you heard, nothing happened."

Paul looked away in disgust. "Come on, man. If nothing happened, then how is she pregnant?"

"What? Britney's pregnant?"

"No, Serena is. You thought I was talking about—"

"Serena?"

"She said you're the father. Old man Haynesworth had me kidnapped. It was a warning to keep my mouth shut."

"Kidnapped?" Brady stood up.

Paul stood. "They knocked me out and took a picture of me with a transvestite."

Brady's mouth dropped open. "No shit. Wait a minute… Did you have your phone with you at the time?"

"Of course."

"Then that's how they found me. You sent me a text about Serena, and they figured out where my burner phone was. Now listen, Paul. Haynesworth didn't kidnap you, Outfit guys did."

"What? Why would Outfit guys kidnap me?"

"Let's sit down." The both sat. "Now don't be talking about this to anyone, okay?" Brady explained the situation at Polyglomerate and Bigham's warning.

Paul leaned back in his chair, taking it all in. "Well then, I may've been kidnapped by the Outfit, but what about Serena? I'm more confused now than before."

"Paul, I did not have sex with that woman." He shook his head. "Sorry, that sounded like Bill Clinton."

"I never really believed you did. You would have told me about it." Paul cringed.

"I would have, and don't worry, I'll take whatever test I need to take. She must have gotten knocked up by some other guy, but wants me to be the dad. She's infatuated with me. Remember her out in the car?"

Paul touched his face. "You may be right, but what about Britney. Why did you think she was pregnant?"

"Did she tell you anything?"

Paul shook his head.

Brady breathed in deep. "Okay, then I'm going to tell you the entire truth, even though I'm risking our friendship. Are you ready?"

"I'm ready. Tell me."

◊ ◊ ◊

Monday Morning
Harwood Heights, Illinois

Polyglomerate Container normally opened its doors at 7:30 a.m. by the maintenance crew. Brady was waiting to go in early and avoid other employees, but his plan didn't work. Right before the doors were unlocked, Lexi pulled into the lot and walked around the corner. She stopped in her tracks. "I can't believe it."

Brady waved her over. "Keep walking, girl. Nothing to see here."

She put her purse over her shoulder and surprised Brady with a hug. "You escaped this place. Why did you come back?"

"I can't say, but I won't be here very long."

"I bet they offered you money to finish the merger."

"That's a good guess." Brady shuffled his feet. "Not to get all mushy, but you're one of the few people I missed."

A janitor unlocked the front door with a click and a clank. Lexi yanked it open. "Give me a break."

Brady followed her inside and headed up to his old office. The door was unlocked, and inside, things were left pretty much the same, except the fan sat on the floor. He would have to rig it up again on top of the wall so his new employee, Spencer, could feel the heat. When his computer booted, his password didn't work, so he wrote a message on a posted note and stuck it on Spencer's door and then went down to get a coffee in the lunchroom. When he got back, Spencer sat in the guest chair. "Jeans and a T-shirt? Not the company dress code."

"Is there a code for kicking the ass of another employee? I'm not interested in following the rules today."

Spencer chuckled. "I'll get you back into the system, and then you'll get the merger done. It doesn't matter what the goon said, I'm not putting up with your shit."

"Awww, that's too bad. I was counting on your great computer expertise."

Brady took his seat, and Spencer moved his chair up next to him to set Brady back up with permissions and passwords. He reactivated his company e-mail. When Brady was ready to work, he turned to Spencer. "How could you get mixed up with Outfit guys? They'll never let you go."

"We couldn't get a bank to bail us out."

"It's your funeral. Now, let me get to work. I'll buzz if I need something."

Spencer stood up. "You do that, hotshot. But one thing, you were right about my piss in your coffee, so don't ask." He left.

Brady inspected the current state of the systems. Someone had started to map connections for the merger but didn't know enough about the tables to do it right. Having designed the structure himself, he didn't need a guide to know where values were kept or how the inner joins worked.

A knuckle tapped on his door. Mark said, "Good, you're here. I'll let Gavin know you showed up."

Brady looked over. "Go away."

Mark walked away without comment.

◇ ◇ ◇

Monday Late Afternoon
Harwood Heights, Illinois

The phone on Brady's desk rang. The caller ID showed it was Sydney Brandenburg.

Brady picked up. "Sydney? How did you know I was here?"

"I got a call from Jolene. Somehow, she knew you were back in town. Why are you working at Polyglomerate again?"

"We can talk later."

"Okay, but you have a hearing Wednesday morning at the courthouse."

"Shit, I only missed two payments."

"You did, but you also invested in a business in Wisconsin, and Jolene wants half. She also wants to take away all your custody rights."

"Will you still represent me, Syd? There's some money left, but they may try to take it."

"I'm your counsel. We'll work things out later. Be at the court-house half an hour early so we can talk things over, okay?"

"Thanks, man. See you then."

Sydney hung up. Brady went around to Spencer's office and banged the door open. Spencer jerked his head up from a line of white powder on a mirror.

Brady smirked. "Breakfast of champions… Did you call my ex-wife?

Spencer shrugged. "Thought your loved ones would like to know you're okay. She was thrilled you were back to work."

Brady figured he could hit him in the face and get away with it, but he resisted the urge. "We'll see what Gavin thinks about your call. Maybe I can get you disappeared."

Spencer frowned and snorted the powder off the mirror.

◊   ◊   ◊

Wednesday Morning
Chicago, Illinois

Brady sat in the witness chair in the courtroom. Judge Jurgons wasn't happy to see him. "Explain yourself, Mr. Witek. Leaving town and missing payments, this does not look good for you."

"The numbers didn't add up, Judge. Paying for the student loan was the last straw—my incoming was less than my outgoing. It's your fault."

The judge glared at him. "I see your bad attitude hasn't changed."

"After my pay was cut by twenty-five percent at work, I couldn't do the math."

"I understand, but you can't take things into your own hands. You should have filed a motion. I'm ordering you to pay the out-standing amount of support." The judge moved some papers. "And I'm removing your custody rights."

Brady stayed quiet.

"Now, where did you get the money to invest in a restaurant in Wisconsin?"

Brady thought about telling her he'd won at Blackjack, but God wouldn't go along with a lie. Brady offered up a silent prayer, asking God for help.

"Mr. Witek, I asked you a question."

"I used the money to pay for kitchen repair and food supplies. I signed an agreement with Sylvia Banner, owner of the Moose and Bear Lodge to become half owner of the restaurant."

"The question was, where did this money come from?"

"I cashed out stock investments."

"Why didn't you reveal this money to your wife's attorneys?"

"They asked the wrong questions. They wanted information on my accounts."

"Then where was the money?"

"I converted the money into certified checks and stored them in a safe-deposit box."

The courtroom rumbled. The judge banged her gavel. Brady noticed a camera trained on him from the spectator seats.

Jurgons turned to Jolene's attorney. "Is this true, you only asked for a list of his accounts?"

Franklin Gaston stood. "Yes, Your Honor, but the implication was for him to reveal all his assets. Hiding the certified checks constitutes fraud."

"Not if you only requested account information. I was there, remember. The settlement is over. Too bad."

Jolene leapt to her feet. "You can't do that. Half of that money is mine!"

"Sit down, Mrs. Witek. You can't blurt things out in my courtroom." Judge motioned to Brady. "Mr. Witek, please step down." Brady went and sat next to Sydney.

"Mr. Witek will continue to make support payments. If he fails to do so, he will be held in contempt." She banged her gavel. "You have my ruling, next case."

◇   ◇   ◇

Sydney and Brady walked down the aisle and into the hallway. A bright light hit Brady in the face. A man wearing a backward baseball cap held a camera, and an attractive woman with perfect makeup and hair stepped up with a microphone. "Mr. Witek, how did you feel when you lost custody of your children?"

Sydney stepped in front of Brady. "We don't wish to comment at this time, thank you."

"Mr. Witek, you testified that you left town due to the burden of your responsibilities, essentially abandoning your children."

"He did not abandon his children. When Mr. Witek felt squeezed by the system, he wanted to find a new way to provide. Maybe he should have done things differently, but he's only human. Thank you."

"Do you think hiding money from your family will somehow help to provide for them?"

Sydney took Brady's arm, pulled him away from the reporter, and directed him toward the entrance of the building. A man in a deputy's uniform stepped in front of them to hand Brady an envelope. The light reappeared on Brady's face. "Mr. Witek, you have been served to appear in court. Can I please have your signature?" Sydney nodded, and Brady signed the receipt. The deputy left.

They started walking again, and another man in a sport coat moved in front of them to hand Brady an envelope. "Mr. Witek, you are served to appear in court. Can I please have your signature?" Sydney nodded again. Brady signed again. The man left.

Sydney and Brady searched around with the camera crew close by. The lady held out her microphone. "Can you tell us more about your continuing legal trouble, Mr. Witek?"

Sydney took Brady's arm. "Let's get the hell out of here."

They went out the front door and down the steps. Mrs. Fitzgibbon's stood waiting with an envelope. Brady went down to her and took it.

"Do you want me to sign?"

"Just pay the bill, darling, or show up in court."

◊ ◊ ◊

In a coffee shop down the street, Sydney opened the first envelope.

"Well, this one is a paternity suit. Serena Haynesworth says she's pregnant with your baby. You know, Brady, I never thought of you as a player."

Brady set down his coffee. "I did not have sex with that woman. There I go with the Bill Clinton routine again."

"Then why would they file the suit?"

Brady twirled his finger next to his head.

Sydney shrugged and opened the next envelope. "Charlotte Fitzgibbons wants all the rent money plus half for breach of contract."

"Okay, I expected those two, but I can't think of what the third would be."

Sydney opened the third envelope. "Cindy Witek is suing for breach of a verbal agreement. She expects to receive five hundred dollars a month from you."

Brady coughed. "She can't be serious."

"From the summons, I gather she's serious. Did you promise to pay her five hundred dollars a month?"

"I've been helping her out, but I don't think I ever promised to do it forever."

"If you promised, she may have a case. Do you remember exactly what you said?"

"No. I started helping her out a while ago."

Sydney crossed his arms and gave Brady a long look. "It's a good thing you have the certified checks. You may be cashing the rest in to pay me."

"Great. Say, do you know where I can sell my blood?"

"Don't bother. I'll drain you at my office."

◊　◊　◊

Thursday Morning
Chicago, Illinois

Shelly LaFortune tapped on the door to Keehn Bennett's office. His head was tilted back as he put drops in his eye. "Come in, whoever you are."

Shelly sat down. "I'm ready to go over the Witek story."

Bennett wiped his cheeks with a Kleenex. "It's not such a hot story. What else do we have?"

"There's the dog who found his way home from Michigan. The quadruplet's in Cicero. Or there's the girl who found a buffalo nickel in her change."

"Hmm. Run the Witek story by me again."

Shelly crossed her legs. "Brady Witek disappeared from town, leaving his four daughters without support payments. We took footage of him on the stand saying he hid money in a safe-deposit box. He then lost custody and was ordered to make the payments. In the hallway, we got a statement from his attorney, and then we got footage of Witek being served with three legal summonses."

"After the judge did her thing?"

"That's right. One is for skipping out on his lease, but the other two are interesting. His sister-in-law says he promised to pay her five hundred dollars a month after his brother left her. Says it was a verbal agreement. The third could be a headliner. Winston Haynesworth's daughter claims she's carrying Brady Witek's baby."

Bennett nodded. "Fine. We'll run with it on Friday."

Shelly jumped up. "Thanks, boss."

◇   ◇   ◇

Friday Afternoon
Burbank, Illinois

In the supermarket, Kacey Farrell observed a young boy, about eight-years old, receive a lecture from his mother about multicolored marshmallows. His dad worked night and day to feed them, and he could have all the marshmallows he wanted when he went to work for himself. The boy quietly took the chewing out. Kacey thought about buying a bag of multicolored marshmallows and handing it to the boy in front of the mother.

As he walked through the meat section, an old lady driving a scooter tossed a pack of strip steaks in the basket. A young man berated her and put them back on the shelf, reminding her that their last name was not "Rockefeller."

Kacey left the store without buying anything and drove back to his apartment building. He checked around for Juan and Bixby, but they weren't out today, so he walked to the bottom of the stairs to gaze at the wall. When he'd stepped back from himself, he went up the stairs, where on the second-floor landing, a door burst open. A man hollered at a woman. The woman threw an apple and hit the man in the forehead. It rolled up to Kacey's feet. Kacey picked it up. As the couple pushed and yelled at each other, Kacey approached. They stopped arguing and turned to him.

The man said, "What?"

Kacey handed him the apple. "I'm Manny Kolinsky, your neighbor from upstairs. It's nice to meet you." He offered his hand.

The man shook. "Ah… We're the Bergdorfs. I'm Glen, and this is Angie."

Kacey shook her hand. "We should have coffee soon to get acquainted."

"Sure, sounds nice."

Kacey headed back to the stairway. "Please continue with your discussion." The Bergdorfs stared at him as he headed up.

Unfortunately, the remodeler had done a nice job on his apartment, restoring the walls to perfect condition. He had to go down the three flights of stairs to use the wall by the landing. He considered altering one of the apartment walls, but the imperfections would have familiarity, not a random quality and would not have worked.

When he turned on the TV to distract himself like most other people, a show was coming back from commercial. A handsome man sat at a desk with a live shot of a downtown street behind him. "Welcome back to *Chicagoland Stories*, I'm Keehn Bennett. Our next story is about a deadbeat dad, one of many in this country, shirking his responsibilities to his children. Some fathers skip town, hoping to find a new life on the road, but for one area father, running away did not work out as planned. Shelly?"

The picture changed to Shelly LaFortune standing in front of the Polyglomerate building. "Thank you, Keehn. Brady Witek once worked at this building, making a good salary as an IT employee, and now, he works here again. Speculation is that he was threatened with a breach of contract suit and had to return. The Polyglomerate Container Company would not comment."

The picture changed to a two-year-old family photo of the Witek family. "Brady Witek, seen here in this family portrait, did not show up for work some weeks back, leaving the company in the lurch, but more importantly, he stopped making support payments for his children."

The picture cut to Brady on the witness stand in court. The exchange between Brady and the judge was edited down. The part where Brady told the judge it was her fault was shown twice.

"The judge ordered Witek to pay outstanding payments and then removed visitation rights to his children."

They played a shot of the judge banging her gavel.

"It was revealed during this hearing that Witek hid a significant amount of money from his wife's divorce team. Because of a technicality, he can keep the money, but Witek did not come away clean."

Footage showed the three individuals serving summons to Brady.

"Brady will go to court for skipping out on his rent, for breach of a verbal agreement with his sister-in-law, and for a paternity suit."

The screen changed to a shot of Serena and Winston Haynesworth walking down a sidewalk on Michigan Avenue.

"The suit was filed by Serena Haynesworth, daughter of Winston Haynesworth, retail magnet in Chicago. Brady Witek is named as the father of her unborn baby."

The shot came back to LaFortune. "We tried to get comment from Witek after his hearing, but he refused to speak. Here is a comment from his attorney, Sydney Brandenburg."

Footage of Sidney played. "He did not abandon his children. When he felt squeezed by the system, he wanted to find a new way to provide. Maybe he should have tried a different way, but he's only human. Thank you."

LaFortune returned to the screen. "The key phrase here is, 'Maybe he should have tried a different way.' After today's hearing, Mr. Witek will suffer the consequences of his actions."

Bennett appeared at his desk. "You can run, but you can't hide, thank you Shelly LaFortune. Our next story involves a young girl who got more back in her change that she bargained for. A near mint condition buffalo nickel—"

Kacey switched off the TV and went down the stairs, leaving the apartment door wide open to take his position in front of the brick wall.

The lawyer on TV had spoken the truth. Brady Witek was only human, but they scoffed at him when he would not submit to authority. Witek did the right thing leaving town to find a new life, one where he wasn't trapped. Now the poor bastard was back where he started.

Kacey squeezed both sides of his head and made a squealing sound, only gazing at the wall after he got back in control. Other residents walked around him to go up the stairs, but he ignored them. Eventually, he headed back up to his apartment.

He booted his laptop on the kitchen table to search for Brady Witek. Maybe he could help the man out.

Chapter 15

Friday Night
Harwood Heights, Illinois

Paul called Brady on his burner phone. "Dude, you're famous."

Brady sat at the kitchen table in the Ghost with his laptop, eating a burger from Larry's Burger Haven. "Thanks, but I won't ignore the little people like you."

"No, really. You were on *Chicagoland Stories* with Keehn Bennett."

"Oh, no." Brady smacked his forehead. "They had a camera at the courthouse. How bad was it?"

"They crucified you."

"You didn't happen to record it, did you?"

"No, but go online. You should be able to find it."

Brady found the story on the station's website. He watched the clip while keeping Paul on the line.

"Where can I go for plastic surgery?"

◊　◊　◊

Saturday Morning
Crystal Lake, Illinois

Jolene nagged Aaron. "We're about to get the support money from Brady, four thousand five hundred dollars, so we can afford to go to Great America."

Aaron walked away from Jolene. "I have to get caught up on the bills, or we're going to miss the next mortgage payment."

Jolene shouted up the stairs. "Girls, get down here."

Footsteps rumbled down the hall and down the stairs. The three youngest girls ran through the living room and into the kitchen.

Jolene asked, "Where's Britney?"

Crissy said, "She doesn't want to be anywhere around Aaron."

Ashley shushed Crissy. "Shut up, baby."

Crissy stuck out her tongue.

"What's she talking about?" Jolene turned to Aaron.

Aaron shrugged. "I don't know. She's a kid."

Crissy said, "Britney said she will never wear a swimming suit around him anymore."

Jolene glared at Aaron.

"I have no idea what that means. All right, everyone, get in the car. We're going to Great America."

They herded out to the garage.

◊　◊　◊

Saturday Morning
Harwood Heights, Illinois

Brady worked hard on the merger to avoid facing all the rest of his problems. Up to now, he had only managed to undo the shoddy work by Spencer and his cheap contractors. Spencer had ignored the instructions and tried to do things the old-school way.

About a decade ago, Spencer stopped staying current and ordered other people to do the tough stuff. He'd focused on driving sports cars and wearing designer shirts. As he fell farther behind, Brady took over systems and became the true administrator.

Despite the situation, Brady had to admit that he wanted to do the merger himself. The Polyglomerate systems were his baby, and he'd always wanted to move the servers into the cloud. Before starting, he asked around about what data to keep, but no one knew enough to answer, so he decided to convert all the data.

Someone tapped on his door.

"Come in."

Lexi came in dressed in jeans, a blouse, and sandals. Her hair was up in a ponytail. She looked beautiful.

Brady stood up. "What are you doing here on Saturday?"

Lexi waved at him. "Sit down, I came to talk." She sat in his guest chair.

Brady pointed to his screen. "That blinking cursor is the future of the company. The servers behind me will soon be gone."

"So there's a future for this company? I have my doubts."

Brady looked around the room. If Lexi wanted to talk, then maybe it shouldn't be in his office. "My program will take a while, why don't I give you a tour of my RV?"

Lexi smacked his arm. "You never stop. No wonder you're in so much trouble."

"Knock it off. That's not what I meant." Brady paused. "So did you see the story about me on television?"

She nodded. "It was harsh. I knew your life had gone to hell, but wow."

"Let's get out of here so we can talk." He pointed at his ears and looked around the room.

Lexi got the message. "All right, but the doors stay open if I get into that camper."

"Just get moving."

Brady led her out of the office to the back of the building where the Ghost was parked. They climbed inside.

Lexi checked it out. "I guess you could live in this if you have to, and I think you will have to after watching the show."

He got water bottles out of the fridge and sat down with her at the table. "I had to skip out on my lease. My landlord wouldn't give me extra time."

"So what about your sister-in-law and the woman you impregnated."

"I didn't impregnate anyone. I did not have sex with that woman."

"Bill Clinton?"

Brady nodded. "I'll take a test and that will be over. We went out on one blind date, and nothing happened."

"So why is she claiming you're the father?"

"I have no idea."

"Interesting. Why is your sister-in-law suing you?"

Brady paused. "You sure you want to hear about it?"

"I won't judge."

He told her about his brother leaving, and how he felt obligated to help Cindy and Lane. He was honest about wanting a relationship with her, even though it would be strange. Then he described walking in on her having sex with another guy.

Lexi gasped and put her hands to her mouth.

"I'd been helping her out every month, and now she's suing me."

"What about missing child support?"

"I can't justify it." Brady shook his head. "But Jolene and the girls live in a huge house with a rich guy named Aaron. I couldn't stand it. A rich guy gets my family, and then I still have to pay?"

Brady looked Lexi in the eyes. "I never wanted to break up my family. Jolene and the judge did it."

Lexi reached over and put her hand on Brady's. "Would you ever take her back?"

Brady breathed out. "No way, but I want my family back..."

Lexi squeezed and then took her hand away to drink some water. They sat in the RV for a few minutes. A cool breeze blew through the screens.

Lexi made a face. "Pee-yew. Is that the garbage dumpster?"

Brady grinned. "Smells like victory. You said you came in today to talk."

Lexi adjusted her seat. "Who are those creepy guys coming around the office? I tried to get information out of Sherry, but she seemed afraid to talk."

"The less you know the better." He looked around his RV, getting paranoid again. "I need to get some lunch. Now, don't give me a hard time. Let me buy you a burger at Larry's Burger Haven."

Lexi got up from the table. "I'll pay so you won't get any ideas."

Brady locked up the Ghost, and they walked to the restaurant where Brady would tell her the truth behind the merger, mainly so she would stop asking questions that could put her in danger.

◊　◊　◊

Monday Morning
Harwood Heights, Illinois

Kacey had purchased a used Ford van, white and inconspicuous. Railings on the top made it look like a commercial van. The motor had good horsepower, and there was plenty of room to haul equipment, or maybe bodies, depending on the situation. He already had one murder charge on him, so why hold back?

He parked in the lot east of the Polyglomerate Container building, searching the area with binoculars. It was a little before 8:00 a.m., a good time to begin surveillance of Brady Witek. Soon after Witek arrived for work, he would leave to work on Witek's problems. Several cars pulled in, but no one went in matching his description.

Movement in the back of the building caught his eye. Brady Witek appeared from the back of a weathered RV, dressed in jeans and a T-shirt, carrying a laptop as he rounded the building and went inside. Witek lived in an RV? The local police must not have noticed. Why wasn't he staying in the apartment? It normally took ninety days for eviction.

Kacey set down the binoculars, put on a hat and sunglasses and got out of the van to amble over to the RV. The vehicle looked in good repair with plenty of tread on the tires. A garden hose and extension cord were attached to the building—Witek really was living back here. Kacey stepped to the back and picked the lock, opened the door and slipped inside. No alarm sounded.

The windows were open, and a garbage smell came in with the breeze. Kacey checked out the loft, went through cabinets, and opened the door to the bathroom. The vehicle would serve its purpose, except for showering. He noticed a bottle of medicated powder by the sink, an alternative to bathing. He slipped out the back, making sure to lock the door.

Back to his van, he drove away while listening to instructions from his GPS. The next destination was Witek's last known address, the apartment building where he stopped paying rent. He found a spot right across the street and waited with a picture of Charlotte Fitzgibbons on his phone. An hour later, she parked her Escalade in the street and walked toward the building. Kacey put on his hat and sunglasses and followed, catching up to hold the door open for her after she used her key.

In the foyer, she stopped and turned to Kacey. "Are you a resident here? You can't just walk in like that."

Kacey smiled. "I am not, but I'm looking for an apartment to rent. Can you help me locate the landlord?"

"Follow me, honey. You just found her."

Kacey went down the hall behind her. She unlocked a door and let him into her office. A cat sitting in her chair greeted them with a meow. Fitzgibbons dropped the cat on the floor and sat down.

Kacey shut the door, went to the side of the desk and picked up the cat. He brought it to a chair and sat, stroking the cat's fur. Fitzgibbons gave him a look. She no doubt thought it presumptuous for him to grab up her cat like that.

"So what apartment size are you looking for?"

"Please don't make a sound, or I break the cat's neck. How much does Brady Witek owe you?"

Charlotte's eyes grew large. "Eighteen thousand in rent and then a fifty-percent penalty for breach of payment."

Kacey sighed. "Tell me how much."

"Twenty-nine thousand."

"You'll agree to twenty thousand, and you'll give me the contract. You will keep no copies for yourself. Does your lawyer have a copy?"

"No, sir. I handle claims myself."

"Then get me the paperwork."

Charlotte sat frozen.

Kacey squeezed the cat's head, causing it to cry out.

Charlotte got up and opened a cabinet drawer. She placed a file in front of Kacey and then opened a side drawer on her desk to take out court filings. "That's everything I have. I swear."

Kacey reached into his coat pocket, produced two bundles of hundred-dollar bills, and set them on the desk in front of Charlotte.

"You should be grateful to have this matter resolved, Mrs. Fitzgibbons—so grateful that you will contact Mr. Witek's attorney and inform him the suit is withdrawn. You will also apologize for humiliating him on television."

Charlotte placed the money in her side drawer. "Why should I apologize? He signed the agreement."

"Why would he sign a new one right before leaving town? You squeezed him."

"The rules are the rules. I didn't get to own this place by being nice."

Kacey looked down at the cat.

Charlotte waved both hands. "Please don't."

"Do not speak to the media, and stay away from the authorities. What is the cat's name?"

"Blue Bell."

"Blue Bell and I will now leave together. If you would like to see it again, let me leave quietly. Understood?"

Charlotte nodded.

Kacey picked up the papers and left with the cat under his arm, making his way down the hall. When he got to the front door, he dropped Blue Bell. The cat dashed down the hallway, and Kacey went to the van.

One down, two to go. His next errand was close by. He drove around the block and parked next to Cindy Witek's building. The house next to the van had a stucco wall with plaster breaking off. There were cracks, vines, and insects. Kacey gazed.

Twenty minutes later, a young man pulled up and walked toward the entrance. Kacey caught up and went in behind him, keeping the brim of his hat low. He went up the stairs, found the correct apartment, and tapped on the door. He waited and tapped again. He picked the lock and let himself in, locking the door behind him.

The smell hit him. Dirty dishes in the sink smelled like spaghetti sauce. A hint of marijuana smoke hung in the air. Underneath was a faint smell of shit. Lint, bits of paper, and small toys lay around the edges of the room as if no vacuum cleaner had been used in weeks. A razor blade and glass tube were set on the edge of an ashtray on the coffee table. Garbage bags were heaped in the kitchen corner.

Voices came from the hallway, followed by a female giggle. The door handle jiggled. Kacey slipped into the kitchen, found the door to the pantry and closed himself in.

The front door opened. Young voices flirted with each other. A woman shrieked in delight, and a man laughed. Kacey waited for a few minutes, came out of the pantry, and walked around to the front of the sofa, still wearing his hat and sunglasses. "Stay quiet and you'll live."

A young man wearing only his undershorts looked up. "Shit." A young woman wore only her panties. The rest of their clothing was scattered on the floor.

"Are you Cindy Witek?"

Cindy nodded and put her hands over her breasts.

Brady noticed a plastic bag on the coffee table, along with a lighter, a spoon, and a needle. He frowned. If she had graduated to heroin, then she was likely a lost cause. "Ms. Witek, where is your son?"

"With friends." Her lip quivered.

"Okay. I'm here to murder you and your friend if you don't do as I say."

The young man sprang from the couch and swung at Kacey. Kacey leaned back, throwing a jab. The young man staggered. Kacey stepped forward and hit him with a combination of punches. The young man dropped to the couch out cold. Cindy whimpered.

Kacey shushed her. "You must stay quiet."

Cindy moved the young man so he could breathe and then looked up at Kacey with sorrow in her eyes. "Tell me what you want." She arched her back to stick out her chest.

Kacey sighed. "You're an attractive young woman, but not for long taking drugs. You'll look like a truck-stop whore in no time. Would be a shame."

Cindy didn't move or speak.

Kacey took a bundle of hundreds out of his pocket. He tore the band, separated out fifty and handed them to Cindy.

"I'm giving you five thousand dollars, although I am afraid of what you'll spend it on. I suggest you take care of your son."

"Come back to the bedroom." She sobbed.

Kacey put his hand up. "The money is not for that. You must drop your suit against Brady Witek, and when you do, I'll deliver you the rest of the money. Ten thousand, total."

"Okay."

"But don't go to the authorities."

Cindy nodded. "Tell Brady to call me."

"Stay away from Brady Witek. You'll only cause him pain."

Kacey left the apartment and got in his van. The first two errands were straightforward enough, but he faced a challenge with the final errand. How would he deal with the pregnant daughter of a wealthy man?

◊　◊　◊

Tuesday Afternoon
Harwood Heights, Illinois

Brady monitored his new installations in the cloud. The database server hummed along, and the new accounting server responded quickly. E-mail accounts were migrated. Conversion tests were next.

Sydney called. "May I speak to Brady Witek, Scourge of Chicago."

"Funny guy."

"Any protestors find you?"

"None yet, which is one advantage of having no permanent address."

"Right. Now, don't fall out of your chair, but for the first time, I'm calling with good news."

"Hit me with it."

"Charlotte Fitzgibbons and Cindy Witek dropped theirs suits against you. I was just notified by the court clerk."

"No shit. Why would they do that?"

"I really don't know, and I don't think we should try to find out. Just enjoy the good news."

"What about Serena?"

"With her, we're in for a battle, and the Haynesworth's have great lawyers."

"Who cares? Get a test done. We'll end it now."

"Serena won't take a test claiming religious grounds. Years ago, a fellow contested the extraction of blood and other body fluids based on his religious beliefs. The court found he had an argument if he truly held those beliefs."

"You've got to be kidding."

"We'll have to look into Serena's records to see if she's ever had blood drawn. For that, I'll have to hire an investigator."

Brady rubbed his face. "What do the Haynesworth's think they can get out of me? I already have five dependents."

"I wondered about that too. If she gets a judgement against you, so what? You can't pay much per month, and they're loaded."

Brady exhaled. "Truth is, Sydney, she's trying to get me to marry her. The lady is not right in the head."

"You did say she stalked you and broke into your apartment."

"Please protect me."

Brady ended the call with Sydney and phoned Paul.

"Serena is fighting a paternity test based on religious beliefs. We all go to your church. Is that something we believe in?"

"No, I think that's the Jehovah's Witnesses." Paul said. "But it's come up a few times. There's a verse in Genesis."

Brady heard flipping noises over the phone.

Paul read, "Genesis 9:6, 'Whosoever sheds the blood of man, by man shall his blood be shed; for in the image of God has God made man.'"

"How does that mean you can't have your cheek swabbed."

"There's other verses about eating blood and how life is in the blood, but it would be hard to argue a DNA sample is forbidden."

"Can't you do something to stop this nonsense?"

"Ah… Remember the picture of me with the transvestite?"

"That probably wasn't Haynesworth."

"Not ready to risk it."

Brady paused. "Then if you're not going to help me, you have to show me the picture."

"Ah, man, I'm screwed either way."

◇   ◇   ◇

Tuesday Afternoon
Evanston, Illinois

Kacey spotted Serena Haynesworth as she walked out of the mansion and drove away in a red Alpha Romeo. He followed her in his van for blocks and then knew something was up when she headed in the direction of Brady Witek's office building. After a few more turns, he had no doubt. Sure enough, she pulled into the lot.

He drove into the next parking lot over and took out his binoculars. Serena sat in her car a few minutes, surveying the area, maybe deciding what to do. He needed to be careful with this one. Her family had resources. Kacey had checked her out online, and rumors suggested her father was connected. Plus, she had several restraining orders for stalking men.

Serena got out of her car and went in the front door of the building. Kacey put down the binoculars. Whatever happened inside would have to play itself out. Brady Witek was on his own.

Kacey brought the binoculars back up when a man came out of the building dressed in an expensive suit, wearing gold jewelry. He had a bald head and a square jaw. An Outfit guy? Witek may be in worse trouble than he thought.

◇   ◇   ◇

Lexi noticed the woman with frizzy hair walking up to the reception area. The woman slapped the counter. "Is Brady Witek here now?"

Lexi smiled politely. "I'm not at liberty to say. Can I take a message?"

"Sure, tell him Serena Haynesworth is here, and she demands to speak to the father of her child."

Lexi's eyes got big. "You're that chick? You shouldn't be here. You filed a suit against him."

Serena searched around, found the staircase, and ran for it.

"Hey! You can't go up there."

Lexi grabbed the phone and dialed Brady's office. "Nutjob lady is on the way up. You better hide."

◊   ◊   ◊

Brady looked down the hallway and then went back to his desk. Serena would find his office in the directory. He wrote a message on a sticky note saying he was in office 313, slapped it on the outside of the door, and then closed and locked it. Footsteps came down the hallway right up to his door. After a few seconds of silence, they left in the other direction. Brady pulled a chair over to the wall and looked over toward Spencer's office.

He couldn't see from that angle, but he could hear pretty well. The top of Spenser's door swung open without a knock. Spencer yelled out in surprise.

Serena asked, "Where is Brady Witek?"

Spencer said, "Try his office."

"You're covering for your male friend." The clattering sound of pens, papers, and a desk-lamp hitting the floor came from Spencer's office as Serena must have cleared off his desk.

Spencer yelled, "What the hell! You bitch!"

Brady jumped down, headed out the door, and ran toward the stairs at the end of the hall. He pulled against the mechanism to shut the door faster, but Serena yelled right before it closed. He turned and took two steps at a time heading down. Serena's voice called his name from above, causing him to take three steps at a time. On the first floor, he dashed out into the lobby, waving at Lexi as he went by.

Lexi laughed and waved back.

He made it out to the parking lot and scanned around. He didn't want to lead Serena to his RV, so went the opposite way toward Larry's Burger Haven to hide and have a burger at the same time. Then he changed his mind and ran toward Ernie's, not wanting Serena to spoil his favorite burger joint.

◊　◊　◊

Kacey saw Brady head out the front door, look around and then run east, stop, and run north. Serena came out the front door searching as Brady disappeared from her line of sight. She jogged west, spun around, and then headed to the back of the building. Kacey got out of his van and strolled in her direction. She made it to the back alley, close to the RV, and stood searching. He walked up, but stayed at an appropriate distance for a stranger. "May I help you miss? You seem distraught."

"Did you see a guy come out the front door and run off?"

"No, I did not. Did he take something from you?"

Serena laughed. "Hah. That's rich. He took my dignity."

"I'm sorry for that. A beautiful woman should be treated with respect."

Serena looked Kacey over, head to toe. "Who are you?"

"Just a stranger, at your service." He bowed.

"You're kinda cute. The bald head and goatee remind me of that guy on the show. What's your name?"

"Call me, Manny." He walked over and held out his hand.

Serena shook. "Would you like to buy me a coffee, Manny?"

"Yes, I surely would."

"I passed a place on the way in called Ernie's, why don't we go there?

Chapter 16

Brady went to the back of Ernie's and found a table. The waitress brought him a menu and water. A few minutes later, the door jingled, and a bald guy walked in and locked eyes with him. Someone with frizzy hair ran into his back, causing him to stumble forward. It was Serena. Brady slid down and dropped under the table.

He looked out from underneath. The waitress's feet were a few tables away, aimed right at him. She must have seen him hide.

Serena spoke by the front door. "Let's sit in back where it's cozy."

Brady saw her feet coming right at him, followed by the guy's feet. He tensed up. The waitress's feet spun around and walked into Serena's path. "You can take this table over here with a good view of the street."

The feet walked to the table next to Brady's and sat. The table cloth was long enough for him to hide under.

Serena asked, "So, Manny, what do you do for a living?"

"I'm between positions, but I have enough money for the time being."

Brady rubbed his chin. Serena met a guy while she was chasing him?

Serena and Manny chatted away for a while, getting acquainted. The waitress's feet came and went. Brady figured he'd need to hide for the duration.

"Won't you excuse me, Manny?" Serena said. "I need to powder my nose." She laughed. Then in a wry voice she said, "That's French for taking a wiz." Manny chuckled. Her feet walked by the table. Brady waited for her to get to the bathroom.

Manny spoke. "Please come out, Mr. Witek. The coast is clear."

Brady crawled out and stood up. "Thanks, man."

The man's expression remained blank. "I'm happy I could be of service."

Brady saluted him and went to the waitress, taking two twenty-dollar bills out of his wallet. "One is for you, and the other is to pay for the lady and gentleman."

The waitress nodded. Brady went out the door and headed back to the building. When he got to the front door, he stopped and turned back. "How did that guy know my name?"

◇　◇　◇

Tuesday Afternoon
Crystal Lake, Illinois

Jolene was at her wit's end after she still hadn't received payment from Brady. Franklin Gaston advised they would have to file for garnishment of wages, which meant more time to wait.

They needed money now. Because the bank would not foreclose on the mortgage until three payments were missed, they decided to skip this month and pay the rest of the bills. Aaron complained about slow traffic at the gym and how his savings had gotten low. His old house still hadn't sold.

She went upstairs. Aaron stood in the hallway as Britney's door slammed in his face.

"What was that about?"

Aaron spun around. "Nothing. Just trying to be interested in the girl's lives."

Jolene led him into the bedroom and shut the door. Aaron kicked off his shoes and unbuttoned his pants.

"Hold on." Jolene held up her hand. "We're not doing that now."

Aaron buttoned his pants back up.

"You must find Brady and make him pay. We're going broke."

"I'll make him pay all right. After that TV show, they'll give me a medal."

Jolene sighed. "But you can't get caught. Give him the facts of life, and yeah, hurt him."

"When?"

"First we have to find out where he's staying, which means we'll have to follow him home from work. Plan for Friday night."

Aaron flexed his muscles and threw some punches in the air.

Jolene watched him move. "Now, unbutton your pants."

◇　◇　◇

Thursday Morning
Harwood Heights, Illinois

Kacey continued his surveillance at the Polyglomerate building. The bald guy's name was Gavin Ricci. He'd found his picture on the internet under known organized crime members in Chicago. Witek shouldn't be involved with a guy like that.

While he waited, he pulled out his phone and searched for restaurants in the area to take Serena on a date. She was a vegetarian, but drank alcohol, so that made it easier. He really had no complete plan for dealing with Serena, and he didn't understand her intentions with Brady Witek, but he would find out more on the date.

His online research suggested Serena began relationships treating men well, but most eventually filed for restraining orders. He might need to arrange for yet another identity.

◇　◇　◇

Friday Afternoon
Harwood Heights, Illinois

Spencer banged open Brady's door and sat in the chair. "Need a progress report."

"Half of the scripts are done. No errors in the tests."

"Will more of your crazy women be coming around?"

"I'll send them to your office." Brady laughed.

"It's not funny. She broke my mirror."

"Snort coke off the back of your hand."

"Like some junkie? Forget it. Have fun sleeping in your truck tonight, loser." Spencer left.

Lexi walked in. "Hey, Brady."

Brady wiggled his fingers and pointed at the chair.

Lexi sat. "You really like hamburgers, I guess."

"I do, and we live in the right town. We have good beef here."

"I've always wanted to try the burgers at Flamer's. Have you ever been there?"

"Yeah, I have. You should go sometime."

Brady typed away on his scripting.

Lexi cleared her throat.

Brady kept typing.

Lexi cleared her throat again loudly.

Brady turned. "What?"

"I'm making it easier to ask me out."

Brady sat back. "Sure, I'll play the game again. Will you go with me to Flamer's tonight for dinner? It would definitely be a date."

Lexi sighed. "Let me think about it, hmmm. Let me see… No better-looking guys have asked me out tonight. Sure, why not?"

Brady went back to typing. "Okay, I gave it a shot. Maybe some other time."

Lexi smacked his arm. "I'll drive. I'm not going on a date in a camper."

◊　◊　◊

Aaron and Jolene watched Brady come out the front of the building and walk around to the RV parked out back. He opened the back and climbed in.

"I can't believe my eyes," Jolene said. "He's staying in a camper behind his office?"

Aaron said, "The guy must really be broke."

"No, he's staying in that thing so he can make another run for it. We need to get him now."

Aaron opened his door on the passenger side. Jolene grabbed his arm.

"No, not in daylight, and we need to watch him for a little while."

After twenty minutes, Brady got out of the RV wearing a fresh shirt with combed hair. Aaron reached for the door handle when an attractive young girl waved at Brady from her car. He got in with her.

"Look at that, he hooked up with a hottie."

Jolene frowned. "But now we know where he lives."

◇　◇　◇

Friday Evening
Burbank, Illinois

Kacey spent extra time in front of the brick wall at the bottom of the stairs. It had been years since he had gone on a date. He got in his car and headed toward the Haynesworth mansion. Maybe he wouldn't even meet the old man, but just in case, he wore an Italian suit that cost a fortune, but no problem, he had a fortune. He pulled into the drive, pushed the button on the speaker and announced himself. The gate opened. After parking, he took a bouquet of flowers to the front door and rang the bell. A maid led him to a room with books and a fireplace. An old man greeted him. "I'm Winston Haynesworth, and who might you be?"

"Manfred Kolinsky, but you may call me Manny."

Winston wobbled his head. "Well then, Manny. I don't often get to meet my daughter's suitors." Winston admired Kacey's new suit.

"I'm a bit old-school, I suppose. And please don't worry. Serena has mentioned her current legal situation."

"Yes, the world has become a complicated place."

Serena entered the room dressed in black with her hair professionally styled. Diamond earrings dangled from her ears. "There you are, Manny. Are those for me?"

Kacey handed her the flowers and kissed her hand. Serena beamed with delight. Kacey held out his arm for her to take. "Shall we?"

As they walked out, Kacey gave a nod to Winston. Winston grinned and nodded back.

◊ ◊ ◊

Saturday, Midmorning
Burbank, Illinois

Kacey stuck his head out of the Bergdorfs' front door. No one was around, so he slipped out, shut the door and went up the stairs to his own apartment. He logged his laptop into the Bergdorfs' wireless router using the password he'd just stolen and connected to the Dark Web. He went to Get-Your-Man and uploaded information, doubling the payment for a rush shipment. Winston Haynesworth would have the resources to deal with a scoundrel like himself.

The plan was coming together, thanks to Serena's mouth. It ran nonstop during their date last night, and while it took time for her to mention her pregnancy, the information eventually flowed. She talked about her father's old-fashioned ideas, her refusal to give a DNA sample for religious reasons, and her wish to not embarrass her family name.

All the information boiled down to one concept. Serena had slept with a man who would not measure up to Winston Haynesworth's standards, so she had accused Brady Witek of being the father instead, despite not actually having had intercourse with him.

Once he came to this conclusion, he'd seduced Serena as part of his new plan, knowing intercourse created an immediate relationship between a male and female, mostly in the female's mind. He was successful, with Serena referring to him as "Moopsie" soon after.

He checked his watch, time to meet Serena for another date. She said being pregnant made her desire sex. "Horny" was the exact term. He logged off the Dark Web and left the apartment, driving to a restaurant called Mom's Kitchen, Serena's choice.

Her dietary standards were confusing. While claiming to be a vegetarian, she ordered pork chops last night, explaining how they were part of an environmentally conscious diet. If he followed her logic correctly, hogs could no longer pollute the air with methane if she consumed them.

He found her sitting in a booth in back. Serena took his hand and pulled him close, his butt sliding across the vinyl seat. "Sit close to me, darling. I want to feel your touch."

Kacey could only get close to her thigh but not the rest of her. "Have you ordered yet? I crave a steak to replenish my manly requirements."

"You're a tiger." She growled. "And my father loves you too. He talked about you during lunch."

"I respect your father."

"Maybe we were meant for each other. It would be so nice to be taken off the market, if you know what I mean."

Kacey frowned and looked away.

Serena took his chin and turned his face back to her. "What's wrong, darling? Did I say too much?"

Kacey paused for affect. "Your paternity suit concerns me. Your family is wealthy. Why would you call more attention to your condition by trifling with a fellow of limited means? Please forgive me, but I believe you are simply trying to rescue your reputation."

Serena's mouth dropped open. "You know me so well. Can I confide in you, Moopsie?"

"Yes, darling, of course you can."

Serena looked around the restaurant. "Brady Witek is not the father of my baby."

Kacey made his eyes open wide. "You must do something about this. Soon, you will embroil a much larger scandal."

Serena looked panicked. "What scandal will I embroil?"

"In the future, Brady Witek will on some occasion have time alone with the child, during which, he will have a paternity test done, and you will be found out."

Serena grabbed Kacey's arm with both hands. "There's more, darling."

"Go on, my dear."

"I hooked up with a guy from an internet site. Have you ever heard of Letsplayinthecity.com?"

"No."

"Well, I met the real father of the baby on that site. In the hotel room, I thought he bent me over to do one thing, but he really—"

Kacey held up his hand. "Spare the details, dear."

"Right. Well, he got me pregnant, and he was…African American."

Kacey paused. He hadn't expected that.

"Please don't judge me, Moopsie."

"I have no problem with your choice of partners, but your attempt to ensnarl Mr. Witek is doomed. When the baby is born, it will be obvious. Don't you see?"

Serena let go of his arm and drank from her water glass. "What am I going to do? Father will boot me out of the house."

"I believe your pregnancy is less than nine weeks."

"No, I can't have an abortion. Father is a deacon in the church."

Kacey turned to the side wall. There were cob webs and a crack in the corner—it would have to do. He allowed his eyes to roam. Once ready, he turned to Serena, took her hand and placed it on the table. "We've only known each other for a short time, but I would be willing to step forward and take responsibility."

Serena sighed. "You're a true gentleman, Moopsie, but it wouldn't work. You're lily-white."

"We can say that due to a medical condition, we chose artificial insemination. And because we are strongly liberal in our politics, we chose to deliver a child of color."

Serena swirled water around in her glass. "It just may work, but what about the TV show? They told everyone about my paternity suit."

"You can say you miscarried. Your father has the resources to change records. He will help us with this plan to preserve his family honor."

Serena smiled and squeezed his arm. "You are so freakin' awesome, Moopsie." She gazed into his eyes. "I think I'm in love with you."

Kacey sensed a kiss coming and pulled back. "But first, you must handle the Witek situation. I will not agree to our plan until he is exonerated. Drop the suit and send a letter to his attorney stating that he is not the father."

She smacked his arm. "You got it, Moopsie. I'll take care of it right away."

They kissed.

◊   ◊   ◊

Saturday Night
Harwood Heights, Illinois

While the server ran a test conversion, Brady had some time. He wanted to call Lexi, but he'd give her some space, even though dinner went well last night. She'd talked about herself for the first time, and she seemed to love burgers as much as he did. Maybe they had a future together.

He strolled out in the hall and made his way to Spencer's office. His door was open. No lines of powder this time, Spencer had a bottle of Johnnie Walker Black open, drinking from a crystal glass. Brady walked in and sat down.

Spencer stared at him. "Can you finish so we can get the fuck out of here? I have a social life, unlike some people who live in a camper."

"The test should be done in thirty minutes, and then I can start checking data tomorrow. We'll probably be all done by the end of next week."

"And then what? Do you really think you're leaving again?"

"What do you mean by that?"

Spencer looked out the window. "Nothing." He poured himself another glass.

Brady got up and looked out the window. Down in the parking lot, a pickup truck looked familiar. Brady came back to Spencer's desk, grabbed the bottle and took a drink.

Spencer snatched the bottle away. "Fucking savage…"

Brady went down the hall to his desk, thought for a moment, and went back to Spencer's office to look out the window again.

Spencer held the bottle. "No more. There's a liquor store around the block."

Brady looked down at the pickup truck again. It had to be Aaron's. Brady returned to his office and dialed Paul's cell phone. It rang and rang and then went to voice mail. He dialed Lexi's number. She picked up. "You're not one of those clingy guys that call all the time, are you?"

"Can you drive to the office? I need your help."

"You know I don't fall for stunts like that."

"I need you to record video with your phone. It's important."

"Are you okay, Brady? Your voice sounds funny."

"I'm about to take a beating, and I really need you to record it. Please."

"A beating? Okay, I have a GoPro camera that'll work better than a phone."

◊　◊　◊

Brady informed Spencer it was time to leave, and they went out to the parking lot. Brady made fun of Spencer's new Volkswagen, and Spencer gave him a good night finger. Brady walked to the back alley, listening for Spencer to drive away. Near the back of the RV, Brady spoke to the bushes. "All set?"

Lexi's voice said, "All set."

Brady turned around, breathing in the city air. A lack of wind kept the garbage smell near the dumpster. He reached up and cracked his neck, trying to look like he was unwinding after a long day. The security light behind the building lit up the area.

Aaron walked around the corner of the building by the dumpster, making a face as he passed. "Fuckin' Brady Witek, you smell like shit."

Brady tried to look surprised. "What are you doing here? Did the zoo run out of bananas?"

"Keep the wisecracks coming, shithead. Won't be so easy when you're taking your meals through a straw."

"In that case, let me start with your mother—"

Aaron came at him down low, but Brady swung up his knee. Aaron's nose broke with a crunch. The two men backed away. Aaron staggered, wiping blood from his lip.

Brady expected more trash talk, but Aaron came swinging. Brady blocked a punch and shot a jab at Aaron's broken nose. Aaron yelled in pain, but swung a fake and connected with his other fist. Brady spun in the opposite direction. They both staggered. Aaron straightened his nose and took Brady's shoulder to spin him around and punch him in the face and stomach. Brady slumped to the ground holding his belly.

Aaron leaned over, breathing in an out through his mouth. "I want to put you in the hospital so bad." He stood up and walked in a circle, pinching his nose.

Brady stayed on his knees, blood dripping from his nose and mouth. "Why don't you call Jolene? You can have a family portrait done now that I prettied up your face. Fucking Fabio wannabe…"

Aaron swung his foot at Brady's head, but held back. Brady flinched but stayed on his knees.

Aaron pointed at him. "What I want is for you to pay. Send the support payments, and come up with the ninety thousand like Jolene told you. Otherwise, the next time we meet, I won't hold back."

"So you get my wife, my kids, and all my money? Kiss my ass, you stupid monkey."

Aaron got close. "You're right, I have your wife. I have her anytime I want, and soon enough, I'll have your daughters. That Britney chick is filling out real nice."

"Son of a bitch." Brady tried to spring up, but Aaron put his hand on Brady's forehead and pushed him backward to the pavement. Brady stayed down.

Aaron left around the corner of the building.

The bushes rustled. Brady held up his hand. "Stay put."

An engine started around the corner and left the parking lot.

Lexi burst out of the bushes and kneeled down next to Brady. She helped him up. He wobbled and put his arm on her shoulders. "Tell me you recorded it."

"I got it, every incredible second."

◊   ◊   ◊

Monday Midmorning
Evanston, Illinois

Serena sat in the library waiting for her father to arrive. He entered from the bookshelf door carrying several printouts. "Can you explain the meaning of this?"

"Brady Witek is not the father of my baby. Manfred has been counseling me, and we decided on another story. Please forgive me for lying, Father."

Winston dropped the papers on the table and sat in his chair. "Who is the real father?"

"Don't worry, it's all taken care of. Manfred and I will get married, and we will explain to everyone how he cannot father children. Instead, we used a sperm bank."

Winston turned. "What's all this now? You only just met the man, and why not just say the baby is his?"

"We're in love, Father. And the baby will not look anything like him. We've thought about it."

"So without consulting me first, you dropped the suit and informed Witek's attorney the baby is not his?"

"Yes, Father. I'm handling the situation my own way. Now, I'm leaving to be with Moop—Manfred."

Winston waved her off.

Serena left and sped away from the house in her Alpha Romeo, heading for Mom's Kitchen. She couldn't wait to tell Moopsie about the progress she made.

Her cell phone rang. "Hello, Moopsie?"

"Hello, my dear. Did you speak to your father?"

"I did. He has copies of the paperwork, including the letter I faxed to his attorney. He can't stop our plan now."

"You did the right thing. I am so proud of you. We'll talk at the restaurant."

Serena hung up and soon pulled into Mom's Kitchen. She raced through the lot with car horns honking at her. She stole a spot from another car and skipped to the front door. Inside, she looked all over the restaurant but didn't see Moopsie. She described him to the waitress and requested the same table they had last time to wait.

She waited.

And waited.

◊　◊　◊

Monday Afternoon
Harwood Heights, Illinois

Sydney met with Brady in his office, surveying Brady's bruised face. "This is a serious matter, my friend. Are you all right?"

"I'll live. What should we do?"

"First, play the video for me."

Brady played video of the fight on his computer screen.

Sydney watched the entire clip. "Looks like you busted his nose pretty good, which is good. He can't deny anything."

"I didn't call the cops. I didn't want to explain why Lexi was in the bushes with a camera."

"Good thinking. We can spin it."

Brady turned to Sydney. "No spin. We tell the truth. I saw his truck outside and thought there would be a confrontation, so I called Lexi to get video."

Sydney put up his hands. "Okay. I say we call another custody hearing and play the tape for the judge. We'll tell her the truth, that you knew what was coming and asked your friend to get video to use against your wife. Now that I think about it, the truth will work better with Judge Jurgons."

Sydney took a letter from his briefcase. "Read this. You won't believe your eyes."

Brady read the letter from Serena. "No shit."

"The suit is dropped, but don't give me any credit, this came out of the blue."

Brady flopped back in his chair. "All the suits are gone. Somehow, I'm off the hook."

"There's a legal grapevine in the court house. Maybe someday I'll find out why all this happened."

They sat for a minute.

"Brady, what do you want to do now? You got yourself beaten up for a reason."

"I want full custody of my girls, and I want Jolene and Aaron out of their lives. And if you can get them thrown in jail, good."

"You're sure about this?"

"I want my girls away from that animal, and I want to call the shots again. I'm their dad."

"The video is disturbing, but it won't undo what you did."

"Let's try anyway, Sydney. Bottom line, Jolene and Aaron need to be out of the picture."

"Okay, you're the boss."

◇   ◇   ◇

Monday Night
Evanston, Illinois

In the library, Winston tossed back scotch and asked Clarice why Serena missed dinner.

"She's in her quarters crying. Should I ask her to join you?"

"Please do." Winston rubbed his forehead. What now? Serena generated constant drama, and this time his reputation was at stake. He had even considered how abortion could solve the problem. He should have dealt with Serena's pregnancy more decisively by having her sent away, like in the old days, but now it was too late, thanks to the scandalous television show.

Serena shuffled in, looking down at the floor as she walked. She plopped down in the chair next to Winston and reached for his scotch glass. "What do you want? I was busy."

Winston took the glass away from her. "You missed dinner. Tell me what's wrong."

Serena grabbed at the glass. "He disappeared. I don't even know where he lives."

"Who did? Manfred?"

Serena sobbed. "After I told him you understood our plan, he disappeared. I sat in the restaurant for five hours. I had four pieces of chocolate cheesecake and then roast ham. Should have eaten those the other way around."

Winston rubbed his chin. "So let me get this straight. The chap convinced you to drop the suit and then vanished?"

"That's right. Can you find him for me, Father? I don't want to be alone again."

"Just a minute." Winston called his lawyer. "I want you to look into something for me. On the television show regarding Brady Witek, there were two other cases against him. Check on the progress of those cases." Winston listened for a moment. "Then call the show and get information. Use my name if you need to." He hung up.

Winston felt his face grow hot. Had the Haynesworth family been the victim of a con artist? If so, the scoundrel better batten down the hatches. There would be hell to pay.

Chapter 17

Gavin drove toward his home, hoping to get some rest. People didn't understand the Outfit still ran this town. They had to be reminded over and over.

His cell rang, and he answered. "Gavin."

"You stupid wop, I want that bastard dealt with."

"Calm down, Mr. Haynesworth. Tell me what happened."

"A man named Manfred Kolinski seduced my daughter and convinced her to drop the suit against Brady Witek. Witek had two other cases against him dropped. My people investigated, and both cases involved women who were visited by a stranger matching the description of Kolinsky."

Gavin thought it over.

"Are you there?"

"Yeah. So you think Witek found a guy to make all three cases disappear? Witek doesn't have our kind of connections."

"It happened, and now he's laughing at me. It's time for you to take action."

"How did the guy get the other two women to drop the suits? Were they smacked around?"

"My people said they were paid, but also threatened."

Gavin thought some more. In his circles, those broads would have been smacked around and not paid. "I'll talk to Sal, but Witek isn't finished with his work yet."

"Listen here, you son of a bitch. I won't tolerate disrespect."

"I'll call Sal and get back to you."

◊   ◊   ◊

Winston heard the phone go dead and tossed his cell across the room. Clarice came in to investigate.

Winston pointed. "Get that phone and give it to me."

Clarice scrambled to the phone and rushed it over to Winston.

"Now, leave me alone. Keep an eye on Serena."

Clarice headed to the guesthouse.

Winston dialed. "Meet me at the usual location in thirty minutes." He ended the call and went to the garage, intending to drive himself.

He arrived at the industrial block on the West Side. Eighteen wheelers got in the way like they owned the road. He pulled into an open garage door and parked inside to wait for his man. A few minutes later, a vintage Camaro drove in and parked. They both got out, and the man shook Winston's hand.

"Lonnie, I need someone dealt with, but it needs to be off the radar. Sal can't know about it."

"Are you sure you want to risk it, Mr. Haynesworth?"

"Sal disrespected me. A man molested my daughter, and instead of taking care of the guy, he's using him to set up a new laundry for his money."

Lonnie rubbed his face. He looked up at Winston. "So if I found you a crew, they would need to mix it up with Sal's guys?"

"I suppose so. We're talking about my daughter here."

Lonnie paused. "Okay, there's a Russian crew that isn't connected to anybody. They have ten guys."

Winston handed Lonnie an envelope with Brady Witek's information. "How much up front?"

"You're good for it, Mr. Haynesworth. We'll settle up later."

Lonnie got in the Camaro and left. Winston drove out of the building. His cell rang, so he pulled to the curb. It was Gavin.

"Mr. Haynesworth, hello."

Winston stayed quiet.

"So Sal says for you to be patient. We'll deal with the matter soon enough. But I need to ask you a question. Are you sure Witek is the father?"

"Are you questioning my integrity, Mr. Ricci?"

"Certainly not, Mr. Haynesworth. We don't want to cause a fuss if we don't have to."

"Okay then. Thank you for calling me." He ended the call.

He'd done the right thing, calling Lonnie. Sal needed to learn a lesson about priorities. Putting money laundering ahead of his daughter's honor was unacceptable.

◊   ◊   ◊

Gavin stared at his phone. Haynesworth would be a problem. He dialed Mark Seiver's number. "Hello, Mark. Are you guys still at the office?"

"No, we all left for the night."

"Is Witek still staying in the camper?"

"I think so, why?"

"It's nothing. Sleep tight."

He hung up and dialed another number. "You and Vinny head over to the Polyglomerate building. Keep an eye on the camper behind the building. You may see some action, so stay sharp."

Gavin listened. "I have a hunch."

◊   ◊   ◊

Tuesday Morning
Chicago, Illinois

Shelly LaFortune walked into Keehn Bennett's office and sat down. "Boss. Yesterday, a lawyer called about Brady Witek. Last night, two more called. I gave them a few details, no big deal."

"Are there developments?"

"According to Witek's attorney, all three suits were dropped. He wouldn't tell me why, so I made more calls. The ladies in two of the suits said Witek paid them. They were careful with their words. I couldn't get ahold of Serena Haynesworth, but she dropped her paternity suit. She even sent a letter stating Witek was not the father."

Bennett frowned. "So Witek took care of everything?"

"Sounds like it. It's an interesting development."

Bennett put his elbows on the desk. "If we were wrong about Witek, we need to follow up."

Shelly nodded.

"Find him after work and get his story."

Shelly got up. "I'm on it."

◊ ◊ ◊

Tuesday Morning
Burbank, Illinois

Kacey loaded bags into his van. "Manfred Kolinsky" was too hot to stick around. The Outfit could show up any minute. His new identity arrived this morning, so "Frank Jones" would make the getaway. He could still drive the van—it was registered to a bogus company. His car would sit in the lot until it was towed.

As he stood at the brick wall letting his eyes wander, a Frisbee drifted by the corner. Bixby ran past, snatched it off the grass, and brought it to Kacey. Kacey rubbed his head.

Juan ran up. "Hey, Manny. You're just in time."

Kacey squatted down and shook Juan's hand. "I need a rain check, Juan." Bixby licked Kacey's hand. "I've enjoyed my time with you and Bixby." Juan and Bixby went back to the lot, and Kacey left in the van.

Things were not settled with Brady Witek. An Outfit guy at the Polyglomerate building didn't add up, so he would continue surveillance. He wound his way through the city streets toward the Polyglomerate building. A strip motel came up on the right, and he turned in.

He paid for a room, and when he opened the door, he shook his head. The room had red carpet, both on the floors and the walls. The bed was round, surrounded by multicolored spot lights with a mirror on the ceiling. He almost went back to the office for another room, but then he noticed the hot tub in the corner.

He soaked in the tub for an hour and then drove the van toward the Polyglomerate building, parking in the street to the north where he could see the front door. The van had a square window on the side in back. He set up a folding chair and took out his binoculars.

The time was 5:03 p.m., but Witek often worked late. Kacey spotted two guys in a car in the next parking lot over. A black sedan pulled up, and Gavin Ricci got out. He saluted the two guys in the car.

Kacey watched for twenty minutes and then climbed out to the sidewalk and the alley between buildings. As expected, the old brick walls had many flaws—bulging mortar, vines, and plenty of cracks. His eyes wandered as he stepped away from himself.

His instincts told him to be ready for action.

◊　◊　◊

Gavin Ricci walked right into Brady's office and shut the door. Brady turned. "What do you want?"

"We need to chat. You can't stay in the camper no more. We'll put you up somewhere more comfortable tonight."

Brady returned to his work. "I'm comfortable enough. Screw you."

"Hey, you're not safe out there."

Brady touched his swollen chin. "I know the guy that did this."

"Right, so I was told, but you may have another problem with Winston Haynesworth. He is extremely upset about his daughter dropping the paternity suit."

Brady frowned. "Whatever, but I'm importing data from Indiana. I need to work for a while."

"No, that's good to hear. The sooner you finish, the better. I'll be hanging around the office until you're ready." Gavin left and shut the door.

Brady stopped typing and stared at the door. How did Gavin know about Serena dropping the lawsuit? Serena and the merger were two different things until just now, and yet Gavin himself, the Outfit Ape, wanted to protect him in a motel tonight.

The other day, Spencer said, "You really think you're leaving again?" He'd wondered in the back of his mind if he'd become a liability after the merger.

He jumped when Lexi barged in. "What the hell? Am I that scary?"

Brady got up and stood close. "Kiss me."

Lexi started to object but then responded.

Brady embraced her passionately. When they separated lips, he held her close and whispered in her ear. "They're going to kill me after I'm finished with the merger. Serena Haynesworth's father wants me dead, and these Outfit guys are going to do it."

Lexi squeezed him and whispered. "We have to get you out of here. What do I do?"

"Leave work like you normally do, and then call the cops. Tell them I'm being held against my will. When they come, I'll leave."

"Okay. You can count on me." She drew back and closed her eyes.

Brady kissed her again.

"I'm going to save you," Lexi said. "I need more kisses like that."

They both jumped at the sound of gunfire.

◊   ◊   ◊

Two rusty vans pulled up across the street from Kacey's van, blocking his view of the front entrance. He was annoyed until ten men climbed out pulling on ski masks and headed toward the building carrying pistols. Two men had AK-47 machine guns over their shoulders.

Kacey unzipped his canvas bags.

Gun fire came immediately from the two Outfit guys in the car. Kacey put his arms through shoulder holsters and jammed in 9 mm pistols. He strapped on a belt full of ammunition and slung the AR15 over his shoulder. He looked down at his ski mask and left it to avoid getting shot at by the Outfit guys.

He wanted to show his face, like when he wore a uniform.

Traffic stopped from gunshots. He sprang out of the van and ran across the street low around the back of the second van. Popping gun noises were continuous. Voices shouted in Russian.

Kacey made a quick assessment. Brady Witek had gotten in the middle of something big, and he had decided to protect him. He would complete his mission. All these men were a threat, and he would neutralize them.

He stepped from the back of the van and located two men wearing ski masks, firing over car hoods. He shot one through the head and the other in the neck. Bullets pinged off the van as he spun around for cover. Voices shouted in Russian, and machine gun fire blasted the van. Kacey withdrew across the street behind his own van.

Two men ran across the street firing shots for cover. Kacey ran to the front of the van and shot one man in the chest. The other dropped down out of sight. Kacey backed across the sidewalk into the recessed entryway of a shop. The man leapt to the sidewalk firing. Kacey waited and leaned out, shooting the man in the shoulder and stomach, dropping him to the cement. He walked over and shot him in the head.

Ricochets chipped the bricks of the building. Kacey ducked down. A scream came from where the Outfit guys were parked. When the next Outfit guy went down, the men in ski masked would storm the building, and Witek would be shot.

Kacey ran down the sidewalk to maneuver south and hit their flank.

◊   ◊   ◊

Gavin yanked the door open and got Brady and Lexi to join the others in the hallway. It was well after 5:00 p.m., so only Mark and Spencer were left. All the other Polyglomerate employees were gone.

Gavin's voice grew excited. "My guys are taking fire. Haynesworth must have hired a crew to take out Witek. We have to run for it."

Brady grabbed Gavin's arm. "Run where? Call 911 already!"

"It's a war zone out there. The cops won't get here in time."

Spencer pointed up. "The roof. I keep drugs up there."

Gavin gave Spencer a push. "Then go."

Spencer led them down the hall to the southwest corner of the building. Inside a metal door, a cement room had a ladder attached to the wall. Gavin shoved Spencer. "Up you go."

Spencer went up the ladder, missing a few rungs in a state of panic. He unlatched a hatch in the ceiling and went up. The rest of them followed. Up on the roof, Brady went over to metal rails leading to the fire escape to inspect the ladder going down the side of the building next to the dumpster.

He turned to Lexi. "Come down after me, and I'll catch you if you fall."

"Just get going, Batman."

Brady climbed down to the bottom of the ladder, still a full story above the ground, inspecting how to drop to the ground. He took hold of the side handles, and when he took his feet off the bottom rung, the ladder dropped, extending down to the pavement. Brady landed on the ground and released the handles. The ladder sprang back up. Lexi climbed down, grabbing the handles and dropping down. Next, Spencer mounted the ladder.

A scream came from the side of the building startling him, causing his feet to slip off. He swung from the ladder by one hand, struggling, trying to wrap his other arm around a rung.

Rapid gunfire became loud from the front of the building, and Spencer lost it. He leapt away from the ladder and crashed down in the garbage dumpster. Papers erupted in the air.

Brady led Lexi to the RV and got her in the passenger seat. She said, "This is the worst getaway car ever."

Brady got in the driver's seat and started the RV. Spencer's hand gripped the edge of the dumpster as he tried to climb out, but he lost his grip in the slime and dropped down. Brady put the transmission in reverse.

Lexi reached over and squeezed his arm. "You have to take everyone. It's the right thing to do."

Brady sighed. "You're right." He got out and went to the dumpster as Mark made his way down the ladder. Lexi led him to the back of the RV when he got to the ground.

◇　◇　◇

Shelly LaFortune and her cameraman Joel were walking away from the TV van when the first shots were fired. Shelly wasn't proud of how she ran like a maniac. Joel skidded up beside her, aiming the camera down on the pavement.

Shelly collected herself. "Joel, aim the camera at the action."

Two guys crossed the street firing at the side of the van to the north. Joel squatted and raised the camera, getting footage of the exchange. He shuffled backward to the back of the van to aim the camera, but then grunted and fell back. Shelly took his arm, pulled him back around the side, and checked the wound to his shoulder. His collarbone stuck out from the top of his shirt, but he would live.

She took the camera and ran east away from the shooting. No one shot at her. She found a spot and risked a peek over a car hood. Six men wearing ski masks were firing at a couple of men in the other lot. She headed back a few rows and climbed on the trunk of a sedan, focusing the camera over the roof and adjusting for a wide shot. The entire gunfight was in the frame.

◇　◇　◇

Spencer's arms were covered with slime. Brady had to grab the top of his shirt to yank him out. He slid over the side. Brady fell back, and Spencer landed on top of him, his face inches away. "Thanks, lover. Buy me dinner first next time."

Brady rolled Spencer to the side, hoisted him up by the collar and tossed him in the back of the RV.

Brady noticed Gavin descending the ladder, wondering if he was about to rescue a man who planned to kill him? Gavin got down to the ground and ran to the back doors. "Get this tub moving!"

Brady closed him in the back and got in the front seat. He backed up the Ghost and headed east down the alley toward Larry's Burger Haven. When he drove past the back of the building, ticking noises came from the side of the RV. Mark yelled in pain from the back.

Gavin shouted, "We're taking fire! Keep moving!"

Brady told Lexi to get down and aimed for the end of the alley, putting his foot to the floor. At the street, he turned a hard right, almost tipping the Ghost over. He recovered and floored the pedal again.

◊　◊　◊

One of the two men in the other lot had taken a hit in the chest and went down screaming. The other got up firing wildly, a gun in each hand. The windshield of the car shattered. Shelly kept the camera steady.

Earlier, she had witnessed a masked man's head exploding and another's neck spraying blood. Vomit came up her throat, and then two men across the street were gunned down.

The remaining man from the car kept raising from behind a door blasting with two guns as the masked men moved up. One masked man raised, and when the man sprang up, he shot him in the left lung. The man screamed and went down. The six remaining masked men got to their feet and headed toward the building. One noticed Shelly with her camera and pointed, yelling at another. They ran toward her, shouting for her to drop the camera.

Shelly slid down the back of the car and ran in the opposite direction, diving for cover as yet another man ran toward her with a rifle. He fired several shots over her. Grunts and screams came from behind. She tilted up the camera to capture footage of the man as he ran past.

More shots were fired near the building. Shelly got the camera up. Four masked men fired at a camper driving down the alley. Holes peppered the vehicle's side. It screeched around the corner, almost tipping over. The masked men turned and raced in her direction. She put down the camera and slid under a car.

Doors slammed. A vehicle screeched away. The man who saved her life ran north, and another vehicle sped away. She got up and checked the camera, knowing she had awesome footage inside, and then remembered Joel and ran to the TV van. He was pushing himself up with is good arm.

"Get in the van, Joel. I'll drive." She hoisted Joel in the side door and handed him the camera. She got behind the wheel and raced in the direction of the other vehicles. She had to record the ending of this fight, however it turned out.

◊　◊　◊

Brady checked the side mirror. A van fishtailed around the corner in pursuit. Another van backed into the intersection and spun around to follow.

"They're still coming." Brady ran through a red light with the horn blaring. Vehicles spun in the intersection behind. "We can't out run them in this boat."

Gavin stuck his head through the vinyl curtain. "Get lost in the neighborhood maybe."

"How are you guys back there?"

"Seivers took a bullet in the hip. He's bleeding. Just do your best and look for a cop car."

Gavin disappeared. Brady took a hard right and headed down Irving Park Road. The Ghost accelerated dreadfully slow. Brady saw the first van fishtail into the road behind him, gaining speed. It would catch up in no time.

Brady turned to Lexi. "They're right behind us. What should I do?"

"When they try to pass, smash into them."

Brady kept his foot to the floor and watched the mirror. The van pulled to the left and surged forward. Brady jerked the wheel and swerved, but they saw it coming and hit the brakes. He swerved back and the Ghost started to tip over. He jerked the wheel back left and headed off the road into a driveway. The Ghost bounced and clipped a metal fence.

Brady found himself driving through a cemetery. He blasted the horn at joggers who jumped into the grass. An old couple shuffled between grave stones just in time. A lady picked up her toy poodle and ran for it. Up ahead, a black hearse parked with pallbearers pulling a casket out of the back. Brady locked the brakes and turned left on a cross path. He stomped on the gas again and checked the side mirror. The van skidded through the crossing behind them, smoke billowing from its tires.

Lexi looked out her window. "Oh, no. They dropped the casket and ran. The van smashed into it."

Brady concentrated on the narrow pathway. "They killed the dead guy?"

"You could say that."

They rounded the circle path and drove in front of the hearse. The crowd ran around hysterically as the Ghost circled. The pastor waved his arms like a bird. The van backed away from the hearse and smashed into something behind it.

"What are they doing?"

Lexi said, "They just smashed into the second van and turned toward where we're going. The second van is right behind them, and now a third van came in the cemetery."

Up ahead, the pathway curved around to where they first entered. The first van, now wrinkled in front, headed toward them. Another cross path appeared going left. Brady tried to turn, but they were going too fast. The Ghost went in the grass and hit a gravestone, bouncing several feet in the air. They slammed to a stop.

Thudding noises came from the back of the RV, followed by a chorus of groans. Behind the Ghost, the van screeched to a stop. Four men got out carrying guns. One man pointed and gave orders. Two men moved toward the second van, the other two toward the Ghost.

◊   ◊   ◊

Kacey skidded his van sideways behind the Russian van, leapt out with his AR15 over his shoulder and dashed to the rear. He spun the rifle into his hands and aimed around the corner. Two Russians charged at him, guns blazing. He pulled back as ricochets sparked off the corner of the van. They would come from both ends to out-flank him.

He backed up three steps, ran past the back of the van, and dove in the air. Bullets puffed in the grass. He tucked in his shoulder, rolled on the ground, and sprung up firing. A round hit the closest man in the shoulder, another hit his chin. Blood sprayed. The farthest man tried to dive in front of the van, but Kacey put a bullet in his ankle.

Kacey went to the first man, shot him through the head and then to the second man. He fired two rounds into his torso while he held his ankle.

A shot was fired behind him. Kacey spun around. Another man had fired through the lock on the back of the RV. Kacey steadied himself, took aim and fired. The top of the man's head disappeared.

A shout came from the other side of the RV. Kacey sprinted by the van and around the camper. A masked man pulled Witek out of the driver's seat. He rolled up against a gravestone. The man grabbed a gun off the asphalt and aimed at Brady. Kacey knew he would not be able to fire in time.

◊　◊　◊

Brady managed to smack the gun out of the guy's hands before getting pulled from the driver's seat. He rolled up to a gravestone and looked up. The guy picked up the gun and turned toward him. Lexi jumped from the RV and landed on the guy's back. The gun fired, puffing the grass next to Brady's foot. The guy bent forward, causing Lexi to somersault up next to Brady. The guy brought up the pistol again. Brady rolled on top of Lexi. A shot fired.

Brady waited. He felt around for a hole in his back.

Lexi asked, "Are you hit?"

"I can't find the hole."

Brady rolled over and saw the gunman lying facedown. His head was the wrong shape. Near the back of the Ghost, another man knelt with a military rifle.

Brady rose and pulled Lexi off the ground. They both raised their hands. The man, bald with a goatee, stood up and walked backward to the back of the Ghost, bringing the rifle up. Gavin and Spencer helped Mark out of the vehicle. They put up their hands. The bald guy motioned for them to get on their knees. Brady ran over, but the man held up a hand. "Please stay back, Mr. Witek. I'm here to protect you."

"Wait. You can't shoot these guys."

"These are dangerous men, Mr. Witek. They need to be eliminated."

"Don't do it. Do you hear that?" Sirens came from all directions. Brady stepped up closer. "Killing these guys would only make things worse. One is an Outfit guy."

A helicopter went overhead. Sirens grew louder.

Kacey held his stare and then nodded slightly. He ejected the magazine from the rifle and emptied the chamber. He tossed the rifle in the grass, followed by two pistols and packs of ammunition. He pulled a revolver from his ankle and tossed it into the pile, and then he held out his hand to Brady. "Promise me you'll end your relationship with these men."

Brady shook his hand. "No problem with that."

"I'm Kacey Farrell. Life has been hard for me after I left the military. Thank you for giving me a purpose."

Brady held on to his hand. "You were with Serena in the restaurant."

Kacey nodded. He took his hand away and stepped back.

Brady bowed to him. "Thank you so much for saving us."

Kacey gave a quick salute before walking to the asphalt path where he got on his knees and put his hands behind his head.

Brady noticed movement. Gavin walked toward the pile of guns. Lexi came from behind and kicked his foot. He fell forward into the grass.

Flashing red and blue lights lit up the cemetery.

Chapter 18

Friday Night
Chicago, Illinois

The lady applied makeup to Keehn Bennett's face. He waved at the assistant director. "Replay the footage, or I'll have to narrate from the seat of my pants." Footage played on the video screen in the studio desk as Keehn watched for the second time with Shelly LaFortune sitting next to him. The show would go live in thirty seconds. Bennett looked at the camera as the theme music played. The director counted down with his fingers and then pointed at Bennett.

"Good evening, I'm Keehn Bennett. Welcome to *Chicagoland Stories*. We have incredible video footage tonight, shot by our own Shelly LaFortune."

The screen cut to a wide shot with Shelly at the desk.

"You are about to witness an intense shootout near the western suburbs. Shelly was in Harwood Heights to interview Brady Witek, the subject of a previous story on our show, when suddenly, shots were fired. Her cameraman, Joel Berg, was shot in the shoulder. Shelly picked up the camera and bravely captured footage of what you are about to see. Please be warned, the footage contains graphic images not suitable for children."

The screen cut to the footage. The two men fired from the car. Masked figures fired back. Men were shot. The camera bounced as Shelly ran, and then came the shot of a bald man with a goatee. An RV took bullets as it raced down the alley. The footage ended with the showdown in the cemetery.

Bennett gave play by play. He explained a group of men wearing ski masks attacked two men in a parked car. The men from the car died, as well as all ten men wearing ski masks. The bald man with the goatee had fired at the masked men, saving Shelly. He confirmed the RV in the alley belonged to Brady Witek.

The screen returned to Bennett and LaFortune. Bennett asked, "At the end, the mystery man who saved you was approached by another man."

LaFortune said, "We have confirmed it was Brady Witek. As you know, Brady Witek was recently the subject of a deadbeat-dad story."

"Why would Witek be involved in this wild shootout?"

"We are still gathering information. We are also trying to identify the mystery man who went to great measures to save Brady Witek's life. He also saved my life. If he had not engaged the masked men, I wouldn't be here now."

"We owe him a debt of gratitude, as we do you, Shelly LaFortune, for having the bravery to risk your life for this dramatic footage."

Shelly smiled. "Thanks, Keehn, I owe it to our viewers."

Bennett turned back to the camera. He described the number of dead and other details. The shootout footage played again while he spoke.

The story went viral. Stations all over the world played the footage.

◊　◊　◊

Monday Morning
Chicago, Illinois

Kacey Farrell sat in an interrogation room in the FBI Chicago office. Across the table, Agent Crenshaw said, "Mr. Farrell, you've been very candid with me today. You've given me so much information that I would like to stop here and organize my notes. Can we please continue our discussion later?"

Kacey nodded. "Of course, Agent Crenshaw." He remained seated as the agent left the room. He was handcuffed to a bar on the tabletop.

The door opened again, and Agent Bessing entered. She sat opposite from Kacey. "Mr. Farrell, it is truly good to see you. I really mean it."

Kacey nodded. "And you as well, Agent Bessing. Call me Kacey, it's like we're old friends. I hope you've fully recovered from your fall."

"I was bruised up a bit, but now I'm one hundred percent. You're probably aware I've been listening in on your chat with Agent Crenshaw. There's very little left for me to ask."

"At this point, there's no need for deception."

"And you will tell us where the money is?"

Kacey leaned forward and spoke quietly. "I could only tell you. My way of making up for your fall."

Verna grinned. "Thanks, but no thanks. Catching bad guys like you is reward enough. But you could do me one favor."

"Go ahead."

"I'd like you to make a phone call."

Kacey's eyebrow went up.

"A few hours after the shootout, Winston Haynesworth was gunned down in his mansion, but you were already in custody." Bessing shrugged. "We believe it probably had something to do with the shootout. Anyway, Serena Haynesworth is a mess. When I questioned her about the shooting, all she could talk about was the loss of her lover, Manny Kolinsky, after she saw you on TV."

Kacey made a grim face.

"The news lady got a great shot of your face after you saved her little ass."

"Luckily, I was arrested. Serena can't get to me in here."

Bessing chuckled. "Why don't you tell her you're a secret agent or something? And that's why you left. Give her some closure." Bessing took out her phone and dialed. She put it on speaker and slid it in front of Kacey. He wobbled his head.

Serena's voice came from the phone. "Who is this?"

"It is I, darling, your Manny."

"Is it really you, Moopsie?"

Kacey gave Bessing a sour look. "It's me. I'm so sorry for leaving you. As you know by now, it's too dangerous for me to be with you.

My profession is extremely dangerous. I could be killed at any time. I only risked being with you before because of what a striking woman you are."

Serena sobbed on the phone. "If only the stars would align, we could be together. How will I go on without you?"

"You must find a way, darling."

The sobbing stopped. "You know what? Don't worry about me. I'll get a load of money from my father. I should be able to just buy another guy. Goodbye, Moopsie." She ended the call.

Verna put her forehead on the table and laughed. Kacey shook his head.

Verna looked up. "We should knock a decade off your sentence for that selfless act." She laughed again.

The door opened, and two men in uniform entered the room. One of them said, "Agent Bessing, we'll be taking custody of Sergeant Major Farrell. Thank you for your assistance."

Bessing stood up. "Who are you guys?"

"NSA."

"Where are you taking him?"

"Let's just say, Sergeant Major Ferrell will be better off with us. His skill set will not be wasted in a prison cell."

"Hold it. A woman died because of him. He shot up a corporate office and stole seventeen million dollars. Many people lost their jobs."

The man nodded. "Understood. Farrell will certainly make up for his misdeeds." The two men went to either side of Kacey to escort him out.

Agent Bessing massaged her chin. "I certainly hope he does."

◊   ◊   ◊

Wednesday Morning
Chicago, Illinois

The sun came in through a crack in the curtains and shone in Brady's eyes. He got up from Paul's couch and went to empty his bladder. When he came out, Paul stood at the doorway waiting for his turn. Brady got dressed, made coffee in the kitchen, and booted his laptop to read more stories about himself in the news, finding he made the Drudge Report. Paul poured a cup and sat down when a knock came from the front door. Brady focused on the computer while Paul went to answer. After a minute, he noticed someone standing over him. He looked up. It was Gavin Ricci.

Brady jumped up. "What do you want?"

Gavin waved hello. "May I sit down and have a cup of coffee with you?"

They sat while Paul got him a cup.

"Relax, Witek," Gavin said. "Nothing's going to happen to you or the padre."

"That's good to hear."

Gavin sipped his coffee. "Very nice." He nodded at Paul. "Witek, can I call you Brady?"

"Why not?"

"Brady, you saved my ass the other day, twice. I saw from the roof you were going to leave, but then you stayed and got us out of there. Then, you stopped James Bond from taking us out. I just want to thank you and to tell you that you have nothing to fear from me, or from my organization."

Brady considered for a moment. "Well, thanks for coming here and looking me in the eye."

"Also, I don't hold nothing against the pretty girl for tripping me up. I got a little excited, and she did me a favor."

Brady chuckled. "You don't want to mess with her anyway."

Gavin nodded. "By the way, who was that guy? I know the Russians, but James Bond was a pro. I'd like to offer him a job."

"I talked to an FBI agent named Verna Bessing. She said the guy is Kacey Farrell, a former army sergeant. He saw a lot of action in Iraq and then snapped when his wife divorced him and he lost his job. He shot up his corporate office, and he stole seventeen million dollars."

"My kind of guy." Gavin chuckled and turned to Paul. "Sorry."

"The rest is weird. Bessing said Farrell saw my story on TV and felt sorry for me. He convinced my landlord and sister-in-law to drop their suits. Then he must have been watching out for me when the shootout started. Bessing called him a psycho, but I call him my guardian angel."

Paul said, "Or he was arranged by God to serve as one."

"What about Polyglomerate Container?" Brady asked. "Do I have to finish the merger?"

"Don't bother." Gavin waved. "After all the publicity, my boss can't use the place no more. Old man Jenkins plans to buy out everything."

"What about Mark Seivers and Spencer Moss?"

"You tell me. Did your accounting program keep up with their unemployment insurance?"

Brady chuckled.

"And my organization is done with those bozos. We won't hurt 'em." Gavin drank down his coffee and reached inside his sport coat.

Brady and Paul's eyes grew wide. Paul set his hands on the table.

Gavin took out two stacks of bills and set them on the table. "Guys, relax. I'm here as a friend. Brady, we agreed on twenty thousand, and here it is."

Brady looked at Paul. Paul said, "Take it, you did the work."

"I said it before, and I'll say it again, thanks for keeping me breathing and standing upright." Gavin offered Brady his hand.

Brady shook. "My pleasure. I'll pray for you."

Gavin paused. "Okay, why not?" He turned to Paul. "How about another cup? I enjoy being around you guys, a couple of good men."

Paul started to get up. "I'll tell you what, let's make a deal."

"Go ahead."

"I'll get you another cup of coffee, and you'll destroy the picture of me with the transvestite."

Gavin and Brady laughed. Gavin banged his hand on the table. "Consider it done."

◇ ◇ ◇

Thursday Afternoon
Chicago, Illinois

Paul drove Brady to the courthouse. Sydney met them out in front. Jolene and Aaron arrived and went straight in. The girls surrounded Brady and mugged Paul.

"Uncle Paul, why are you here?" Crissy asked. "Are you going to jail?"

Everyone laughed.

Laurie said, "You're going to jail for being too short."

"They can put me in jail during the hearing," Ashley said. "It's so boring."

Britney said, "It may not be so boring this time."

Sydney got everyone moving, and they assembled in the courtroom. Lexi came down the aisle and sat behind Brady's table. Brady winked at her. The bailiff announced Judge Jurgons and they all stood up.

The judge told everyone to sit and banged her gavel. "Why are we here today?"

Sydney stood up. "We are petitioning the court to remove all custody rights from Jolene Witek, and to give full custody of all four children to Brady Witek."

"Now, why would I do that? I just removed custody from Brady Witek."

"Your Honor, we call Lexi Dean to the stand."

Lexi walked to the witness stand carrying a tablet computer. She was sworn in.

Sydney walked over to the stand. "Ms. Dean? Did you shoot the footage we're about to see?"

"I did."

Franklin Gaston stood. "Objection, Your Honor, we have not seen the footage. And we cannot see it from here now."

The judge waved. "Come up close. We'll watch it together."

Franklin led Jolene and Aaron up to the stand. Lexi played video of the fight between Aaron and Brady. Afterward, Franklin led them back to the table. Aaron glared and showed his teeth to Brady.

Judge Jurgons pointed at Aaron. "This is clearly you in the video." She took the computer from Lexi. "You're excused." She pointed at Aaron. "Get up here."

Aaron was sworn in and took the stand.

The judge played the footage again. "Explain what you meant when you said Britney was filling out nicely."

Aaron opened and closed his mouth a couple of times.

"Never mind. This was a bad idea. Go sit down. You're disgusting."

People talked to each other in the courtroom. The judge banged her gavel. "Quiet!"

Jurgons continued. "Jolene Witek will lose custody of her children if she remains in a relationship with Aaron Gilbert. Mr. Gilbert is hereby ordered to have no contact with the Witek children. An officer of the court will be assigned to check on the living conditions of the family, and if it is determined Mr. Gilbert is having contact with any of the family members, custody will be revoked, and the children will be remanded to the state."

Sydney stood. "Your Honor, do you intend to leave the children with a mother who sent a thug to assault her ex-husband?"

"Do you have proof Jolene Witek was involved?"

"No, Your Honor."

"Assault charges will be dealt with in another court. Jolene Witek is innocent until proven guilty."

"Brady Witek can take custody of the children."

Jurgons chuckled. "That ain't gonna happen."

Sydney rubbed his chin. "I need a minute with my client, Your Honor."

She banged her gavel. "We'll come back in twenty minutes."

◊ ◊ ◊

Sydney escorted Brady out to the hallway and around the corner. Paul followed. They stopped in a dark area.

"Now what?" Brady asked. "Jolene still has the girls."

Sydney nodded. "That's why Paul and I need to talk to you. We didn't want to take the next step."

"What are you talking about?"

Paul took Brady's arm. "Britney wants to testify."

Brady shook his head. "No way. Leave her out of it."

Paul squeezed his arm. "She came to us and wants to tell the truth. You need to let her do this, Brady. It's a turning point for her."

Brady paced down the hall and back. "She came to you guys?"

Sydney nodded. "She wants to make things right."

Brady looked at the ceiling and prayed. "Then give her the chance. You're right, Paul. This is a big thing for her."

They went back into the courtroom.

◇ ◇ ◇

Aaron no longer sat with the family. The judge banged her gavel. "Mr. Brandenburg."

Sydney stood.

"Aaron Gilbert has been arrested on assault charges. He will not be joining us for the rest of the hearing."

"No problem, Judge."

Brady looked at Britney. She held his stare and smiled. Brady turned forward and wiped a tear from his eye.

Sydney said, "Your Honor, we call Britney Witek to the stand."

Jolene got up and reached for Britney's arm. Franklin pulled her away. Jolene pushed Franklin in the chest, and he sat down hard. The judge banged her gavel. Britney slipped around the railing and walked to the stand. Jolene came around the desk, pointing at Britney. "I do not give her permission to testify. She is under eighteen. Come down from there."

The bailiff got in front of Jolene. The courtroom became loud with people talking.

The judge banged her gavel. "Mrs. Witek, you will restrain yourself or be removed from the courtroom."

The bailiff forced her to the table. Franklin made her sit down.

The judge turned to Sydney. "Please continue."

"Miss Witek. Your father, Brady Witek, adopted you eight years ago. Correct?"

"Yes, he did."

"Has he treated you like his own daughter?"

"He has." She looked at Brady.

"During your last visitation with him in Roger's Park there was an incident, wasn't there?"

Britney's face reddened. She nodded.

The judge said, "Please speak up, dear."

"There was."

Sydney walked to the right of the stand and put his hands behind his back. "This will not be easy for you, Miss Witek, but I need you to describe what happened."

Britney adjusted her seat. She glanced at Brady and then at the judge. "During the night, I got into my father's bed with him. He was asleep. I rubbed his chest and kissed his ear. He started to moan and rolled over too me. I kissed his lips. His eyes opened. Then he rolled backward and fell on the floor. He was very angry."

"What were you wearing?"

Britney looked down. "I was naked."

The courtroom rumbled. The judge banged her gavel. "Everyone, shut up."

Jolene stood up and sat down.

Sydney stayed where he was with his hands behind his back. "Britney, please tell the court why you did this."

Britney turned to the judge. "My mother told me to do it. If my dad did something bad to me, he'll have to give us all his money. My mom said she knows I've already had sex with boys, so it won't be a big deal for me."

Jolene jumped up. "You little bitch, I never said that. Take it back!"

The bailiff walked over and took out his handcuffs. Jolene saw him and backed up. The courtroom got loud again.

The judge sat with her mouth open, letting the courtroom get out of control. The mayhem continued for several minutes before dying down.

She picked up her gavel and banged. "I want the husband, the wife, and their attorneys in my chambers, now."

◊ ◊ ◊

The lawyers and clients sat in front of the judge's desk in her chambers. The judge made them wait while she wrote on a pad. Brady thought it was a tactic to show them who was in charge. When Jurgons looked up, everyone sat up straight in their chairs. She made eye contact, starting with Brady, making her way to Jolene. Jolene squirmed.

"I've been on the bench for nearly twenty years, and this is a new one on me. A mother urges her daughter to entrap the father with sex." She tented her fingers and rocked back and forth. "Jolene Witek, you will lose custody of your children."

Jolene cried. Franklin raised his hand. "Your Honor, we object to the change in custody. There is no evidence Jolene Witek participated in either the beating or the blackmail attempt. She remains the best option for the children's custody."

"No, she isn't. You heard the daughter. I believed every word she said."

"Surely Brady Witek is not an option for custody. He stopped making payments and left town. He's been on a TV show."

Sydney spoke up. "Notoriety should not be a consideration in a custody matter."

Jurgons smacked the top of the desk. "For this case it is."

"My client didn't ask for trouble. His own daughter tried to have sex with him. He felt obligated to leave town."

"I understand the events, Mr. Brandenburg, but your client operated outside of the law. Regardless, he doesn't even have a place to live right now."

"Then what will become of the children?"

"They will enter the system and be placed in foster care. There's no other choice. Both parties have no immediate family living nearby to place them with."

Brady raised his hand. "Excuse me, Your Honor. Can I get a five-minute recess? I have an idea."

"We're not in court, Mr. Witek. But go ahead, take five minutes."

Brady told Sydney to stay put and left the chambers. He went into the courtroom, spotted Paul and waved him over.

Brady asked Paul, "Could you handle four foster children in your place? They're all girls, and you know them already."

"Seriously? I thought you would get custody."

"The story is too hot, and I have no place to live."

"Then, absolutely I'll take them."

"And you'll take the twenty thousand for them."

Paul nodded. "There you go."

Brady took Paul by the arm and led him to the chamber. They walked up behind the lawyers.

"Judge, my friend Paul is an associate pastor, and he's already set up to take foster children. Please, let him take care of my daughters."

Jurgons turned to Jolene. "It would be very good if you agreed to this."

Jolene had tears streaming down her face. She nodded toward the judge. "Paul should take the girls. He's a good man."

"All right then. I'll get it arranged. Sorry, Mrs. Witek, but you will have no contact with the children while your case is pending. I have instructed the bailiff to place you in custody after we conclude here today."

Jolene nodded.

"Furthermore, I will be changing the support payments." The judge turned to Brady. "Once you get a job and a place to stay, ask for another hearing. But for now, you can visit the children as long as Pastor Paul is present. Okay?"

"Thanks, Judge."

"You're welcome. Try to stay off television."

Sydney turned. Brady exchanged a glance with him.

The judge raised her eyebrows. "Now what?"

Brady said, "I'll stop going on television after my interview on *Chicagoland Stories*. Okay?"

The judge waved him off. "Whatever, now get out of here."

Chapter 19

Saturday Night, One Week Later
Chicago, Illinois

Brady pulled the Ghost up in front of Lexi's apartment building. She walked down the sidewalk and paused to look at the repair work. Brady met her by the passenger door to let her in. "What do you think?"

"The old barge looks even shabbier than before. I hope you cleaned the blood out of the back."

"That and Spencer's garbage stink."

Brady opened the door for her. Lexi surprised him by allowing it.

He pulled out into traffic. "I drove here straight from Frost, Wisconsin after the lunch rush."

Lexi leaned over and sniffed. "I'm hungry for dinner, so your hamburger smell is better than cologne. Where are you staying tonight?"

"Keehn Bennett got me a hotel room. A car will pick me up tomorrow."

They drove near the church and pulled down the alley to Paul's house. Crissy led the pack of girls out of the back of the house. Brady got out and caught her as she dove into his arms. The other girls gave him a group hug. He introduced them to Lexi.

The girls climbed into the freshly cleaned and repaired Ghost to explore. Brady planned to take them out for stuffed pizza—he'd had enough burgers lately.

Crissy climbed in the passenger seat. Laurie poked her head through the vinyl curtain. "Isn't this the house on wheels Crissy pointed to that one time?"

Brady's stuck his head in the window. "It is. I bought the exact one. In fact, I should name it the 'Crissy.'"

Crissy turned. "No, Daddy, please don't do that."

Paul chatted with Lexi in the drive. "You're going out with Brady, eh? How did he fool you into it?"

"Yeah, how did he do that?"

Brady spotted Britney behind the Ghost and walked over. "Ready to fatten up on some deep dish?"

Britney looked down. "Things are weird between us."

Brady took her in his arms. "You're right, but time will take care of it. I'm so proud of what you did in court."

Britney gave him a squeeze.

Brady got everyone in the RV and started the engine. "Crissy, this camper just got a new front suspension, so you can eat all the pizza you want, and you won't break the axel."

Crissy giggled. "Then I'll eat dessert too."

◊　◊　◊

Sunday Evening
Chicago, Illinois

Brady sat next to Keehn Bennett on the set of *Chicagoland Stories*. Bennett recapped the latest on the shooting. When he finished, he turned to Brady. "Brady Witek. You survived a dangerous ordeal. What was it like getting shot at?"

"It was terrifying, to say the least."

"The involvement of Kacey Farrell turned your affair into a sensational story."

"I can't thank him enough," Brady said. "The guy saved me out of the blue. He may have done some bad things in Kentucky, but he took care of some bad guys here in Chicago."

"What have you learned from your ordeal?"

"Well, going off the grid didn't solve anything, but God was looking out for me, despite my choices. And…"

"Go ahead, Mr. Witek."

"When I lost my family to another man, I had a hard time sending them money. I didn't think it was fair when they had plenty already."

"Was this your primary motivation for leaving town?"

"It was a big reason, but I'll have to admit, when everyone kept demanding things from me, I wanted to teach them a lesson."

"What was the lesson?"

"Someday, the people you demand things from may decide enough is enough, especially when there's no longer enough to go around."

"Did you mean to include your daughters in that lesson?"

"No way. I had assumed the guy my wife left me for would take care of them. Now that the circumstances are different, I'll focus on raising them. I never wanted my family broken up in the first place."

"What are your plans for the future?"

"I own half of a restaurant in Wisconsin, and I'll find contract work so I won't get tied down. Eventually, I'll buy a house to raise the girls in, or maybe we'll travel."

"Very nice. On behalf of *Chicagoland Stories*, I wish you well. Our first story portrayed you as just another dead-beat dad, which was unfair. The story was much more complicated."

"Thanks for letting me tell my side."

The screen changed to a shot of Keehn Bennett with a live city street in the background. "That concludes our show for tonight. Thanks to the audience for watching *Chicagoland Stories*. I'm Keehn Bennett. Good night."

The End

Steven W. Smidesang, author of the *Chicagoland Stories* series, lives and works in the Chicagoland area. He currently runs the IT Department for a chain of retail stores, and before, he drove an 18-wheeler over the road for seven years—this after obtaining a bachelor's degree in journalism at the University of Oklahoma. Recently, he dusted off his degree to try his hand at writing novels, and *Chicagoland Stories* is the result. More books are to come!